# THE HANGED MAN

Being the Fifth Volume of the

**Memoirs**

of

**Madame Seraphina Fox,**

Spiritualist,

Describing Her Worldly and Otherworldly

Experiences

## Edited by Joy Reed, M.A., B.Sci.

ISBN: 9780578530307

Books by Joy Reed

Seraphina Fox Mysteries

*The Ghost in the Machine*
*Poison in Jest*
*All Hallows' Eve*
*Night Music*
*The Hanged Man*
*Ministry of Angels*

Published by Unconsidered Trifle Publications

## Historical Romances

*An Inconvenient Engagement*
*Twelfth Night*
*The Seduction of Lady Carroll*
*Midsummer Moon*
*Lord Wyland Takes a Wife*
*The Duke and Miss Denny*
*A Home for the Holidays*
*Lord Caldwell and the Cat*
*Miss Chambers Takes Charge*
*The Baron and the Bluestocking*
*Lord Desmond's Destiny*
*Lord Yates and the Yankee*
*Mr. Jeffries and the Jilt*
*Catherine's Wish*
*Emily's Wish*
*Anne's Wish*

Published by Zebra Books

# CHAPTER ONE

"I s there a disembodied Spirit in the room?"

In the silence that followed my question, the room seemed to hold its breath. Mr. and Mrs. Clarke sat motionless, their hands clasped and their faces turned toward me. Overhead, the lantern shed splinters of light over the table. It left the corners of the room in darkness, but here and there you could glimpse the sheen of brass or the paler gleam of marble where statues of Greek, Roman, and Hindoo gods and goddesses stood against the black-draped walls. I waited a full minute and then repeated the question:

"Is there a disembodied Spirit in the room?"

Once again, the only response was silence. Not a breath stirred in the Spirit Parlour—which was airless enough in the heat of a summer evening. The heavy draperies of black velvet hung motionless in the bay at the end of the room, masking the windows that gave on the street. The only light—the only move-ment—came from the candle in the lantern above us. But there *should* have been more movement than this. Frowning, I spoke the words one last time:

"Is there a disembodied Spirit in the room?"

For a moment it seemed as though this inquiry, too, would go unanswered. The Clarkes looked anxious, obviously wondering if our Spiritual Summoning would be for naught. But then a breath of air swept through the room, coming so suddenly and powerfully that it nearly extinguished the candle.

It didn't come from outside. That was manifest from the scent of it, which held nothing of the odour of London—that mixture of coal smoke, dust, horse, and inadequate sanitation that characterizes our great city. No, this breeze carried a much more rarefied scent, a subtle mingling of floral essences that hinted at a celestial origin.

"At last," Mrs. Clarke told her husband in exultant undertone. "At last they have come. The Higher Beings!"

"Seemed a bit reluctant to show this time," said Mr. Clarke, with a glance in my direction.

I thought there was a hint of criticism in his words. Addressing him sternly, I reminded him that those Higher Beings had come a long way to meet us—all the way from the Seventh Sphere, in fact, where they dwelt in conditions of Perfect Harmony, Ineffable Beauty, and Eternal Wisdom. "And they are ready to speak to you now," I added.

The chime of a bell gave confirmation to my words. It came from the table in front of us, on which stood a wooden box about two feet in length and half as wide. Its edges were bound and studded in brass like a steamer trunk. On its top surface was a large dial with the alphabet inscribed around its circumference.

Mrs. Clarke was gazing raptly at this box. "Speak to us," she implored in a passionate voice. "O dear Spirits, speak to us and shed the light of your wisdom on our unborn child!"

The dial began to move: "T-H-E T-I-N-Y S-O-U-L G-E-R-M I-S N-U-R-T-U-R-E-D A-M-O-N-G U-S," it spelled, "M-E-A-N-W-H-I-L-E Y-O-U-R T-E-N-D-E-R C-A-R-E P-R-E-P-A-R-E-S T-H-E L-I-T-T-L-E O-N-E-S E-A-R-T-H-L-Y H-A-B-I-T-A-T-I-O-N."

The Clarkes exchanged pleased glances, their faces alight with the fervency of True Belief.

As for me, I tried not to roll my eyes.

This was a typical sitting with the Clarkes, a young couple expecting their first child. They were a good deal alike in appearance—fair-haired, fresh-faced, and intensely youthful to my jaded, middle-aged eyes.

They were alike, too, in being fervent believers in Spiritualism. At our first meeting, Drusilla Clarke had made this very clear: "When we learned I was carrying the future Hope of the House of Clarke," she said, laying a hand on her as-yet unthickened abdomen, "we vowed not to limit ourselves to taking medical advice. It is not merely the *physical* welfare of our developing child that concerns us. No, indeed!"

Here she and her husband had exchanged looks of pride and exaltation before she took up her narrative again. "Alfred and I are both believers in Spiritualism, and it seemed to us that the Spiritual welfare of our unborn child was of equal importance—perhaps of *more* importance—than the physical."

Being a Spiritualist, I naturally congratulated them on this sensible attitude. They looked pleased and exchanged glances once again. Mr. Clarke took his wife's hand in his, as though it were made of spun glass, and she bent a loving look upon him before returning to her explanation.

"You know many people believe that mothers can foster artistic talent in their offspring," she said, "simply by studying painting or music while they are in a delicate condition."

I agreed that they did, Dear Reader. Some people will believe anything. As a Spiritualist, I have reason to know it.

"That would seem to indicate that the unborn child may gain not only *physical* nourishment from its mother, but much more besides," she went on. "And if mere *earthly* attainments may be gained through such means, it seems to me that the soul of the unborn child might likewise be elevated through *Spiritual* nourishment provided by Higher Beings."

"Higher Beings," I repeated.

My voice must have held a question, because Mr. Clarke hastened to clarify the matter. "Beings from more advanced worlds," he explained. "Souls strong in light and understanding. Higher Beings."

"Oh, yes," I said. "But are we talking about purely Spiritual beings? Or—er—formerly human ones?" Spiritualism embraces all kind of crackpot theories, Dear Reader, concerning multiple spheres and astral bodies and so forth. I wanted to make sure I knew exactly what kind of Spiritual company they were seeking.

Fortunately for me, it turned out they were a little vague on the subject themselves. They only knew they wanted Higher Beings, and they looked to me for guidance about the sort most likely to do Mrs. Clarke good in her delicate condition. I suggested a regular course of sittings, taking place on a weekly basis, at which we would summon the Wisest Entities from the most Advanced Spheres to commune with their offspring *in utero*. We also settled what my payment would be, which was a matter of rather more interest to me.

Happily, the Clarkes were a wealthy couple, well able to afford their little fancy. For the past six months, we had been meeting every week in an atmosphere redolent with rare perfumes and enlivened with the tinkle of celestial chimes as the Spiritograph spelled out the most uplifting messages I could devise.

Between you and me, Dear Reader, I was getting a bit tired of it. It wasn't what you could call hard labour, but I nonetheless found myself looking forward to Mrs. Clarke's own labour, which would bring a close to these sittings. I have nothing against Light and Beauty and Understanding, I hope, but as a steady diet I found that such lofty sentiments tended to pall. Besides, it was getting harder and harder to invent original messages after going over the same ground so many times.

At the moment, the wheel was spelling out my latest effort, which Mr. Clarke read aloud in a suitably reverent voice: "We rejoice at your little one's growth in wisdom, grace, and understanding. The time draws near when soul and body shall be joined together and entrusted to the couple bound together in love to receive this most precious being."

These last words were accompanied by the sound of chimes, coming not from the Spiritograph but from somewhere overhead. Three high-pitched notes rang out in an ascending series that shivered briefly on the edge of hearing before fading away.

Mrs. Clarke, at the séance table, shivered in response. "Oh," she whispered. "How beautiful! It's enough to make me forget all the discomfort of this past week."

Mr. Clarke, for his part, threw me a look of gratitude. "Don't know what we would do without these sittings," he said. "They're the only thing that seems to bring Drusilla comfort right now."

I smiled and bowed my head, modestly acknowledging the compliment.

It is always a pleasure to have one's achievements recognized, Dear Reader—even if Higher Beings get the credit for them. And of course I get credit, too, by-the-by. It was I, after all, who invented the Electrical Spiritograph, my patented device to communicate with the Other World. It's one of the things that has helped make me London's most successful Spiritualistic Medium.

My name, Dear Reader, is Seraphina Fox.

Now if you have read my previous memoirs[1], you will know that Seraphina Fox is not the name I was born with. Nor was I born a Londoner. Given that I have practiced Spiritualism for more decades than I care to own, this is hardly surprising. In my

---

1 *The Ghost in the Machine, Poison in Jest, All Hallows' Eve,* and *Night Music.*

business, a change of names and locales may be not only a useful boost to trade but sometimes a positive necessity, when one's activities bring one into conflict with the Law.

In my early career, I was unfortunate enough to experience conflict with the Law of several countries. It is a sad fact that policemen, whether French, British, or American, are inclined to look unsympathetically upon some of the little deceptions we Spiritualists practice. Thus, it is a matter of no small wonderment to me that I have lived in London close on a dozen years now without undergoing any real conflict with the Metropolitan Police. Indeed, over time I have developed a surprising rapport with at least one member of that body, which will appear in due course. For now, let me simply say that though my past is not stainless (nor, indeed, my present), I pass as a respectable woman nowadays as well as an authentic Medium.

Of course, I am no more one than the other.

Like most Spiritualists—I might indeed say *all* of them—I achieve my effects through fraud. This I take care to conceal from my clients, naturally enough. But as I have stated in my previous memoirs, there will be no concealment between you and me, Dear Reader: at least none excepting what touches upon purely personal matters. So let me state again that I am a fraud—but a very successful one. And the key to my success has been the Electrical Spiritograph.

As you may or may not know, Spiritualism has many variants, most of which I have practiced during my long career. Some are quite risky to the practitioner—materializing full-figure apparitions, for example. However spectacular the phantom form, it takes only one skeptic to grasp the ghostly figure as it drifts about the séance room and unmask it as a human being draped in phosphorescent gauze.

That is the genius of the Electrical Spiritograph, Dear Reader. There is nothing for the skeptic to grasp or unmask, no simple way to connect the Medium with the message. My hands rest on the table in full view of my clients while the bell rings and the alphabet dial turns to spell out its messages. In fact, the machine appears to work by magic, although I assure my clients it is rather a matter of *Science*: that personal and particular branch of Science I call *Spirit Energy*.

Spirit Energy, like the Electrical Spiritograph, is a thing of my own invention. As the theory goes, electricity pervades all life and persists past death in a spiritual form.[2] Like its more material brother, Spirit Energy can be harnessed to run a device, but only if one is able to channel it out of the Ether in the first place. I was the first to do so—and my success has brought me a commensurate amount of worldly fame and fortune.

As a result, I have a group of devoted clients who believe wholeheartedly in me and my machine. I do not require that *you* do so, however, Dear Reader. Indeed, if you have read any of my previous memoirs, you already know that the Spiritograph and I are both frauds. My device runs on ordinary electricity, obtained from batteries originally, though recently I have upgraded to a steam-powered dynamo system. To make the bell ring or the wheel turn, I merely operate one of a pair of simple switches. As a precaution, there are two sets of these switches, one which I can operate with my feet, and another, less convenient set that I can operate with my thumbs in situations of extremity.[3] Thus, I am able to spell out messages without the means being evident to my clients.

---

2 In positing that energy is not destroyed but only transmuted to another form after death, Madame Fox ingeniously draws upon the conclusions of her scientific contemporaries regarding the Law of Conservation of Energy and the First Law of Thermodynamics. —*Ed.*

3 The Spiritograph is bolted to the table on which it sets. This table has four apparently solid legs and a central pedestal base, studded at intervals with brass studs. Madame Fox wears Turkish slippers with a surface of pure silver metal inset beneath their upturned toes. By pressing the toe of a slipper against a particular pair of the metal studs on the pedestal base, the connection is completed. Metal rods running up through the table legs take the power to the box—and the end result is that the bell rings (in the case of the left slipper) or the wheel turns (in the case of the right). –*Ed.*

And where do those messages come from, you may ask? *Not* from Spirit Sources—far from it. Rather, I employ agents and informers who bring me information about my clients, which I then dole out at the séance table to the wonderment of all.

Not all clients are looking for the same information, of course. Broadly speaking, they come seeking one of three things: either *consolation*, *entertainment*, or *enlightenment*.

The Clarkes, though falling into the enlightenment category, were seeking enlightenment of a very specialized sort. It was a sort obtainable not through private investigation but rather esoteric research. In poring over tomes dense in Spiritualistic cant and cobbling together suitable messages, I felt I was earning my money quite fairly.

"Have courage," spelled the wheel now, addressing Mrs. Clarke's confession of weakness. "Those who dwell in the light surround you at all times. We endeavour to strengthen you and ease your burden."

Once again the triple chime rang out, shivering in the air around us. But this time, instead of shivering in response, Mrs. Clarke let out a little gasp. Her husband leaned forward with a look of concern. "Is something wrong, my darling?" he asked.

I looked at her, too, and saw that her face was beaded with sweat. With an effort, she smiled and laid a hand on her abdomen. By this time, Dear Reader, it had swollen to a most impressive prominence. "Nothing wrong at all," she said. "It was only the baby's way of approving the Spirits' words! He gave such a kick just now—quite the strongest I have ever felt. He must be an Enlightened Soul already—or she must be, of course," she added punctiliously.

Her husband did not look quite satisfied with this reassurance. "Perhaps it would be as well if we ended the sitting now," he said, glancing at me. "The circle has been broken in any case, has it not, Madame Fox?"

"Oh, yes, I did break the circle," cried Mrs. Clarke, before I could speak. "How silly of me to take my hand off the table! I daresay it is no use our going on now."

Despite the penitent words, there was an almost hopeful expression on her face as she looked at me. And I could see that the perspiration was now running down her face in little rivulets. Her husband drew out his handkerchief and began to dab at it tenderly, murmuring words of concern and endearment.

No Medium succeeds who cannot read the mood of her clients, Dear Reader. Rising to my feet, I announced that our sitting had already reached a satisfactory conclusion, signaled by the baby's movement within her. "He—or she—is in closer communion with the Spirit World than we are," I said with authority. "You will do best to follow your own instincts in the matter."

Mrs. Clarke was happy to follow her own instincts, which led her out of the Spirit Parlour and into my Sitting Room, where I threw open the windows and helped her arrange herself on the sofa with her feet on a hassock. Her husband took a seat beside her and began fanning her with her own fan. "I will go fetch you something cool to drink," I told her, then left them together, as pretty a picture of conjugal devotion as you might find in the whole City.

# CHAPTER TWO

J ust outside the Sitting Room door, I encountered Susan. She was standing in the corridor with her hands clasped in the folds of her apron and a look of strong emotion on her face.

I felt no surprise at seeing her there, Dear Reader. Or if I did, it was only surprise that she had not appeared sooner. Susan is my chief assistant in the Spiritualism business. Of all the members of my household, she is the most essential as well as the most senior, having worked with me the whole time I have lived in London.

In appearance, she is a respectable-looking middle-aged woman whom you might pass in the street without a second glance. But she has hidden depths, Dear Reader. Lately there had been some roiling in those depths, which had been disturbing the course of my ordinarily smooth-running business. I hoped we might soon get to the bottom of them, but now was hardly the time, with our clients still in the house and needing attention.

I said as much when she tried to apologize for having missed her cue with the breeze.

"I'm sure I don't know how I came to do it, ma'am," she said. "I got there in plenty of time and had the equipment right there by the ventilator—"

"Never mind, there was no harm done," I said briskly. "We can discuss it later. For now, I need a restorative beverage for Mrs. Clarke. Something cool and soothing—barley water, perhaps, or lemonade."

Susan said she thought she had some lemons in the larder and went off to see. As if to atone for her lapse, she returned in a remarkably short time bearing a glass of lemonade on a silver tray. I took it into the Sitting Room and administered it to Mrs. Clarke in sips.

"Oh, that was wonderful," she sighed, as I set aside the empty glass. "I feel so much better now! This warm weather has been very trying in my condition."

"I am sure it must be," I agreed. "I wonder that you do not go into the country, or to the seashore." For the past week, London had been sweltering in a heat wave, with the thermometer standing above eighty during the day and scarcely subsiding even at night. Most of my clients had fled along with the majority of the better-off populace. Of course there were those like me, whose business obliged them to stay in Town and sweat it out. But Mr. Clarke was a gentleman of means who only dabbled in business when he grew tired of sport or the social round. I could not see any reason why he should not take himself and his pregnant wife to greener pastures forthwith.

The Clarkes exchanged glances—rather embarrassed glances, I thought. "I have been urging that very thing," said Mr. Clarke. "But my wife feels uneasy at the idea of leaving Town now that she is drawing close to her confinement."

That seemed natural enough to me, and I said so. "I suppose her doctor is here in London, and she wants to remain near him," I suggested.

"Yes," agreed Mr. Clarke. "But it is not only that." Again he looked at his wife. She fastened her eyes on me—the large, light eyes so typical of Spiritualistic enthusiasts.

"It's you," she said. "These sittings are such a comfort to me, Madame Fox! Now that my time draws near, I cannot help thinking about what is to come and being a little *afraid*. But when I am here, I seem able to put it aside . . . or perhaps rising above it would be a better way to describe it."

I told her I was glad our Spiritual visitors had soothed her. She agreed that they had, but in a way that told me there was more to it than that. Once again, Mr. Clarke took it upon himself to explain.

"My wife feels you have been of use to her in a *personal* sense, Madame Fox," he said, "quite apart from your work as a Medium. You know Drusilla had the misfortune to lose her mother at a very early age."

Mrs. Clarke nodded, looking wistful. "I never knew Mother," she said. "But I feel she must have been a great deal like you, Madame Fox. Spiritual, that is, and with such a *comforting* presence. When you speak, your voice is so calm and uplifting!"

"It is," agreed Mr. Clarke earnestly. "Very calm—very uplifting."

"And now, when I am about to become a mother myself, it is a comfort to me to have you here, and to fancy that my real mother would have spoken to me in just the same way."

I was old enough to be Mrs. Clarke's mother, Dear Reader, although not pleased to be reminded of the fact. Still, she obviously meant it as a compliment. And the compliment to my voice I was very happy to accept. Quite a few people have praised my voice over the years, and not without reason, I think.

"Well," I said, smiling, "I must thank you for a very high compliment, Mrs. Clarke. But indeed, I am not sure you ought to let such a consideration weigh with you. Not when it is a question of your health."

Although this sounded admirably disinterested, Dear Reader, it was not quite as disinterested as it seemed. Mrs. Clarke's pregnancy had another six or eight weeks to run according to her own and her doctor's reckoning, but she was so enormously swollen now that I suspected there had been a miscalculation somewhere. I thought it unlikely that we would be able to get in more than one or two more séances before she gave birth.

Then, too, there was the responsibility of the thing. Her pregnancy had been going well so far, and I didn't want anything going wrong now because of my advice. That would have been bad for business, even setting aside the humanitarian aspect.

In the silence that followed my words, the Clarkes looked at each other again. "I *feel* the heat, but I don't believe it is *harming* me," said Mrs. Clarke. "In any case, such extreme heat as we are having now is sure to break soon." Smiling sweetly, she added, "I would rather stay here in London where I can be near to you, Madame Fox. And to my doctor, too, of course."

Mr. Clarke threw me a look, Dear Reader—a look that seemed to plead for my assistance. "But there are other doctors, dear," he said. "Down in Hampshire, near our country place, there are several medical men of fine reputation."

He paused, still looking at me. I wondered if he expected me to suggest there were other Spiritualists, too, down Hampshire way. That was a little more disinterest than I was prepared for. As I hesitated over the best way to respond, his next words took me by surprise.

"And perhaps Madame Fox would consent to come with us and be our guest in Hampshire? For a week or two, at least?"

"Oh, yes, please do!" urged Mrs. Clarke. "That would be wonderful! And we would do everything in our power to make you comfortable."

"It's very kind of you," I said. "But I am afraid it is impossible."

I spoke with real regret, for a week or two in the country just then sounded like paradise. But there were pressing reasons why I could not accept their hospitality. Chief among them was the fact that I could not take the Spiritograph into the country with me, or the Spirit Parlour either. They weren't exactly portable. And without them, I would be liable once more to all the risks of exposure I had been so glad to leave behind.

I didn't put it that way to the Clarkes, of course. Instead, I explained in a hushed voice that my Spiritual sensitivity rendered me vulnerable to malign as well as beneficial Spirits, making it essential for me to remain here at the Temple of Spiritualism where I could be assured of an environment that was carefully cleansed and protected from negative influences.

The Clarkes, as True Believers, were forced to accept this. "We would not want you to run any risk, of course," said Mr. Clarke.

"But is there *no* way we could make it safe for you to accompany us?" asked Mrs. Clarke wistfully.

I told her that I could not accept the responsibility, since her unborn child seemed so receptive to Spiritual influences.

That shut her right up, of course. Yet I felt a bit guilty as I watched her making her way down my front steps, her dress mottled with patches of sweat and her head bowed over the weight of her belly. I had done what I had to do, but that didn't make me feel any better about it. With an inward sigh, I went upstairs to change out of my own sweat-stained dress.

In the Spiritualism business, appearances are very important. This applies not only to the décor of one's séance room, but to one's personal appearance.

At the séance table, I appear in full evening dress, tight-laced and décolleté, with a veil on my head and a discreet amount of paint to shadow my eyes and give my complexion an interesting pallor. Thus arrayed, I appear quite an impressive figure, but I am always glad to change into more comfortable attire at the end of the evening—especially on such a warm evening as this.

After scrubbing my face, brushing out my hair, and exchanging my black silk dress for a cambric wrapper, I went downstairs to the Sitting Room. There, I found Susan and Jenny waiting for me with supper on the table.

I have already described Susan, but Jenny also requires a word of explanation. I would call her my housekeeper if mine were an ordinary household. Since her duties include helping me create supernatural effects in the Spirit Parlour when Susan is not around, that title doesn't fully express her function. She is a young woman as tall and powerfully built as most men, and she has been married for the past year to Sam, my coachman. The two of them, along with Susan, comprise the whole of my staff.

Sam was not there that evening, being away on an errand in another part of the city. In any case, he seldom supped with us. It is my custom to critique the day's sitting during our evening meal, and to solicit suggestions for improvement. Since Sam didn't play any rôle in that part of the business, it was usually just Susan and Jenny and I. Often these suppers were very convivial affairs, but I feared it would be otherwise tonight.

I was right, too. As Susan shared out the veal-and-ham pie, she spoke hardly a word. Jenny told a funny story about the Clarkes' coachman, whom she had entertained in the kitchen during our sitting, and I spoke of my invitation to Hampshire and how pleasant it would have been to escape the London heat for a week or two. But the silence from the third member of our trio was formidable.

This nettled me a bit, Dear Reader. I felt it was I who had cause for resentment, not she. During séances, Susan is stationed in the room that adjoins the Spirit Parlour. There is a ventilator that gives communication between the two rooms, and among other duties, she is supposed to create a breeze that can be felt in the Spirit Parlour the first time I inquire whether there is a disembodied Spirit in the room, introducing a suitable scent to the breeze on my second inquiry.

Tonight, she had missed the first cue altogether and come close to missing the second. Fortunately, it hadn't materially affected the sitting. I might have let it go at that, seeing she had already made an effort to apologize, but her attitude of sullen silence now did not incline me to leniency.

Nonetheless, I followed my usual strategy of beginning with the positive. "Your work on the chimes was splendid, Susan," I said. "It sounded perfectly heavenly in the Spirit Parlour. Indeed, I would say the sitting tonight went very well overall, wouldn't you?"

She had been sitting with her eyes on her plate, crumbling the crust of her pie with the edge of her fork. At my words, she looked up with an air of recalling her mind from a great distance.

"The Clarkes?" she said. "Yes, I thought so, ma'am. Very well indeed, apart from my almost forgetting the breeze and the flower scent." She shook her head. "I do beg your pardon for that, ma'am. I'll be forgetting my own head next." Her mouth quivered. "The fact is, I received a bit of bad news just before the Clarkes arrived, and that put me off my work."

I told her I was very sorry to hear it, Dear Reader. In fact, I felt more of a sense of relief. Since the previous spring, something had obviously been troubling her—troubling her so badly that it had affected her usually impeccable work. Not only had there been several lapses like tonight's, she had also requested extra days for personal business in addition to her usual days off. Once, it had been a whole week.

I had not minded giving her extra days off, but I would have been glad to know they had done some good. Every time I had inquired about her and her affairs, she had shut me up with a snap.

Thus, for her to admit anything was wrong seemed progress of a sort. "I hope it is not news that affects you personally," I said.

"What kind of news was it?" asked Jenny, who approaches these matters more directly.

For a moment I thought Susan was going to snub us both, but at length she spoke in a heavy voice. "It's my sister," she said.

Dear Reader, I didn't know she *had* a sister. It seemed almost inconceivable. Susan is such a fixture in my household that it was like hearing the kitchen pump own to a twin. "Your sister?" I repeated, and added cautiously, "She is not ill, I hope?"

"No, not ill," she said, "at least, not physically. I reckon you'd better hear the whole story, ma'am. You might be able to help her—you and the Inspector."

"Inspector Harper?" I exclaimed.

At this, she threw me a look that held a momentary flash of amusement. "I don't know what other inspector I'd mean." she said. "The only inspector that runs tame in *this* household. And the only one you'd be likely to give the time of day to. Or night, as the case might be."

I tried not to blush and (I believe) succeeded. "Yes, of course," I said. "What I meant was, is the matter that serious? A matter for the police?"

The flash of amusement faded, giving way to a bleak expression. "I'm afraid it is," she said. "See what you think, and then you can tell the Inspector if you think it'll do any good."

"You don't mind me staying too, do you?" asked Jenny.

Of course she was as eager to hear the story as I was. I was glad that Susan made no objection to her staying. "I don't mind your telling Sam, either," she said. "He's no talker, as we all know. But apart from him, I'd rather it didn't go any further."

With this proviso, she embarked on her explanation. "My sister Ellen is a good bit younger than me," she said. "She's in service, too, down in Dorset. She's a widow now, but there was a child born while her husband was still alive. That was my niece Rebecca—Becky, we called her."

"*Called* her?" I repeated, emphasizing the past tense.

"Yes, she's dead now," said Susan, answering the unspoken question. "Becky took sick and died, all in a matter of a month or two."

"Oh, what a shame," said Jenny, who has a notably soft heart. "That's a hard thing, that is—losing a child. Hard for her mother, and hard for you, too, Susan. She was your niece, after all. I don't wonder you was upset to get the news."

Susan shook her head. "That's not why I was upset," she said. "Not today, at any rate. Though that was bad enough by itself. But that was only the beginning." Looking at me, she added, "It was earlier this year, in the spring, when Becky died. You remember my asking for some days off then. That was to go down and help Ellen nurse her, when first she fell sick. And then when she died, I took a week off to go help bury her."

"I am so sorry," I said. "I wish I had known. I might have helped somehow."

"Nobody could have helped," said Susan, with emphasis. "I did what I could, but it's not in nature that a mother can lose a child and not feel it. For a while there, Ellen was nearly out of her mind. And she's never been the same since."

Jenny and I exchanged glances. We seemed to be getting to the heart of the matter now. "Of course there's nothing much you can do to ease the pain of that kind of loss," Susan went on. "At best it's a work of time. And even time don't always help much. *You* know," she said, looking at me again.

I did know, of course. A fair proportion of my clients have suffered the loss of a Loved One. "You think Spiritualism might help your sister?" I asked.

It does help some people, Dear Reader. Just because I am a fraud, it does not mean I do not sometimes perform a genuine service. Susan, as my long-time helper, knew this as well as I did. But she shook her head now.

"It wouldn't help Ellen," she said. "She's a Christian, one of the sort that doesn't hold with séances and talking Spirits. Anyway, that's not the trouble—not the real trouble, I mean. Unless she really *has* lost her mind, and that I'll not believe until I'm forced to it. There's got to be another explanation."

"Another explanation for what?" I asked, as she paused.

"For the children that have gone missing," she said. "There's three of 'em gone now, vanished without a trace. And they think Ellen's responsible."

# CHAPTER THREE

O f course Jenny and I were agog to hear more about the mysterious disappearances. But Susan said there wasn't much more to tell.

"Naturally there's all kinds of rumours going about. It's a small place, just a village, where Ellen lives, and there's nothing like a village for gossip. Everybody in Ainsworth knew she was near out of her mind about losing her daughter. So it wasn't such a stretch to suppose she was out of her mind plain and simple, and taking it out on other people's children."

"They think she is a murderess?" I exclaimed.

Susan's face was set in lines of misery. "That's what it amounts to," she said. "Though not everybody thinks so, mind. The people at the Vicarage where she works—Reverend Douglas and his sister—they've been nothing but kind to her. She tells me they've stuck up for her in the face of the rumours right along. And there's others, too, that've stuck up for her—most of the better sort of people in the place, in fact. But some of the lower sorts there, they hold she's done away with those children who've gone missing. It's got so she can hardly set foot out of doors without getting hissed or spat at. Not even to go to church."

Jenny and I made sounds of shock and dismay. "What do the local police think about these disappearances?" I asked. "Do they believe Ellen is responsible?"

"No, I don't reckon they do. They've talked to her, but then they've talked to most people in the place. From what she tells me, it sounds as though they don't have any idea who's responsible. If she's telling me the truth, that is." Susan made a helpless gesture. "All I know is what she tells me. And that's little enough, God knows."

I was frowning, trying to remember. "I don't recall seeing anything in the newspapers," I said. "You'd think if three children have disappeared, there would have been some mention of it."

Susan explained that when the first two had disappeared, they had been thought merely to have run away. "They were both boys and a bit wild-like. Nobody thought too much about it when they disappeared. It wasn't until the third one went missing that people began to get the wind up."

"Was that a boy, too?" I asked.

"Yes, a lad about ten or so—the same age as the others."

"Then that ought to vindicate Ellen," I said. "If losing her daughter had prompted her to make away with other people's children, surely it would be girls rather than boys."

"So it would be, if lunatics thought like regular people," said Susan shortly. "But that's what neither you nor I can be sure of, and neither can the police."

On reflection, I could see her point, Dear Reader. "But do I understand you to say that they have found no trace of these boys at all?" I asked. "In that case, maybe they *did* run away—all three of them."

Susan shook her head. "They might think that of the first two, but not the third one. He was lame, you see, and could hardly get about even with a crutch. And it wasn't just his legs that was wrong, but his mind, too. He was a bit of a natural. Ellen was sorry for him, and often gave him a cake out of her baking, or a few nuts or raisins. That's partly what's caused the mischief. People recalled him hanging around the Vicarage the day he disappeared, and from that, it didn't take long for the whole story to get started."

"Such wickedness," said Jenny indignantly. "Just because she was kind to the boy!"

I thought over what Susan had said, trying to see the matter from every angle. "The local police must have some theory," I said. "We know they are investigating the matter because they have talked to Ellen. And we know they do not have evidence to prove her guilty, because they have not arrested her."

"Yes," said Susan. "But unless they find who's guilty pretty soon, it's not going to matter. She's had about all she can stand." Her eyes filled with tears. "She talked about suicide before, when Becky died. Now she's talking about it again. Just today, in the letter I got from her, she was saying as how she felt it'd be easier just to put an end to herself rather than endure it any longer."

"She mustn't do that," exclaimed Jenny in horror.

"No, indeed," I agreed. "That would only convince everyone that she *was* guilty, including the police."

Susan nodded, her eyes streaming. "That's what I told her. I sat down and wrote her straight off, then sent it off by special messenger, but I can't be sure it'll do any good. That's why I thought you might have a word with Inspector Harper, ma'am. He might know of something they could do at Scotland Yard to get to the bottom of it."

Unfortunately, police etiquette does not allow the central branch to participate in local investigations unless invited to do so. I explained this to Susan. "But I will certainly have a word with Inspector Harper," I said.

"And in the meantime, maybe you could invite Ellen to come here for a visit," suggested Jenny. "To get her away from Ainsworth for a while."

It was a good idea, Dear Reader, and I was willing to endorse it, but Susan explained that her sister refused to leave Ainsworth. "Because of Becky," she said with a despairing gesture. "She's buried in the churchyard down there, and Ellen can't bring herself to leave her—says she'd rather join her. That's how bad the situation is. So if you'd speak to Inspector Harper as soon as you can, ma'am, I'd be very grateful."

I promised to do so, a promise that seemed to cheer Susan somewhat. At any rate, she took an intelligent rôle in the discussion that followed, concerned with the details of that evening's sitting and the one scheduled for the morrow. After settling all this business, the three of us adjourned for the night.

━╡· ·╞━

Later, upstairs in my bedroom, I got into bed and pulled the sheet over me, leaving the counterpane folded at the foot of the bed.

Although it was nearly midnight, the room was still tropically warm. There was no need for a fire in the hearth, which gaped black and empty at the end of the room. I had both windows open as wide as they would go, and the streetlamp's glow filtered through the curtains, making the wardrobe on the wall opposite a dark mass of shadow. A lighter patch beside it represented the pitcher and basin on the washstand. Beyond that, an empty stretch of wall extended to another shadowy mass that was a Turkish divan filling one corner of the room.

As I contemplated these things, I thought I heard a faint sound coming from somewhere nearby. It was a scraping noise that might have been a hidden latch stealthily drawn back.

Suddenly, a section of the paneling swung out, just beside the washstand. A rectangle of light appeared, in which was silhouetted a tall figure.

I regarded the phantom form steadily.

"My God, what a day," it said.

"It must have been, to make you so late," I agreed. "Put out the light, Tom, and come to bed."

Some women have secret lovers, Dear Reader. I had a secret husband. He was, in fact, none other than Chief Detective Inspector Thomas Harper of Scotland Yard, making his usual clandestine entrance to my bedroom under the cover of darkness.

This might be thought an eccentric approach to matrimony, but it was a sensible one for a couple like us. In some future and better world (we are told), the Lion may safely lie down with the Lamb, and so it may be with the Policeman and the Spiritualist. In this world, however, such an alliance is likely to prove embarrassing. For the good of our respective careers, I thought it better that our marriage should remain a secret.

Of course, one might argue that it was better not to marry at all under such circumstances. I had originally argued this viewpoint but ended up being convinced otherwise—for better or worse, as one might say.[4] So far, I am happy to report, it had definitely been for the better.

I say this to you, Dear Reader, among friends, but it was a trifle embarrassing to admit it publicly. Not only was there my career to think about, I had been an outspoken critic of men and matrimony for a long time. So that was another reason for keeping our

---

4 See *Night Music.*

marriage a secret. Inspector Harper was good enough to humour me in the matter, though the deception was not to his taste.

"I always feel a bit of a knave, coming into your room this way," he complained as he shut the panel behind him.

"You must comfort yourself with the purity of your intentions," I told him. "As we are legally married, it is all perfectly proper and aboveboard."

"Proper perhaps, but not aboveboard," he retorted. "I feel certain that your servants must be wondering. My living right in the building now, and the wall of your bedroom adjoining mine. And that hidden door isn't as hidden as all that. You can't tell me they haven't worked it out by now—seeing that they work in the Spiritualism business."

I told him I didn't know what he meant.

"That they are up to every trick in the book," he said sternly. "And so are you. For my part, I blush whenever I meet Jenny's eye. I don't see why you don't just tell them we are married."

"It's more interesting for them this way," I said. "And it ought to be more interesting for you, too. Everyone knows men like danger and intrigue."

He said he got quite enough of that in his job, groaning slightly as he sat down on the bed.

"Poor Tom," I said sympathetically. "Does it still hurt very badly?" A ruffian with a cudgel had fractured his collarbone a few weeks ago, Dear Reader. Bad as that was, it would have been worse if the blow had struck its original target, which had been his skull. I might easily have been a widow rather than a wife.

He said the pain wasn't too bad anymore. "Anyway, it was worth it, just to see you weeping like Niobe and wringing your hands over me," he said reminiscently. "I didn't know you had it in you."

"I didn't either," I said. "But remarkable as it seems, I find I would rather have you than your pension."

This led to an exchange of still warmer sentiments, Dear Reader. We had to be careful of his collarbone. Eventually, the conversation returned to the subject of his work.

"It's been a beastly day," he said. "A river rescue—which failed, unfortunately. Two more of those smash-and-grab robberies in H Division. And just when I thought I was done for the day, I had a visit from a Member of Parliament with some helpful suggestions about improving the force."

"Were they good suggestions?" I asked.

"Very good, if we only had about a thousand more men and ten times the budget."

"Well," I said, "as a rate-payer, I can't condone *that*. Unless he means to pay for it out of his own purse, of course."

He said it was not very likely, Dear Reader. In fact, he used stronger language than that, but I edit it for your benefit.

There was a slight pause. "My day wasn't as beastly as yours," I said, "although it had its moments. The Clarkes have invited me to go down to Hampshire with them."

"Well, that doesn't sound beastly," he said. "In fact, it sounds pretty damned good. Wish I could go with you!"

"Ah, but I can't accept their invitation," I said. "The Spirits can't be depended on to communicate in Hampshire as they do here, you see."

I could see his grin in the darkness. We both paid lip service to the idea of Spiritual Communication, to avoid the conflict that might arise if it were openly admitted between us that I committed fraud on a regular basis. "That's too bad," he said. "Very inconvenient."

"So it is," I said. "But that's only a minor matter. The greater issue is that I've found out what's troubling Susan."

"Have you?" he asked, stifling a yawn.

He knew, of course, that Susan's behaviour had been concerning me these last few months. "Yes," I said. "And it's more serious even than I feared. She wanted my advice on the matter and yours, too."

He had been looking sleepy before, but at these words he grew suddenly alert. "*My* advice?" he said. "It's a criminal matter, then?"

"It appears so," I said. As concisely as possible, I told him the whole story about Susan's sister, the death of her daughter, and the disappearance of the three boys.

"That's bad," he said, at the conclusion of my tale. "Very bad indeed. Children gone missing—the villagers up in arms—taking it out on a poor soul who's nothing but a scapegoat, like as not. All policemen hate that sort of thing."

"But can you do anything about it?" I asked. "Susan seems to think her sister might kill herself if the persecution doesn't stop soon."

"I've known it to happen," he said somberly. "We hate that sort of thing, too." He thought a minute, frowning in the darkness. "I can't interfere in a local investigation," he said at last. "Not unless I'm asked."

"Yes, I know," I said. "I already told Susan that. Is there anything you *can* do?"

"I can put out a few discreet inquiries. If the local force is hesitating on the brink of calling in the Yard, that might be enough to tip them over the edge. At the very least, I can find out if they have another suspect in mind. And I can urge them to give Susan's sister some protection against these louts who are persecuting her."

That seemed fair enough, Dear Reader, and I thanked him for it. "What's the name of the village where this is happening again?" he asked.

"Ainsworth," I said. "It's somewhere down in Dorset, I believe. I'm not sure exactly where."

"Southeast corner," he said. "Near the Hampshire border."

"Hampshire," I echoed. "That's a bit of a coincidence!"

He looked at me sharply. "You're not thinking of going down there, are you?" he asked in a voice of strong foreboding.

"I wonder if I shouldn't," I said. "It's clear *somebody* ought to go. And it seems *you* can't."

With only a slight tightening of the jaw, he said he was perfectly willing to go if he was invited. "Yes, but I have already *been* invited," I said. "It seems like a sign."

"I thought you turned the invitation down."

"I did," I acknowledged. "But I left a loophole."

He snorted. "Of course you did. I suppose the Spirits are even now preparing an urgent message that will call you down to Hampshire in the very near future." In a milder tone, he added, "Of course you must go if you feel obliged to. But let me make my inquiries first. It might save a lot of trouble all around."

I agreed that it might be as well to do this. Marriage sometimes involves compromise, Dear Reader, not to mention humouring one's spouse in his or her fancies. I haven't been married very long, but quite long enough to know that.

# CHAPTER FOUR

The Inspector, after making his inquiries, reported the result a few days later. By that time, I had already packed my trunk, purchased a smart new hat and a couple of summer dresses, and informed the Clarkes that I was able to accept their kind invitation after all.

I managed it this way, Dear Reader.

I told them that I did not care to risk any sittings in Hampshire, with my Spiritual sensitivity being so high. But it had occurred to me that if Mrs. Clarke merely wanted me there as a motherly companion rather than a Medium, that objection need not apply. I added that I had friends in Dorset whom I also thought of visiting, and that I could do this quite conveniently while staying with the Clarkes— assuming they were willing to accept my counter-proposal.

Dear Reader, they jumped at it. They even wanted to pay me for my time.

I have a great deal of effrontery, but not quite that much. I told them they didn't have to pay me. As they were allowing me to escape the heat of the City for a week or two, not to mention feeding and housing me *gratis*, I reckoned that was payment enough.

I hoped the Inspector's inquiries might result in his accompanying me, but it didn't turn out that way. "The Ainsworth constabulary thanked me for my interest," he said. "But they assured me they had the situation well in hand. I gather they are about to make an arrest, or at least that they have identified a person of interest in the case."

"That's wonderful," I said, "assuming it isn't Ellen."

"It isn't," he assured me, then paused.

"Who is it, then?" I asked.

"They didn't mention a name," he said. "That might be merely prudence on their part, of course, but . . .."

"But what?" I asked, as he paused again.

"It might mean they're talking through their hats," he said reluctantly. "It's possible they don't really have anybody in mind at all, but don't want to admit it. I've known it to happen, unfortunately. There's always pressure for the local men to solve a case themselves. They feel that if they call in the Yard, we get all the glory and they come off looking no-how. So they stall, hoping to find a clue that will lead them to the truth. And sometimes they stall so long that when they finally *are* forced to call us in, the trail is completely cold, and no one gets any glory at all."

"That mustn't happen," I said. "If they haven't made an arrest by the time I get there, I shall take steps to resolve the situation."

He looked amused, Dear Reader, but also a little apprehensive. "What do you mean to do?" he asked.

"I don't know yet," I said. "I'll know better when I have looked the ground over and talked to the people concerned."

⊷⊶

My Hampshire idyll began well. The Clarkes had a comfortable modern home set in the midst of extensive grounds. There were gardens and terraces and nicely graveled walks ideal for the kind of gentle stroll suitable to a pregnant woman. I passed a week there very pleasantly, reading to Mrs. Clarke, walking with her in the gardens, and performing the few little services that were not already being performed by her husband and servants.

"This is so kind of you," she told me, on the eve of my departure. "It has meant so much to me, your being here!"

Her husband, as always, endorsed her sentiments. "Drusilla and I cannot thank you enough," he told me. "Indeed, we've been talking the matter over, Madame Fox, and the two of us are in complete agreement. When the baby is born, we want to name it after you."

"If you don't mind, that is," said Mrs. Clarke anxiously.

I said I did not mind at all, Dear Reader. In fact, I was extremely flattered. Of course the compliment could be only a provisional one, seeing that the baby might be a boy rather than a girl. But I had never been paid such a compliment before. I told them so; and at dinner that night we drank a toast to my unborn namesake.

"To Baby Seraphina," said Mr. Clarke.

"To Baby Seraphina," echoed Mrs. Clarke and I.

It was good champagne, Dear Reader: rather better than what I normally drink. I went to bed slightly tipsy, but very pleased with myself and the world in general.

The next morning, I took my departure for Ainsworth. The Clarkes let me go only with extreme reluctance and after extracting a promise that I should return within three days at the utmost. They even wanted to send me there in their own carriage to ensure my speedy return.

That did not suit my plans, however. I meant to shed my identity as Madame Seraphina Fox, Spiritualist, on the way, and arrive at Ainsworth with a name and title that would help in my inquiries rather than causing question.

The name part was easy enough. For years, I had transacted business under the name of Letitia Blackwood whenever it seemed prudent to eschew my professional name. The title was easy, too. There had been much discussion in the newspapers lately about societies for the prevention of cruelty to children. There aren't many areas in which women are admitted to have any knowledge or authority, Dear Reader, but children form the rare exception.

I assumed my new identity, along with a stern mien and imposing hat, as I emerged from Ainsworth's tiny railway station. There weren't many buildings of size in the place, and I identified the church immediately, situated on rising ground at the far end of the village. It was surrounded by a churchyard and flanked by a rambling grey stone building that I took to be the Vicarage. It was no distance from the station at all. Carrying my own small bag, which contained a change of linen and other necessities, I set off on foot.

It was Ellen who opened the door to me. This I knew not because she looked like Susan—there wasn't any great physical resemblance—but because she sounded like her. It was disconcerting to hear the familiar voice issuing from an unfamiliar face. "How may I help you, ma'am?" she asked.

"Good morning," I said, and presented her with my card. "May I speak with your mistress, please?"

She took the card and gestured for me to enter. I noticed that she did not even look at the card. One would have expected her to show some curiosity about a stranger on her mistress's account, if not her own. But her expression was dull and distant. It was no stretch of the imagination to suppose it the expression of a woman worn down with suffering.

I was shown into a draughty parlour, crammed with the output of someone's industrious needle. Ellen went to summon her mistress and presently returned with not only Miss Douglas but with a man in a clerical collar who proved to be her brother the Vicar.

For some reason, Dear Reader, I had assumed that he and his sister must be elderly people. But in this I was mistaken. Miss Douglas was no more than forty and her brother a good decade younger, a handsome man with a square jaw, Roman profile, and wavy golden hair. I felt sure he must be wildly popular with his lady parishioners. His sister wasn't as good-looking as he was, but she still seemed a pleasant person with an engaging smile and eager way of speaking.

"Miss Blackwood?" she said. "You wished to see me?"

Glibly I launched into my explanation about the Society for the Prevention of Cruelty to Children. "Am I correct in believing that several children from your village have recently disappeared?" I asked. "And that they haven't yet been located?"

The Douglases, exchanging glances, agreed that I was correct.

"Then this would seem a matter that falls within our society's province," I said. "If crimes against children are being committed, we naturally wish them to stop, and to see that whoever is responsible is brought to justice."

Reverend Douglas was regarding me quizzically. "But wouldn't that be a matter for the police, Miss Blackwood?" he asked. "I don't question your society's aim, which is certainly admirable. But I can't see what good it does for you to duplicate the efforts of our local authorities."

With a slightly patronizing air, I explained that he had misunderstood my society's intentions. "We do not wish to duplicate the police efforts, but only to assure ourselves that they are appropriate and rightly directed. Too often village constables are unaccustomed to deal with any crimes more challenging than petty theft and public drunkenness."

"That is true," he agreed. "But again, it seems to me there is a duplication of purpose here. For if our local men need assistance, then the proper procedure would be for them to call in Scotland Yard."

He wasn't making it easy for me; that was certain. "Of course," I said cordially. "And one would suppose they would have done so long ago, given the seriousness of these crimes. I made inquiries on the matter before I ever left London, Mr. Douglas. And I have it on unimpeachable authority that your local police have not only refrained from asking the assistance of Scotland Yard, but have refused it when it was offered."

A silence followed my words. It was Miss Douglas who broke it. "You are saying exactly what I have said myself, Miss Blackwood," she said, in a voice that trembled slightly. "Scotland Yard ought to have been called in long ago, whatever the consequences."

At these words, her brother threw her a look—a look which I thought held a hint of warning. "Naturally we are eager to find the missing boys," he said. "Any unsolved mystery looms large in a place like this. Especially when it involves children."

"Yes," cried Miss Douglas. "That is what I find so unbearable. Think of the families of those poor boys! Not that Mrs. Hubbard is a very *conscientious* mother, of course. One cannot call her that, though possibly she had some small excuse. Indeed, I know she had, for Georgie often tried her sorely."

"Georgie tried all of us sorely," said Reverend Douglas dryly.

"Yes, Julian, but one must be charitable. Ten is a difficult age. And he hadn't much guidance at home, poor boy. He was a dear little baby," she added in a sentimental voice.

"Yes, to be sure," said her brother without enthusiasm. Glancing at me, he added, "But I doubt that fact is of interest to Miss Blackwood."

I assured him that everything was of interest to me. "In your position—in *both* your positions—you are able to see much that is hidden from others. And you possess influence in the community also, which is equally important."

"I don't know about that," said Reverend Douglas, sounding rather rueful.

"But you must," I protested, ladling on the butter with a heavy hand. "As a clergyman, you naturally occupy a position of authority. It is your influence, and that of others like you, which we must bring to bear upon the local police. In my experience, local pressure often leads them to try to solve crimes on their own rather than seeking assistance. We want to bring local pressure on the *other* side of the question."

I was happy to see that this speech seemed to convince him. His sister, of course, had been convinced long ago. "What can we do?" she asked eagerly.

"You can begin by telling me who else hereabouts might help advance our cause," I said. "The principal families, large landowners, and so forth." I thought this a good place to begin my inquiries, Dear Reader.

The Douglases said there weren't many such families in Ainsworth. "The Priory is the only property of size," said Miss Douglas, with a glance at her brother.

"Who lives there?" I asked.

I saw her look again at her brother before answering. "Lord Rodney Pierce," she said. "He is one of the Lincolnshire Pierces and a very well-off gentleman."

"Who does a great deal of good hereabouts," added Reverend Douglas, with what I felt to be unnecessary emphasis.

Producing a notebook and pencil from my bag, I wrote down the name. "Is Lord Rodney a married gentleman?" I asked.

"Oh, no," said Miss Douglas with an emphasis quite equal to her brother's.

I made a note of it. "And is there anyone else you might recommend my visiting?"

"There is Sir Owen Lecker," said Reverend Douglas, sounding a little doubtful. "He is our local magistrate. But I'm not sure whether it would do you much good to speak with him, Miss Blackwood. By all accounts, he is on the opposite side of the question: one of those who wish the local police to continue the investigation themselves."

On further inquiry, it turned out that Sir Owen lived some distance from Ainsworth within the precincts of a neighbouring town. In light of that fact and Reverend Douglas's comments, I thought I would omit him from my inquiries at present, or at least reserve him till later. "Is there no one else?" I asked. "What about that pretty place I saw across the fields as the train was coming into the station?"

"Oh, yes: Cincinnatus," said Miss Douglas. "General Whitmore's place. Certainly he is one of our local worthies. But his health has fallen off badly in recent years. I doubt whether you would be able to speak with him, Miss Blackwood."

"You might speak to his son instead," suggested Reverend Douglas.

"His son-in-law," corrected Miss Douglas. "Yes, you might do that, Miss Blackwood. Although I question whether the Major could decide any issue without reference to his papa-in-law! From what I understand, the General still holds the reins in that household, bad health or no."

I made notes of all this, and then suggested they tell me more about the boys who had disappeared. "You mentioned the name of Georgie Hubbard earlier. Was he the first child to disappear?"

"Yes, he was," said Miss Douglas. She obliged me with several anecdotes about Georgie, most of them involving some kind of property damage.

Reverend Douglas looked as though he did not relish this conversation. When he did speak, it was to moderate his sister's comments, or to stress that they had nothing to do with the matter at hand. "The fact that Georgie stole apples from his neighbours' orchards can have nothing to do with his disappearance."

"You think not?" I asked. "I have always understood the character of the victim to be very important in solving a crime."

He looked a little flustered, Dear Reader. "Not necessarily—or at least not in this case. Indeed, it is my belief that no crime was committed at all."

"You think the boys simply ran away?"

He agreed, but without much conviction. His sister, meanwhile, was shaking her head. "I could believe it of Dan or Georgie, but not of poor little Peter," she said. "Someone must have spirited *him* away, if not the others. *Spirited away*," she repeated with significance.

I was about to ask what she meant when her brother addressed her sharply. "That is enough, Cecilia," he said.

She looked at him, then at me. "Miss Blackwood is here in the interests of justice, Julian," she said. "I think she ought to have all the facts."

"All the *facts*, perhaps," he said, "but not gossip and surmise."

Of course he was dead wrong about that, Dear Reader. I wanted all the gossip and surmise I could get. "I do appreciate your reservations, Mr. Douglas," I said earnestly. "But I would be very much interested in what your sister has to say. Talking to me is not the same as talking to the police. You need have no fear of my being indiscreet."

"Still, I don't think—" he began.

"But I do," retorted his sister. "And I will not be silenced, Julian! For the sake of those poor boys, I must speak, even if it does jeopardize the belfry restoration."

This seemed a complete non-sequitur to me, Dear Reader. I looked from one of them to the other and back again. "Belfry restoration?" I repeated.

Neither of them answered me. Reverend Douglas was regarding his sister more in sorrow than in anger. "You can't think such a motive would keep me from speaking out, Cecilia," he said. "Not if I thought a crime had been committed."

"We differ on what constitutes a crime, Julian," she retorted. "I do not think being wealthy and well-born makes up for what is, after all, an abomination in the eyes of the Lord."

"*Abomination?*" I repeated.

Again, neither of them answered me, being too busy castigating each other. "Rumour and surmise!" thundered Reverend Douglas. "Servants' tittle-tattle!"

"Servants' tittle-tattle is very often true," returned his sister with spirit. "You would know that if you had as much experience of the world as I do, Julian."

I quite agreed with her, Dear Reader.

"And if the boys' disappearance should prove to have some connection with the goings-on at the Priory . . . no, it would be criminal not to speak."

Her brother got up from his chair and walked back and forth across the room. I hoped he might walk right out of it, Dear Reader, for it seemed to me we would get on better without him. But after taking a couple more turns back and forth, he returned to his chair.

"Very well," he said. "But I beg you will be charitable in your turn, Cecilia. 'Judge not, that ye be not judged,' you know, and 'he that is without sin, let him first cast a stone.' I don't believe Lord Rodney can help how he is made. And it's certain that he gives very generously to our local charities."

Between the two of them, they filled me in on the rest of the story. It was much as you might expect, Dear Reader. Lord Rodney, now in his fifties, had never shown any inclination to marry, but instead gave clear evidence of preferring his own sex. There had been parties of an unspecified nature at the Priory, from which all servants had been barred and which had given rise to the most lurid of rumours. Reverend Douglas was inclined to discount these rumours; his sister to give them full credence.

"And such conduct *is* an abomination, condemned by scripture," she finished with triumph. "You know that as well as I do, Julian."

Reverend Douglas, with a doggedness that suggested the subject had often been discussed between them, pointed out that if one went merely by public behaviour, Lord Rodney embodied Christian principles to an exemplary degree. "He is a kind master, a good neighbour, and invariably generous to those in need," he said. Turning to me, he added, "When our church belfry was damaged during a storm last winter, it was Lord Rodney who led the drive to have it repaired, and it is he who has pledged the greatest amount for its restoration. I hope that circumstance does not weigh with me, in believing him innocent of the charges my sister imputes to him. But indeed, I cannot think he had anything to do with the disappearance of those boys." He looked sternly at Miss Douglas.

"I only thought it was *suggestive,* Julian," she said. "Their being *boys,* you know. One naturally supposes his tastes might lie in that direction. Especially since he is also an exponent of paganism and black magic."

Reverend Douglas sighed loudly. "A man is not a pagan simply because he gives the village a bonfire party at Midsummer," he said. "It was a tradition here for centuries and only discontinued some fifty years ago. I have seen the village records myself." To me, he explained, "Lord Rodney is an antiquarian. It amuses him to see old customs revived."

"Perhaps it does," said Miss Douglas. "But it was on Midsummer's Eve that Dan Pyle disappeared. And Georgie Hubbard disappeared around the first of May—and you remember Lord Rodney had arranged for a Maypole dance and a lot of other heathen festivities about that time. Oh," she exclaimed, her eyes going round as saucers. "There was a bonfire then, too! Oh, good heavens!"

In the silence that followed, we were all free to imagine the horrors her words suggested. "Are you suggesting the boys may have been victims of *human sacrifice?*" I asked.

At these words, Reverend Douglas shook himself like a man awakening from a dream. "Not at all," he said. "My sister, in her enthusiasm to condemn Lord Rodney, has forgotten an important point."

We both looked at him, I inquisitively and Miss Douglas skeptically. "If you will exercise your memory, Cecilia," he said, "you will recall that the police investigated the remains of the Midsummer's Eve bonfire after Dan's disappearance. Not, indeed, from any such theory as you have hinted at, but out of fear that he might have been playing too near the flames and met with an accident. There were only wood ashes found and nothing else."

"Very likely there *was* nothing else by the time the police got around to looking," she retorted. "Who knows what might have been there earlier?"

Even she seemed to think this a little far-fetched, however, for she added, "Not that I think Lord Rodney is as bad as that. Indeed, I am sure I hope he is not. But it does seem rather a coincidence. His proposing a bonfire on both those occasions. His love for pagan rituals. His *perversion*. And of course he dabbles in necromancy," she added matter-of-factly.

"Necromancy?" I exclaimed.

Her brother made a weary gesture. "Spiritualism," he said. "My sister calls it necromancy, but most people would call it Spiritualism."

# CHAPTER FIVE

M y pencil skidded off my paper. There was a little silence, and then I spoke, very carefully. "You equate Spiritualism with necromancy?"

"Yes," said Miss Douglas. "It's all the same thing in *my* opinion. Table-turning, and talking with the dead, and pretending to see into the future. All wicked, heathenish nonsense and clearly condemned by the Bible. 'Thou shalt not suffer a witch to live,' you know."

It is said that the Devil can quote scripture, Dear Reader. So, too, can I. "But did not Saul pay Samuel to divine the whereabouts of his father's lost asses?" I inquired in an innocent voice.

This momentarily threw her.

In the silence that followed, her brother spoke again. "My sister and I do not quite agree on that subject, Miss Blackwood," he said, "just as we disagree on others. Although I am not personally a proponent of Spiritualism, I tend to think there is no great harm in it."

Miss Douglas said darkly that that was as may be. "There might be no harm in it as *some* people practice it," she said. "But one has only to look at that creature staying at the Priory to know that he and all his works are *anathema*. An oily, smirking, unprincipled sort of person, Miss Blackwood—and, if I mistake not, of the same persuasion as Lord Rodney."

Reverend Douglas did not attempt to dispute with his sister on this point. Instead, he addressed me directly. "Mr. Alexis is, I believe, rather celebrated in Spiritualistic circles," he told me. "And there are plenty of local people besides Lord Rodney who have availed themselves of his services. General Whitmore had him at Cincinnatus for some months before he moved to the Priory."

"Yes, but the General has lived in the East for many years, Julian. It is natural that *he* should have an interest in mysticism."

It was easy to see that whereas Lord Rodney was an abomination to Miss Douglas, General Whitmore was rather a favourite. She went on in an excusing sort of voice: "And of course the household at Cincinnatus must needs be a bit irregular, without any woman to rule over it. If the General's daughter had lived, *she* would have kept them all up to the mark. But with nothing but men in the house, it's not wonderful things should go awry. I pity that poor little boy, growing up in such a household."

"Little boy?" I asked. It struck me that there had been a regular motif of little boys throughout this business.

"The General's grand-son," explained Miss Douglas. "David is the offspring of the marriage between the Major and Lily Whitmore, the General's daughter. She died giving birth to him, poor little fellow. That's what they call him at Cincinnatus: the Little Fellow. One forgets that he has a Christian name."

I was more interested in pursuing the subject of Mr. Alexis, Dear Reader. "This Spiritualist who is staying at the Priory," I said. "Is Alexis *his* Christian name? Or is that a family name?"

The Douglases seemed a little doubtful on this point, agreeing only that they had never heard him called by any other.

"Mr. Alexis," I repeated. The name seemed familiar, and after a moment I placed it. Some years ago, the Spiritualistic press had been full of stories about the wonderful Mr. Alexis, who had astounded the crowned heads of Europe with his psychic powers.

If this was the same man, he had certainly come down in the world. It was a long way from the courts of Paris, Vienna, and St. Petersburg to a Dorset village. But ironic as this circumstance was, I was more struck by its inconvenience. I had worried earlier that the Clarkes might seek a local Spiritualist while they were staying in southern England. Now here one was—and one, moreover, who had astounded the crowned heads of Europe. I hoped the Clarkes would not get to hear of it.

Aloud, I said, "I believe I might have heard of Mr. Alexis. Does he not claim to levitate at his sittings?"

Miss Douglas said she didn't pretend to know what went on at such unholy gatherings. "Sitting around in the dark," she said. "Pretending to talk to the dead. One can only imagine the tricks the creature gets up to."

Indeed one could, Dear Reader. One could imagine very well. "Was Mr. Alexis staying in Ainsworth when the boys disappeared?" I asked.

Miss Douglas said he was. "Although I don't believe he moved to the Priory until late July or early August. Yes, it must have been about the first week of August when he left the General's house. Still, I know he was at Cincinnatus for at least six months before that. So that puts him in the village at the time of the first disappearance—Georgie Hubbard's, that was."

She was obviously struck by this circumstance, Dear Reader, which seemed not to have occurred to her before. It was clear she would have been happy to pin the guilt on Mr. Alexis as an alternative to Lord Rodney. Even Reverend Douglas was willing to consider this idea, since it did not directly involve his wealthiest parishioner. "It is true that Mr. Alexis arrived here before the first disappearance," he said. "And it's true also that he was here during the period that the other boys disappeared." Rather regretfully, he added, "But it's not as though there was any real coincidence of date. I remember him attending our spring festival last year, so he must have been in the neighbourhood then, too—which makes it quite a year that he was with the General. No, I doubt whether there can be any connection. Besides, the police would have already found it out if it were as obvious as that."

I agreed that they would, but added I would like to speak to Mr. Alexis anyway. "Surely you don't credit him as having any occult powers, Miss Blackwood?" asked Miss Douglas, looking as though she would be sorry to believe this of me.

I assured her with sincerity that I gave him no such credit. "But since he was here at the time of the disappearances, I would be remiss not to speak to him along with everyone else. One never knows. The least fact may be helpful in forming a theory that would explain the whole matter."

I saw Reverend Douglas exchange looks with his sister. "As to that," he said, "I may as well tell you that there are theories circulating in the village which involve our own household."

"*Which* are complete nonsense," added Miss Douglas. "But my brother is right, Miss Blackwood. It is better that you should hear them from us rather than from other people."

Of course it was the rumours about Ellen that they meant. I was happy to listen to their version of the business, Dear Reader, and happier still to find that, much as they differed on other issues, they were united in her defence.

"My brother and I are convinced that Mrs. Mason had nothing to do with the boys' disappearance," said Miss Douglas. (She and her brother referred to Ellen by her married name and title, as is correct for one's housekeeper.) "Indeed, the very idea is ludicrous. Or it would be, if it hadn't added to the burden of suffering she already bears. To lose a child, especially such a dear child as

Becky, is a terrible thing. It is no wonder if she were distraught about it, or even a little—" she glanced at her brother, "even a little *unbalanced,* for a time. But that she would harm someone else's child, even in that state, I will not believe."

"Nor I," said Reverend Douglas firmly. "Unfortunately, the fact that she suffered a mental breakdown at the time of her daughter's death is widely known in the village. And it was enough to convince some of the lower elements hereabouts that she must be responsible for the boys' disappearance. More especially as she had been on friendly terms with one of the boys and was seen talking to him on the day he disappeared."

"That was Peter Dray, I suppose," I said. "The third boy."

"Yes, it was he. An unfortunate coincidence, but nothing more. My sister and I are convinced of it."

"Indeed, I cannot imagine *anyone* harming Peter," said Miss Douglas. "The poor boy was a bit simple, of course, but he had the sweetest nature."

"Quite the reverse of Georgie and Dan," said Reverend Douglas.

There was something in his voice as he spoke—a kind of ironical detachment that might almost have been amusement. I regarded him with interest. "Yes, I had gathered it might be a case of good riddance with those two," I said, "from the standpoint of some people, at least."

"From the standpoint of *most* of us," he said, with the slightest of smiles, "though as a Christian it ill behooves me to say so."

Miss Douglas shook her head. "You are thinking of their disrupting the service last Whitsuntide, Julian," she said. "And indeed, that was very bad. But boys will be boys, and one must remember their upbringing left much to be desired. I for one hope they will be found to have come to no harm."

"And so do I," said her brother. "And so it will prove to be, I have no doubt. A year or two hence, we shall find that they ran away to be cabin-boys on a China clipper, and that they have been sailing the South Seas all the while we have been fretting about their disappearance."

"But not Peter," I said.

His expression clouded. "No, not Peter," he said. "That's a deeper mystery."

"But one that doesn't involve *our* household," reiterated his sister. "It is most unjust that poor Mrs. Mason should be suspected in the matter. Not that most people *do* suspect her, but unfortunately there are some who do."

"Very unfortunate," I agreed. "Er—are there others whom the villagers suspect?"

I was afraid the Douglases might refuse to tell me, on the grounds of Christian charity. Fortunately, they had no such scruples. Miss Douglas explained that General Whitmore's servants were mostly foreigners, and that there had been some talk about them as well as Ellen. "One of them is a *black* man," she explained in a hushed voice. "And naturally there are those in the village who would suspect him on those grounds alone."

"Especially as some of them were already inclined to think he was the Devil," put in Reverend Douglas dryly. "There is much ignorance and prejudice hereabouts, I am sorry to say."

"But I believe the General also employs a Turk," said Miss Douglas, "and it is he on whom most of the local suspicion rests. Because of its being *boys* who have disappeared. One remembers Lord Byron and his Turkish travels, Miss Blackwood. Not a subject one likes to allude to, but the practice is well-known."

It struck me that she did a lot of alluding to that subject, what with one thing and another, but I wrote it down in my notebook just the same. "I suppose the police have investigated the General's household?" I asked. "Seeing that there are rumours about his servants?"

"Oh, yes," she assured me. "They have investigated, and they found no evidence that any of the staff at Cincinnatus were involved. But like our Mrs. Mason, they bear the burden of village suspicion."

I said I would like to speak to Mrs. Mason myself, in order to get her own views on the subject. They were very loath to let me do this, Dear Reader. But I finally convinced them that I had no suspicion that she was guilty of any crime, and that I would handle her with kid gloves regardless. So Miss Douglas rang the bell, and then she and her brother tactfully withdrew as Ellen appeared in answer to their summons.

# CHAPTER SIX

E llen entered the parlour with downcast eyes and dragging step. I bade her sit down, then studied her in silence. She seemed content to endure my scrutiny without remark, Dear Reader. It might be that she did not even notice it. She sat quietly with her hands folded as in prayer and her eyes cast down: a *Mater Dolorosa* in cap and chintz gown.

I spoke at last, in the gentlest of tones. "First, Mrs. Mason, I must say how sorry I was to hear about your daughter. You have my deepest condolences."

That made her look at me for the first time. There was something like resentment in her eyes, and I thought I understood. I have suffered a bereavement or two in my own time and remember very well the stab of pain one feels when the subject is alluded to— the more so when it is merely some well-meaning stranger mouthing platitudes. Still, I felt she might resent my ignoring her loss altogether, given that it was linked with the local disappearances.

"I am acquainted with your sister in London, and it was from her that I learned about all that has happened," I went on. "Of your initial loss, that is, and of the way it is now being used to torment you."

She was looking at me squarely now, Dear Reader: staring at me, in fact. "You know Susan, ma'am?" she asked.

"Very well," I said. "Enough to know how worried she is about you."

There was a pause, and then Ellen spoke, rather hopelessly: "Yes, I know she is."

"Is the situation still as unbearable as when you wrote her last?"

"Yes," she said, her voice very low. "Yes, it is." Then, in a sudden change of tone, she added, "No, maybe not. Not so bad as that, at least. My master and mistress here—Reverend and Miss Douglas—they've been very good to me. I don't go out except with one of them now, and nobody dares say a word when they're by. But folks are still thinking it. Thinking I had something to do with those boys going missing."

"Some people might think it," I said. "But surely not all."

"No, not all," she agreed, but did not seem to find any comfort in the idea. I thought it might help to stress that her situation was not unique.

"I understand you are not the only one suspected in the boys' disappearance," I said. "Your mistress seems to think Lord Rodney Pierce might have played a rôle."

"Him?" she said, sounding faintly surprised. "Wouldn't have thought he would harm a fly, myself."

"She hints that he might have a—er—predilection for his own sex. Which might lead him to—er—prey upon young boys."

"Oh! Oh, that's dreadful." She was shocked out of her lethargy now, Dear Reader, and considered the idea with real concern on her face. "Of course there's been rumours about Lord Rodney for years," she said, after a pause. "But I don't believe he'd do a thing like that, ma'am. No, that I don't—not to a child."

"Do you have any idea yourself about the disappearances?" I asked. "Any theory or suspicion?"

She shook her head with a hopeless air. "I can't think who would steal away one child, let alone three of 'em."

I remarked that it was the kind of crime for which Gypsies were traditionally blamed. Ellen said there weren't any Gypsies hereabouts, and that she didn't suppose there was much in those kinds of stories anyway.

"But someone must be responsible," I said. "Unless you hold with the idea that all three boys ran away."

"They couldn't have," she said. "Not Peter, at any rate. He was that lame, he could hardly walk."

"You were very kind to him, by all accounts," I said. "Which makes it all the worse that you should now be suspected of harming him."

"Yes, ma'am," she agreed, her voice dull once more.

"Especially since you hadn't much to do with the other two boys who disappeared. You hadn't, had you?"

"No," she agreed. Her voice still sounded dull, but it was decided, too, Dear Reader. "I knew 'em, of course. Everybody did."

"It sounds as though almost everybody found them rather a nuisance," I remarked.

For a moment I thought she would not respond. At last, however, she nodded. "Yes," she said. "There's plenty might find them that. Georgie, especially. He was a regular bad boy." Her face darkened. "Wicked cruel he was to the smaller children. My own Becky included."

This, to my mind, was a more substantial motive than the one that had been imputed to her. I looked at her with dismay. "If he was as wicked as that," I said, "do you suppose someone thought he *deserved* to disappear?"

"I don't know what to think," she returned. "At first it seemed as though he might have just run away, back when it was just him. Even when Dan went missing, that was what most of us thought. But with Peter, it was different. Nobody could believe he'd gone on his own."

"Yes," I said. "That seems the most baffling part of this business—that he could have disappeared so completely that the police could find no sign of him. But it is a circumstance in your favour, Mrs. Mason. For if you *had* made away with him, some evidence of it must remain."

She nodded, her expression resentful. "That's what the police thought. They spent the best part of a week poking around the churchyard and garden and all the outbuildings here at the Vicarage. I know that's what they were looking for: evidence that I'd killed Peter and the others and buried them somewhere hereabouts."

Rather sententiously, I said that since they had failed to find any such evidence, suspicion must soon pass from her. "You must not let it wear on you," I urged. "I shall be here another day or two, looking into the matter. Please let me know if there is anything I can do to help."

With dull resignation, she said there was nothing. I made a second offer, which only provoked her to resentment once more.

"I don't know what you *can* do," she retorted. "You or anybody else. Unless you're willing to help me dust and sweep and make up the fires." With a touch of asperity, she added, "Our last house-maid left two weeks ago, because her mother wouldn't hear of her working with a murderess. Since then, Miss Douglas and I've been doing all the work between us. We haven't been able to find anyone else willing to come here."

It wasn't an area where I felt I could be of much help, Dear Reader, but of course she did not mean her invitation literally. "Well," I said, as cheerfully as I could, "if I can do nothing else while I am here, I might be able to find you a new maid. I shall keep my eyes open for a suitable candidate."

This offer seemed to make her ashamed of her previous outburst, for she said that would be very kind of me. "Though I doubt you'll be able to do it, ma'am," she added with a shake of her head.

"You'd have an easier time if we had the smallpox and cholera in the house combined."

I told her I counted on being able to improve the situation while I was here. "In that regard, could you recommend a place I might stay?" I asked, picking up my bag. "Is there an inn or hotel here in Ainsworth?"

She said the only inn was the Hound and Huntsman at the other end of the village. "But it's rather a low place, ma'am. Not fit for a lady like you, I'm sure," she said, looking me over.

"Needs must," I said cheerfully, moving toward the door. "I daresay I can endure the Hound and Huntsman for a night or two."

As I spoke, I swung open the parlour door, revealing Miss Douglas in a crouching position. Her head, bent low, was tilted at just the proper angle for applying an eye to the keyhole.

It was an embarrassing situation for us both, Dear Reader. Once I recovered from my initial shock, however, I didn't think any the worse of her for it. She was merely being protective of Ellen, according to her lights.

She got to her feet in a flustered manner. "I—er—dropped a half-penny somewhere hereabouts, Miss Blackwood," she said, "and I can't seem to find it."

I joined in the search, for the look of the thing. After we had made a decent pretence of looking for the mythical half-penny, she called off the search and turned to me. "It occurs to me that since you are planning to stay here in Ainsworth, you might need a place to stay," she said, as if the idea had just occurred to her. "My brother and I would be very pleased if you would be our guest here at the Vicarage."

I told her I didn't wish to put her out, seeing that she was already short-staffed. She waved this objection away, however. "Indeed, we would welcome your presence here," she said, "especially since you are working to resolve this terrible situation with Mrs. Mason."

It suited me to accept her invitation, Dear Reader. Being a guest at the Vicarage would give me an official status in the village, and it would also imply that my mission had the sanction of the Vicar and his sister.

Since I meant to call on some of their neighbours, I asked where I could hire a conveyance and driver. She said they could provide me with those, too. "William, our outside man, will drive you, if you don't mind riding in a gig."

I have ridden in many worse vehicles than a gig, Dear Reader. I said I would be very pleased to have William drive me. And in fact I was, for I reckoned I could question him during the drive and get his opinion about the disappearances, too. Since he was another of the Vicarage servants, his opinion seemed worth having.

In that matter, however, William defeated me. I put question after question to him in my most ingenious manner, but could get no opinion from him that was not expressed in grunts. "Very well, then. At least you might tell me whether it would be better to call at Cincinnatus first, or the Priory?" I inquired acidly.

He grunted. "Cincinnatus is closer."

"Very well," I said. "Let us go to Cincinnatus, then."

⭇ ⭈

The glimpse I had from the train seemed to show the General's home was a pretty place, Dear Reader. In fact, it was beautiful. The house was square and white, with green blinds at the windows, a porch covered with vines, and a gabled roof. One scarcely noticed the house, however, for the glory of the gardens that surrounded it. There were flowering shrubs and ornamental trees, a rose garden with a sundial, and a flourishing kitchen garden. Behind this lay an orchard, neatly and symmetrically laid out in rows. Other trees spread their branches flat against the orchard wall—espaliered is, I think, the proper term. Peaches and apricots glowed like flame-coloured jewels among the trees' leafy boughs. Further off was a hothouse as large as the house itself and in a rather better state of repair.

In the arch over the garden gate, the word "Cincinnatus" was chiseled in Roman lettering. I recalled that Cincinnatus was a Roman general who had laid down his sword to take up farming. The name seemed appropriate enough, though it appeared General Whitmore ran more to gardening than farming *per se*. It crossed my mind also that he appeared to be a bit of an egotist, in comparing himself to one of Rome's military heroes.

As I opened the gate, I saw in the distance a stocky man wearing breeches and a blue apron. He was tying up some vines, but stopped when he saw me and stood watching as I approached the door and rapped firmly upon its panels.

The door opened to reveal a giant. He was nearer seven feet tall than six, with a skin black as coal. As if to emphasize this last point, he wore a dazzling livery of scarlet and gold that bore more than a passing resemblance to a guardsman's uniform.

The effect was simply stupendous, Dear Reader. I am afraid that I was guilty of staring at him with something like desire in my eyes. Not desire in a physical sense (though there might have been an element of that, too—he was undoubtedly a very handsome and masculine figure). But it was mainly in a professional sense that I desired him. I found myself thinking how beautifully he would harmonize with the exotic décor of my Temple. And if it had still been the fashion to materialize Spirit Guides of foreign extraction, what a splendid appearance he would have made, with no need to resort to burnt cork or similar shams.

Obviously this must be the black servant Miss Douglas had spoken of—the one whom the villagers took for the Devil. The idea wasn't as laughable to me now I had seen him. There was nothing actually satanic about him, but a more formidable figure could scarcely have been envisaged, or one that would appear more out-of-place in a rustic village like Ainsworth.

He looked back at me calmly, his dark eyes revealing nothing. At length he spoke, in a sonorous voice: "May I help you, madam?"

His voice was as good as his appearance. I had to damp down another wave of desire. "I would like to see General Whitmore, please," I said, handing him one of my Letitia Blackwood cards. "I understand his health is rather uncertain, however, so if it is more convenient, I would be pleased to speak with Major Whitmore instead."

"Major *Phelps*-Whitmore," he corrected. "Please come in and take a seat, madam, while I inquire."

I was shown into a small parlour just off the entrance hall. It was neat as a pin but rather bare. There was a Bokhara rug on the floor, but no pictures or ornaments of any kind. The sofa was shiny black horsehair without any cushions to soften it, and the few chairs were all plain wooden ones. As I sat looking around me, a small boy appeared in the doorway.

He was a very little boy: no more than three or four years old. He gazed at me with round eyes and his mouth wide open: probably the same expression I had worn on beholding the black servant.

"Hullo," I said, giving him a friendly smile.

He let out a whoop and ran off. I tried not to feel offended.

As I sat looking after him, another figure appeared briefly in the parlour doorway. I caught a glimpse of a villainous dark face beneath a white turban and another scarlet and gold livery, before he, too, passed out of view.

I felt as if I had wandered into the *Arabian Nights*, Dear Reader. The figure I had just glimpsed might easily have been one of Ali Baba's forty thieves, judging by his physiognomy alone.

It occurred to me that this must be the Turkish servant Miss Douglas had spoken of. Having seen him, I could not wonder that he was favoured as a suspect in the boys' disappearances. It was only too easy to visualize him as an assassin complete with bow-string and scimitar.

As I was just reflecting on this, the turbaned man appeared again in the doorway. He was holding the hand of someone who proved to be the small boy. "Come along," he said, "and make your apology to the lady. Is this how a gentleman behaves in a civilized house?"

"I am sorry, Sandeep," said the boy, in an abject voice.

"And so you should be. But it is to the lady you must apologize."

The servant gestured toward me with a smile that invited me to share his amusement. The smile transformed his face, Dear Reader. He no longer looked villainous at all, but perfectly kindly, while the look he bestowed on his infant charge was warm with affection.

I smiled back, feeling rather ashamed of myself. It is the first rule of Spiritualism that appearances can be deceptive. I knew this as well as anyone living, and yet here I was, judging the book by the cover like any fool.

"No apology is required," I said. "I expect the young gentleman was merely surprised at finding me here."

The boy had been keeping his face hidden in the skirts of the servant's jacket while we spoke. Now he turned so that a single china-blue eye appeared, along with one-half of a cherubic mouth. "I'm sorry, ma'am," he said, very rapidly, then hid his face once more.

"It is well," said the servant with an approving nod. "Let it be a lesson to you, young sir, to treat ladies with the respect they merit."

It was a lesson to me, too, Dear Reader. Clearly I had fallen into the habit of taking things at face value. So when Major Phelps-Whitmore finally appeared in the doorway, I made a point of appraising him with open mind and unfettered judgment.

# CHAPTER SEVEN

The first thing I noticed about the Major was his size. He was almost as tall as the black servant, although not nearly as striking. He had the erect posture of a military man, a sun-browned complexion, and close-cropped hair not yet showing any grey. His size would have made him intimidating had not his demeanour been so self-effacing. In conversation, he would hunch his shoulders and duck his head, as though seeking to bring his dimensions into line with the rest of us, and he had a tendency to diminish his own authority, too. It showed in his first words, spoken with an air of apology.

"Miss Blackwood? Phillipe said you was wanting to talk to the General. Hope I'll do instead. Fact is, the General's not a well man. He has his good days and his bad days, and I'm afraid today's not a good one."

"I understand perfectly, Major Whitmore," I said. "Or no—it is Major Phelps-Whitmore, isn't it?"

"Aye, that's right. The General's my father-in-law. I took his name when I married his daughter. I wasn't worthy of her," he explained matter-of-factly. "I'm quite an ordinary fellow—no family to speak of, and no money except what I've made myself. But Lily was willing to have me just the same."

His face softened almost to the point of fatuity at these words, Dear Reader. For a moment he sat shaking his head as though still bemused at having won so much more than his just deserts. "The General didn't like it, of course—why would he? But he came around in the end. Only he made it a condition that I take the name of Whitmore when I married Lily. Well, I didn't mind *that*." He flashed me a smile. "Mean to say, I was nothing but a new-made lieutenant at the time, and his name's a pretty powerful one. Between you and me, I'm not sure I'd have got as far as I did in the ranks without it."

There was something very charming in being made the recipient of these confidences, Dear Reader. I found myself liking Major Phelps-Whitmore very much indeed. I had to caution myself again not to hurry to judgment.

"I am sure you can assist me quite as well as your father-in-law," I said, and went on to explain about the Society for the Prevention of Cruelty to Children and my crusade to solve the mystery of the missing boys.

The Major shook his head and opined that it was a bad business. "Can't think how such a thing could happen in a place like this. Poor little fellows, I hope they haven't come to any harm." With an air of thinly-disguised pride, he added, "I'm a father myself—got my own Little Fellow to think of. And what I say is, the sooner we find out what's happened to those boys, the better."

"Exactly my feeling," I said. "Especially since the mystery is having such a terrible effect on the lives of those suspected of playing a rôle in the boys' disappearance. You may have heard that the housekeeper at the Vicarage has been harassed so she daren't set foot alone in the village?"

The Major had *not* heard and expressed indignation at the idea. "Ridiculous," he fumed. "Louts and cowards, the lot of 'em. Treating a lady that way!"

I was interested to hear him call Ellen a lady, Dear Reader. The British, in general, are so class-conscious that though a housekeeper might be described as a good, genteel woman, most people wouldn't put her in the lady category. As I don't myself subscribe to the British Class system, it made yet another reason to like the Major.

"I understand you have suffered from suspicion yourself," I said. "Or at any rate that your household has."

He looked puzzled. "Don't know about that, ma'am. We've had the police here, of course, like everybody else. Asking questions and poking around and wondering if we'd seen anything suspicious. But the General sent 'em to the right-about pretty quick." He grinned. "It was one of his *good* days."

"Still, I understand suspicion lingers around one of your servants."

"Phillipe?" said the Major, grinning yet broader. "I don't doubt it. Mean to say, most of 'em have never seen a Black before in these parts, and they don't quite know what to think. But Phillipe can take care of himself."

I asked if Phillipe was the servant who had opened the door to me. The Major said he was. "Saved the General's life in Africa," he explained. "Phillipe's a very superior fellow. Speaks French as well as English, not to mention his own tribe's lingo. The General thinks a lot of him—so do we all."

"Ah," I said. "Then it is not Phillipe I mean. I was given to understand that suspicion centred rather around a servant who is a Turk."

The Major looked puzzled. "That can't be, ma'am," he said. "We haven't any Turks here at Cincinnatus."

I was taken aback by this statement, Dear Reader. "No?" I said. "But I saw a servant earlier, in company with—I believe—your son. An Eastern-looking person wearing a turban?"

"Sandeep? Oh, but Sandeep's no Turk. He's a *Sikh*," said the Major, looking shocked at my ignorance. "From India, that is. Been in the General's service these twenty years."

I apologized, explaining that I had been misinformed. "But I am afraid it is rather a general misunderstanding, Major. Miss Douglas mentioned his being a Turk, so doubtless there are others who think so, too."

The Major agreed it was very likely. "They're an ignorant lot hereabouts," he said. "We've had trouble before with some of the village boys hanging about making nuisances of themselves. They used to hoot and make cat-calls at our poor cook whenever he'd set foot out-of-doors. Made it jolly inconvenient for him to pick the greens for dinner. He's a foreigner, too—a Chinaman."

I pricked up my ears at this. "Were George Hubbard and Dan Pyle among the boys who were harassing him?"

The Major said they might have been. "There was a regular gang of them, that I do know—trampling the cabbages and causing no end of commotion. But they went away pretty quick once the General spoke to 'em. And no wonder, too." The Major smiled reminiscently. "He's broken up rougher crowds than that, I can tell you!"

I said I didn't doubt it. "But that may explain why the villagers suspect your servants of playing some rôle in the boys' disappearance. If the boys were harassing one or more of them, they might be considered to have a motive."

Although I had striven to word this statement as tactfully as possible, I was afraid the Major might still be offended by it. But he seemed wholly dismissive of the idea that his servants could have taken any vengeance on their harassers.

"Can't believe any of 'em would do such a thing," he said with decision. "Certainly not Sandeep. He's a thoroughly trustworthy fellow, and he'd never hurt a child. Why, I trust my own Little Fellow with him."

This, to the Major, was clearly proof enough. It did not quite satisfy me, Dear Reader, but his assurance was convincing nonetheless. I moved on to my next idea. "I understand there is also some feeling that Lord Rodney Pierce may have played a rôle in the boys' disappearance."

The Major made a noise that was half disparaging and half amused. "Him?" he said. "Why on earth would anyone think that?"

As delicately as possible, I alluded to Lord Rodney's predilection for his own sex. The Major allowed it was a possible motive, but said that he, for one, would be very much surprised if Lord Rodney had had any hand in the boys' disappearance.

"It'd be an ugly business," he told me. "And frankly, I don't see it of him. He does a deal of good hereabouts. Then, too, he's a rich fellow, one who can pay for his pleasures. Not to be indelicate, ma'am, but I've seen enough of the world to know that most anything's for sale if you can pay for it—if not here, then on the Continent or further abroad. Why would Lord Rodney want to go fouling his own nest right here in Ainsworth?"

I suggested that he might have some form of lunacy that drove him to commit crimes against his own inclination. The Major said he didn't believe there was such a thing.

"Most men are pretty consistent types," he said, "even men of Lord Rodney's stamp. I've seen a fair bit of him with us living here in the same village. And I'd say he's all about—well, art and beauty and poetry—that kind of thing." He gestured vaguely in a way that suggested these were foreign concepts to him. "This business of the boys—that'd be ugly—about as ugly as it gets. I don't see it of him."

I said I was glad to have his opinion, Dear Reader. "I gather there is another circumstance against Lord Rodney, however. He seems to have arranged for a couple of bonfire parties in the village, which more or less coincided with the disappearances of two of the boys."

The Major made a disgusted noise. "Now *that's* all nonsense," he said. "Not about him and the bonfire parties, of course—he was behind those, right enough. But I mean to say, they were *parties*. The whole village was there! What's he supposed to have done—killed the boys and then burnt 'em like a heathen sacrifice?"

I said it did seem improbable. "And I gather the police even investigated the ashes of the second bonfire and found nothing suspicious."

"There you are, then," said the Major. "Nothing to it."

I agreed he was likely correct. "Still, the mere fact of Lord Rodney having sponsored such parties has been enough to arouse the prejudice of some of the more rigidly Christian types in the village," I said. "That, and the fact that he practices Spiritualism. In fact, I gather he has a well-known Spiritualist staying with him right now."

I was unprepared for the effect of these words, Dear Reader. Up till now, Major Phelps-Whitworth had been remarkably charitable in his speech—charitable almost to a fault. But his whole demeanour changed at the mention of Mr. Alexis. "*That* fellow," he said. "I tell you, ma'am, if I had to pick a villain in this business, based on probabilities alone, I'm damned if I wouldn't pick him. If he could get any profit out of it, that is. Begging your pardon, ma'am—I shouldn't use such language in front of a lady. But I've had a bellyful of Mr. Alexis and no mistake."

Of course I encouraged him to tell me more. "I did hear that Mr. Alexis had been staying here at Cincinnatus before he went to the Priory."

"You heard right," said the Major with emphasis. "He was here for the best part of a year, battening like a tick on the poor old General all the while."

I said I had gathered that the General was a believer in Spiritualism. The Major nodded, looking as though the admission came hard. "I suppose it's natural enough. He's getting to be an old man, and the past is more real to him than the present. He likes being able to talk to other old generals—compare notes, so to speak."

"Bonaparte, I suppose," I said, "and Wellington." I have quite a few retired military men among my own clientele, Dear Reader, and Bonaparte and Wellington are the two most frequently summoned generals at my séance table.

The Major, however, said that his father-in-law was more partial to generals of the classical era. "Hannibal, and Julius Caesar, and Alexander, and so forth."

It made perfect sense, Dear Reader. Indeed, I felt I might have guessed it, given that he had named his property Cincinnatus. "And Mr. Alexis summons these ancient generals to speak with General Whitmore?"

"So he *says*," said the Major with a darkling look. "You couldn't prove it by me."

"You don't attend the séances?"

"I sat through one or two of 'em in the beginning, but as a regular proposition, I couldn't stomach it. A lot of nonsense, in my opinion. Fellow's smooth, though—not a doubt of that. He's got the General completely fooled."

Rather timidly, I inquired whether the deception were such a bad one, if it brought comfort to the General. It was my profession, after all, Dear Reader, and I felt obliged to defend it.

"I wouldn't care for his being deceived," said the Major, "but that Alexis fellow was bleeding him dry. He'd have ended by bankrupting the poor old man. The only thing that saved him was Lord Rodney jumping in when he did and offering him a better proposition." He shook his head. "Of course the General's got a right to spend his money how he likes. I don't dispute it, and I wouldn't dream of interfering—not on my own account, at least. But where the Little Fellow's concerned, that's a different matter. I hate to see the General squandering money on a smooth villain like Mr. Alexis when he's got a perfectly good grandson." He shook his head again, his expression mournful. "If Lily was still here, I don't doubt she'd have put a stop to it long ago."

I couldn't help feeling a little guilty, Dear Reader. In my own practice, I choose only clients who can easily spare my fees, but there had been a time when I wasn't so scrupulous. In any case, I didn't like the idea of being bracketed with Mr. Alexis, for whom I was fast conceiving a dislike. I will admit, however, that there might have been an element of professional jealousy involved. The man had been very successful, by all accounts, and I was curious to know how the trick had been played.

"What does he do at his séances?" I asked. "Does he materialize full-figure phenomena?"

This concept had to be explained to the Major, who was unfamiliar with Spiritualistic terminology. As nearly as I could determine from his account, Mr. Alexis was an advocate of the classic dark séance, meaning that he extinguished all lights in the room beforehand and then ran around in the dark playing tricks. It's a good old dodge if you can find clients who will still tolerate it, Dear Reader. I raised my eyebrows on hearing that Mr. Alexis was accustomed to float around the room, addressing his audience from the ceiling.

"From the ceiling?" I repeated.

"That's right, ma'am," affirmed the Major.

"Did you actually *see* him floating around the room?"

"Couldn't see anything, ma'am. The room was completely dark."

"Then how did you know he was there?"

The Major rubbed his mustache in a puzzled manner. "It *sounded* like he was there. Aye, and I did see something—something like a mist, up there by the ceiling. The General could tell you more about it than I could. He was sitting next to Mr. Alexis at the time and says he actually felt him float off the ground."

My expression must have betrayed my opinion of this infantile deception, for the Major looked at me curiously. "You seem to know a lot about Spiritualism, ma'am," he said.

In a reserved manner, I admitted that I did.

"Are you a believer in spooks and spirits like the General, then?"

With a mental glance over my own career, I said truthfully that I believed there were more things in heaven and earth than our philosophy dreamed of. "But if you ask me whether I believe in Spiritualism as practiced by the likes of Mr. Alexis," I said, "then no, I don't."

The Major was regarding me with new attention. "No more do I," he said. "And I tell you, I'd give a good deal to see the fellow unmasked as a fraud. Do you have any idea how he plays his tricks?"

I allowed that I did have an idea or two, as it happened.

"You wouldn't be willing to sit in on one of Mr. Alexis's séances and see how he does it? It'd be a real service to me, ma'am—to me and the Little Fellow. Aye, and to the General, too, for he can't afford to keep running through the ready like he's been doing. This place is expensive to run. Not the house so much—we're nothing but a lot of men, and don't want much in the way of household doings. But it takes a devil of a lot of work to keep up the gardens. Especially now the General's too frail to do much himself."

"Who's too frail?" demanded an imperious voice from the doorway.

# CHAPTER EIGHT

I t was comical to see the consternation on the Major's face when
he saw his father-in-law standing in the doorway. I noted it only
in passing, however, for I was more interested in seeing for myself
the great General Whitmore.

I had visualized a stern, commanding figure—old, perhaps,
but still impressive. What I saw was a little dried-up puppet of
a man leaning on a stick. Even in his prime he must have been
a bantam figure compared to his massive son-in-law. As he was
now, bowed over with some rheumatic complaint, his head hardly
reached the level of the fireplace fender.

He shuffled over to where we were sitting, his stick tapping on
the floor. His back was so bent that, in order to see where he was
going, he had to cock his head sideways. I could see the glint of
a shrewd blue eye beneath the thatch of white hair overhanging
his brow.

The Major sprang to his feet and stood at attention, further
emphasizing the elder man's diminutive size. "Sit down, sit down,"
said the General irritably. Switching to an exaggeratedly courtly

manner, he addressed me with a bow that nearly overset him. "Good day, ma'am. Sorry I wasn't here to receive you. The Major should have let me know."

The Major protested that he had only been trying to spare him trouble. The General snorted. "Nonsense, nonsense! I'm fit enough, even if I *am* a bit elderly." Adopting once more his courtly manner, he turned to me again: "I tell you what it is, ma'am. He's got an eye for a good-looking woman and wants to keep you to himself. Hey, Major?"

The Major protested this statement, too, but to little effect. The General had meanwhile been casting an eye around the room. Now he turned on his son-in-law with sudden ire. "Where's the tea-tray? What the devil do you mean, entertaining a lady and not offering her any refreshment?"

The Major said feebly that he had not thought to offer me tea. I assured him I didn't want it. We were both overruled.

"*Phillipe!*" roared the General. For all his apparent decrepitude, there was clearly nothing wrong with his lungs.

With magical promptitude, Phillippe appeared in the parlour doorway. The effect was heightened by the imperturbable calm of his face. "Phillippe, tea for the lady," ordered the General. "And tell Jian to make some cakes or somethin'—bread-and-butter—that sort of thing. It's not often we have a lady to tea, what?"

Something in these orders *did* seem to cause Phillippe a momentary perturbation, but he quickly mastered it. "Yes, sir," he said, and vanished as quickly as he had come. I resigned myself to tea at Cincinnatus, not sorry to see what they would make of it.

It was a peculiar affair altogether, Dear Reader. For one thing, the tea came in three different pots—one a long-spouted brass affair that gave off a strong odour of spice. At least I assumed it was tea, until the General enlightened me. "Coffee, ma'am, made in the Arab way. I had a Lascar servant years ago, and dashed if I didn't get so I preferred it to tea. Care for a cup?"

I said I preferred tea, glancing uncertainly at the other two pots. The General seemed puzzled, too, for he rounded on Phillipe, who had remained in the parlour to serve us. "What's this, what's this?" he asked. "Why are there two pots here?'

"Jian felt the lady would prefer China tea to Indian," said Phillipe, with a wooden expression.

"Of course he would," snorted the General. "Of course he would." He seemed of two minds whether this might constitute an insult to his own chosen beverage, but the Major said hastily that it was dashed generous of Jian to offer up his cherished Longjing, and I added quickly that I was very fond of China tea. So the General let it pass, devoting himself instead to plying me with cakes and bread-and-butter.

The bread-and-butter was ordinary enough, but the cakes were distinctly odd. They were pure white, triangular in shape, and possessed of a strange, gelatinous texture. I couldn't imagine what they were made of.

As I sat nibbling dubiously at one of them, the turbaned Sandeep came into the room. The small boy was with him, and at the sight of the tea-tray he let out a whoop and made a beeline for the cakes.

"Hold the line there, sir: hold the line," ordered the General, albeit in an indulgent voice. Addressing the servant, he said, "Sandeep, see the Little Fellow gets some tea and a cake or two. Have some yourself if you've a mind to." To the boy himself, he said, "Mind your drill, sir, mind your drill. Barrack room manners won't do when there's a lady present. Make your bow, say 'how d'you do,' and retreat in good order."

"We have already met," I said, and was rewarded with a flash of a shy smile. The boy sidled a step closer to address me in a confidential voice.

"We don't usually get cakes for tea," he said. "Jian makes them, but mostly just for himself. And he gets very angry if I take any without asking."

"Quite right, too," said the General, with a nod. "Too many sweets ain't good for a Little Fellow like you."

I thought this explained Phillippe's discomfiture when the General had given the order about cakes. Evidently the cook had been obliged to dip into his own private store, which he was accustomed to defend against all comers. I made a mental note to thank him later, if I got the chance.

Sandeep, meanwhile, had set about preparing two cups of tea (one rather more milk than tea) and a plate of assorted delicacies. I studied his face as he went about the work, and also that of Phillipe, standing calm and immobile against the wall in his splendid red-and-gold livery. I wondered how they felt, strangers in a strange land, serving a foreign race in this curious quasi-military fashion. The cook was apparently a foreigner, too. As I looked around the parlour, so bare of the usual Benares brasses and stuffed elephant legs and tiger-skin rugs of the returned British ex-patriate, it struck me that the General had chosen rather to bring home men as souvenirs.

Sandeep and the Little Fellow did not remain for tea, but withdrew to some nursery precinct where the Little Fellow might enjoy his refreshments in greater freedom. I noticed, however, that he managed to cram one of the cakes whole into his mouth on the way out the door. He seemed to have no objection to its texture.

The General, fortunately, had missed this manœuvre. He was telling me his daughter's tragic history (which I already knew from the Major).

"Great shame poor Lily isn't here to see him," he said. "A boy that age wants his mother, ma'am—there's no getting around it. But the Major and I between us are doing our best to bring him up. And the servants, too, of course. We're all fond of the Little Fellow, aren't we, Phillippe?"

"Yes, sir," said Phillippe. Though his expression was immobile as ever, I thought I detected a slight softening in his voice.

"Although I say it who shouldn't, he's growing up a fine little fellow," continued the General. "Does us all credit."

The Major expanded visibly at this praise, Dear Reader. For my part, I said that he appeared to be a delightful child and that children were a particular interest of mine. From there, it was an easy step to the subject of the missing boys and the Society for the Prevention of Cruelty to Children.

The General listened with interest, carrying his coffee cup to his mouth every now and then, and blotting his lips afterwards with a napkin. "Yes," he said, "of course it's not wonderful that there should be a to-do over these disappearances. I feel the local police have been very slack in the affair, ma'am: woefully slack. There's no doubt our local constabulary wants stirring up. Only I wonder at your society sending a lady to do it."

I was not surprised at his words, Dear Reader. Men of his sort typically have very traditional ideas about the things women should and should not do. But when I pointed out that the welfare of children fell naturally within the female province, I found I had misinterpreted his reservations. "I don't question your concern in the matter, ma'am. It only strikes me that in an affair of this sort, where there might be danger, a man would be a more suitable agent."

"You think there might be danger?" I asked.

The General looked somber. "It strikes me as possible, at least," he said. "You'll say I'm an old fool, getting the wind up over nothing."

He paused here, obviously expecting to be contradicted. The Major and I hurried to oblige him, whereupon he looked pleased. "It's true I've seen some queer things in my time," he said. "And this business has got some very queer features, no doubt about it. I'm not altogether sure it's a human agency we should be looking for."

The Major was once again looking pained. Clearly we were approaching once more the touchy subject of Spiritualism. I made my voice as respectful as possible as I addressed the General. "Do you think these disappearances might be supernatural in origin?"

He did not answer directly, but repeated that the business had some queer features. The Major cleared his throat. "It seems some folks think Mr. Alexis might have had a hand in the boys' disappearance, sir."

The General turned on him sharply. "They do, do they? What makes 'em think that?" And then, before the Major could answer, he added, "He's an amazing fellow, Mr. Alexis. Got powers beyond anything I've ever seen. Stands to reason that kind of a power comes at a cost."

"You think he—er—used the boys to gain power?" I asked.

"Certainly not," said the General.

I was confused, and my expression must have shown it, for he smiled at me a bit sadly. "Forgive me, ma'am. I'm wandering in my mind—not making myself clear. Hazard of old age, I'm afraid." In a brisker tone, he added, "I don't think Mr. Alexis knows a thing about the boys' disappearances, but I daresay he could tell us what happened if we asked him. Doesn't seem to have occurred to the police to do it." He snorted. "Maybe they'd rather not! Might show 'em up, what?"

"Well," I said, "I mean to call at the Priory after I leave here. And I hope to speak to Mr. Alexis as well as Lord Rodney Pierce. You may be sure that I, at least, will ask him what he thinks."

"You couldn't do better," said the General warmly. "Wonderful fellow, isn't he, Major?"

"Wonderful," echoed the Major without enthusiasm.

I was all for excusing myself at this point and heading off to the Priory, but the General wasn't letting me go that easily. "You haven't seen the gardens, ma'am," he said. "I may not be able to do much of the work myself nowadays—" he threw a dark look at his son-in-law that showed he had overheard and resented the latter's words, "—but I flatter myself they're still worth seeing."

I saw them very thoroughly, Dear Reader. As the General could only limp, our progress was necessarily slow and further limited by his pausing to find fault with much of what his gardeners had done while he was recuperating from his latest bout of illness.

"Look at this, look at this," he growled, as we paused beside an espaliered peach tree. I looked at it but could see nothing to growl about. The tree appeared absurdly productive. Its branches were so loaded with fruit that they could not have remained upright had they not been firmly tethered to the wall. To my astonishment, the General raised his stick and began striking at them. Unripe peaches pattered around our feet.

"What are you doing?" I exclaimed.

He shook his head angrily. "Shows what happens when I'm not here to see to things," he said. "These should have been thinned out weeks ago."

"But why should they be thinned?" I asked. "Won't there be more fruit if you don't?"

"Aye, but it won't be half the quality," he explained. "Or half the size, either. It's the same with roses. Unless you thin 'em down to just a few buds—the best of the lot—you get a lot of inferior flowers that aren't worth having."

It seemed a wasteful proceeding to me, Dear Reader. But I am not a gardener, and there was no denying that he was. The work might be done by others nowadays, but the overall vision had been his, and it was an impressive vision even to my inexperienced eyes.

As you may know, the English climate is both a curse and a blessing to gardeners. It is a blessing owing to its regular rains and generally moderate temperatures; a curse because the sun often fails to shine for weeks on end even in the summertime, making the ripening of all but the hardiest crops problematic. The General had laboured hard to overcome these obstacles. Besides the usual cloches and cucumber frames, he had fitted his hothouse and warm walls with a system of his own devising, in which heated water was circulated through pipes embedded in the brickwork. By supplementing the sun's rays with this artificial warmth, he boasted of growing the earliest fruits and vegetables in the county.

As proof of this, he personally bestowed on me a fine melon of the Persian variety. He also went into the rose garden and cut a dozen of its choicest blooms, making them up into a bouquet that was very beautiful to look at but (as it subsequently developed) very prickly to hold. I found both melon and bouquet very much in my way as the tour continued.

Although the General monopolized the conversation, I nonetheless managed to get in a question now and then on my own subject. I ran through my list of suspects and theories as I had done with the Major, and the General heaped contempt on all of them indiscriminately. "Have you no theory of your own, then?" I asked, letting a note of exasperation creep into my voice. Realizing it too late, I tried to sweeten my words with a bit of flattery: "With your experience, I daresay you can suggest an avenue or two that the police have neglected."

The General responded to the flattery readily enough. "Ah, and so I could, ma'am, if I were consulted," he said. "But the police haven't seen fit to make me their confidant. They think I'm too old, no doubt. You probably think I'm too old, too." He accompanied this statement with a sidelong look.

"If I thought that, I wouldn't be asking your opinion," I said.

It was a true answer as well as a diplomatic one, Dear Reader. He might be old and a tremendous egotist, but I didn't see any signs of mental decline. My words obviously pleased him, for he took my arm in a little tighter grip (we had been walking arm-in-arm about the garden under the pretence of his supporting me, though really it was more the other way around). "It takes a woman to see what lies beneath the surface," he said. "Wonderful creatures, women. See a lot we men don't."

There was a musing tone in his voice, such as had been there when he was speaking of his daughter. Taking my cue from this, I said again how much he must miss her, and what a superior woman she seemed to have been. He agreed, albeit in a preoccupied manner. "Lily was a clever girl, right enough. A pretty girl, too. In fact, you put me a bit in mind of her, ma'am. *And* of her mother before her. Ginger hair and a lively manner." He regarded me with a speculative eye.

I thought I knew where this was going, Dear Reader. "I am sure the Major must miss his wife, and your grandson his mother," I said, "but—"

The General cut ruthlessly through my words. "I can't help worrying about what'll happen to 'em when I go. I've had some health concerns this past year, though you mayn't think it to look at me." He threw me another sidelong look. "*Miss* Blackwood. That's the name on your card, ain't it? You're not married, then?"

You can imagine what an awkward question it was, Dear Reader. Rather than answering it, I sought to divert him. "The Major is a very handsome man," I said, "but he seems rather a *young* man to me. In any case, I doubt he has any thought of marrying again at present."

The General gave an exasperated snort. "Damn the Major," he said. "It wasn't him I was asking for. I was asking for *myself*." He glared at me beneath his crest of white hair.

I had a hard time controlling my jaw, Dear Reader. It kept wanting to drop open. "Oh," I said, inadequately. "Oh, I see."

"You're a good-looking woman. Still young, too," pursued the General. "My wife's been dead a couple decades now. In all that time I haven't thought of marrying again, but I'm not so old that I couldn't think of doing it yet."

I supposed I *was* young from his perspective, Dear Reader. It was flattering to be desired, but between you and me, I would have found it more flattering if his desire had been based on something more than an hour's acquaintance and something deeper than admiration for my (comparatively) youthful looks. Women are often called vain and shallow, Dear Reader: I have been often called so myself. But in our hearts, I think most of us would rather be desired for our true selves rather than mere externals.

This might have led me to reflect upon my relationship with Inspector Harper, and the associated pleasures thereof, had not the General been waiting for me to say something. Obviously it could not be the truth. I was in no position to accept his putative proposal, even had I wanted to. It suited me to keep him as an ally, however, if not as a husband. So I searched for a diplomatic way of temporizing.

"You honour me, sir," I said gravely. "But at present, I really cannot think of anything except those unfortunate children. I must at least discover what happened to them, even if I fail to bring them home safely. After I have done my duty, it will be time enough to consider *personal* matters."

Since he was a military man, I supposed the concept of duty would weigh with him, and so it did. He said my feelings did me credit. "Mind you, I don't see a quick end to this business," he said, with a shake of his head. "Or a happy one, either, if it comes to that."

"Don't you?" I asked, looking at him. His profile was toward me as he inspected the leaves of a rose tree. It was a fine, military–looking profile, though the pallor of his complexion made it look as though it were sculpted out of something less substantial than human flesh. If I had really been wanting to marry him, Dear Reader, I would have proposed eloping immediately, lest he might not live to marry me in a more formal fashion.

"No," he said. "Mind you, it might be just the croaking of an old man who's seen a lot of sad things in his time. Caused 'em, too," he added matter-of-factly. "You send men to their death pretty often in my business."

"You think the boys are dead, then?"

He shook his head, but not in a way that negated the question. "It wouldn't surprise me," he said, after a pause. "Again, though, it might just be the croaking of an old man."

"Is there any theory the police have failed to consider? Any person you yourself might suspect?"

Again there was a pause. "If I had any advice for the police," he said, "I'd advise 'em not to waste time on my poor servants, or Mr. Alexis, or any other foreigner about the place. I'd tell 'em to look closer to home."

"Closer to home," I echoed. "What do you mean?"

He made an impatient gesture. "I mean that villages like Ainsworth might look pretty on the surface, but there's a deal of ugliness if you only know where to look. I've seen cannibal savages that look civilized next to some of your English villagers. You can see it for yourself if you look for it. Weakness, ignorance, and prejudice, all aggravated by inbreeding."

"I suppose that *might* be so," I said cautiously. "I haven't seen a lot of cannibal savages to compare."

This caused him to embark on a lengthy disquisition on the influence of blood and breeding. "It's blood that tells every time," he said conclusively. "You hear a lot of talk about the white race being superior to the coloured, but that's all nonsense in my opinion. Why, look at my own servants, Sandeep and Phillipe—aye, and Jian, too. Best of their types, all of 'em, and worth a hundred of your pasty-skinned English lackeys. And why?"

"Because of blood?" I said obediently.

"Exactly! It's the blood that tells. Good breeding's good breeding, whatever the colour of the skin."

I suggested mildly that whatever the merits of the blood, education and upbringing might play a rôle, too. The General said that was exactly his point. His arguments here became a little confused, but I gathered that if the blood were good enough, the other qualities were magnified in proportion.

"I see," I said. "So in that case, one might suppose that the native Ainsworth culture would breed a lesser sort of man. One prone to violence or debauchery, perhaps."

"It might," said the General somberly. "Or if not that, weakness generally. Look at the boys themselves, ma'am. You said yourself one was a cripple. And the other two—well, if they weren't criminals, then at least they were criminally inclined."

Now I felt we were getting somewhere, Dear Reader.

"You believe the character of the boys played a rôle in their disappearance," I said. "That is what I myself believe. The Vicar thinks otherwise, however."

The General snorted. "The Vicar! What does he know of men? Or of boys, either, for that matter?"

As spiritual leader of the parish, I thought he might know quite a lot, Dear Reader, but I refrained from saying so. "I wonder how much investigating the police have done on that score," I said. "Of the boys' own friends and families, I mean."

The General said he doubted they had done very much. I took his words with a grain of salt, however. He might have been a power in the neighbourhood once, but as he himself had noted, the police hadn't made a confidant of him in this affair. And I couldn't really blame them, Dear Reader. Even in his prime, he would have been the kind of man who would insist on having things all his own way and make a lot of trouble in any joint endeavour.

Still, I was grateful to him for having given me an idea or two. I wasn't quite so grateful for the melon and bouquet, which I had been lugging around for an hour now and was quite ready to lay aside. So I thanked him profusely and said I must be heading to the Priory if I meant to call there that day.

My departure was delayed by the General, who insisted on escorting me to the gig and handing me in as though it had been a state carriage. The Major and Little Fellow attended on this ceremony, and so did all the servants. Among them was a white-clad figure with a face the colour of old ivory and a long pigtail. Presuming this was Jian the cook, I paused to say a word of thanks for the tea and cakes before stepping into the gig. His English wasn't as good as Phillipe's or Sandeep's, but he made up for it by bowing and smiling repeatedly, like an automaton. He then pressed a small package into my hand.

It proved, on inspection, to contain more of the glutinous cakes.

As the gig rattled down the drive, I glanced back at Cincinnatus in its verdant setting of fruit and flowers. Near the hedge, an apron-clad man was working with a set of clippers. I identified him as the same servant I had seen earlier tying up vines. Unlike the house servants, he appeared to be a native Englishman. Apparently, the General's prejudice did not extend to his gardening staff.

As he had done before, the man stopped working and stood watching until the gig and I had passed out of sight.

# CHAPTER NINE

The Priory was a wholly different proposition from Cincinnatus, Dear Reader. It was a much larger and grander place, for one thing. And rather than being Spartan in its appointments, it was furnished with taste and an apparent disregard for anything as mundane as cost.

In the same way, Lord Rodney Pierce was a wholly different proposition from General Whitmore.

He was around my own age—well along in his middle years—a plump gentleman with fair shoulder-length hair and long-lashed eyes of a vivid blue. His mouth was beautiful, too, delicate and clear-cut. He had a habit of twitching it into a nervous smile as a preliminary to speech, then shutting his eyes and opening them very wide, as though he were astonished by the words coming out of his mouth.

I thought it was a happy circumstance that he had been born a gentleman of means. He seemed too shy and sensitive a creature to make his way in a world that is notoriously unkind to men of his predilection. I refer to his predilection for his own sex, Dear

Reader, for that was a matter about which I had no doubt within seconds of meeting him. One cannot always judge by externals, of course—but then again, sometimes one can.

"You have a most beautiful home, Lord Rodney," I told him. It was no empty praise, Dear Reader. Every chair and table and cabinet was a museum piece, every room a miracle of color and proportion. As a whole, it argued strongly against Miss Douglas's contention that a home without a woman's touch must necessarily be lacking.

Lord Rodney accepted my praise with a flash of his nervous smile. "I am glad you admire it, Miss Blackwood," he said. "I have laboured long and hard on it, certainly. Although it has been a family holding for centuries, the Priory was in a neglected state when I assumed care of it. My elder brother's seat is in Lincolnshire, and it is there that my family has naturally concentrated their efforts through the years. But I always thought this place offered possibilities for someone with the imagination to see them."

I warmly complimented him upon his imagination. This had the effect of relaxing him somewhat, for his speech became less mannered and the trick of his eyes and mouth less pronounced. "May I offer you tea?" he asked.

I had just had tea with the General, Dear Reader, but that did not stop me from accepting Lord Rodney's offer. I can drink tea anytime. In any case, I was curious to see how this, too, might differ from Cincinnatus.

Tea at the Priory turned out to be a ritual closely resembling a high church sacrament. A series of trays containing the tea service, cakes, and supplementary dainties was brought into the drawing room by a stately procession of footmen, all immensely tall and all (I could not help noticing) extremely good-looking. The tea service was a magnificent blue-and-gold set which, Lord Rodney modestly noted, had once belonged to Catherine the Great.

As I was the only lady present, it fell to me to make the tea, which I did in fear and trembling lest I accidentally damage one of his museum pieces. It was a relief to set my cup and saucer aside and proceed to business.

My business was already known to Lord Rodney, as it happened. "I have been expecting you," he said. "You must know that gossip flies about very rapidly in a village like Ainsworth." With feeling, he added, "I wish it were some happier cause that brought you here."

"I wish it were, too," I said. With some curiosity, I added, "Do you mind telling me how you knew I was coming?"

"I had a note from the Vicar," he explained, readily enough. "He said you were working to influence the local populace in favour of calling in Scotland Yard. It is a measure that should have been taken long ago, in my opinion."

"Then I am surprised that your opinion should not have prevailed, given your position here in Ainsworth," I said. Indeed, Dear Reader, it struck me as a suspicious circumstance, now that I had seen the style in which he lived.

Lord Rodney stirred his tea with a moody air. "Probably it might, if I cared to assert myself," he said. "But I have been uncertain how far I am entitled to do so. I have no real experience with crime or criminals. It is true that my family have played the rôle of squire hereabouts—but that is more of an assumed authority than a real one. It is very difficult."

I said I could see the difficulty. "Have you yourself any theory about the disappearances?"

"No, none," he said at once. "Indeed, I could not imagine one child disappearing under such circumstances, let alone three. Neither could I imagine that the police would utterly fail to uncover any clue to the crimes—if, indeed, there have been crimes."

"Do you think the police have been lax?" I asked, the memory of the General's denunciation vivid in my memory.

Lord Rodney said he did not think so. "If I have any qualms about calling in Scotland Yard at this point," he said, "it is only because I cannot imagine what more they could do that has not already been done. I have followed the matter personally, you understand, even suggesting additional measures the police might take. It was I, for instance, who suggested bloodhounds might be of use in tracing George Hubbard when first he disappeared."

"That sounds like a good idea," I remarked.

"It proved better in conception than execution," he said ruefully. "The wretched hounds led us in a circle, all around the village and right back to the Hubbards' cottage. Having first detoured to every orchard and berry patch in the village from which Georgie was accustomed to steal fruit!"

"Including your own?" I asked.

"Oh, yes," he said. "My head gardener was accustomed to wax eloquent on the subject. To hear him tell it, Georgie was more destructive than the ten plagues of Egypt."

I looked at Lord Rodney closely. To all appearances, he was oblivious to the implications of this speech. "You can't have appreciated that," I said.

"No," he agreed. "But it is understandable behaviour, given the boy's upbringing. If you saw the condition these people live in, Miss Blackwood! One does what one can, but I have learned through bitter experience that philanthropy must be tailored to the individual. There are individuals on whom one may confer benefits without hesitation—people who will receive them gratefully and use them wisely. And then there are people like the Hubbards."

I nodded to show my understanding. Lord Rodney went on, with another dramatic closing and opening of his eyes. "One of my earliest acts of philanthropy was to rebuild the whole row of cottages that stands near the mill. The Hubbards' was among them and quite the worst of the lot. I employed a good architect and consulted with the Vicar and others in authority, to determine what would best suit the needs of their inhabitants. I strove to incorporate features that would make their lives easier and more comfortable. And what has been the result?"

Once more he shut his eyes, then opened them wide in his habitual gesture of incredulity. "In the case of Widow Turwell, or old Mr. Blaine, my work was not wasted. If you go by their cottages today, you will find them beautifully kept and looking quite as good as when they were first built—better, even, in some cases. But if you go by Mrs. Hubbard's—well, you might be forgiven for supposing pigs lived there rather than human beings."

"It's a difficult problem," I commented.

"It is," he agreed with feeling. "In retrospect, I sometimes wonder if we ought to have removed George from that environment early on. It might have been better for the boy, and certainly there were factors that would have justified it. But one hesitates to remove a child from his mother's care, however unsatisfactory that mother may be."

I agreed that this, too, was a difficult problem.

"And there is another aspect to it as well," continued Lord Rodney. "George's presence, problematic though it may have been, still seems to have served as a check on Mrs. Hubbard's worst excesses. She *drinks*," he explained with another widening of his eyes. "And her son's disappearance has prompted her to drink all the more. Last time I called, she stormed and wept in the most maudlin way, begging me to bring her little boy home. One would like nothing better, of course, but how does one manage it?'

I said it sounded as though he had been very conscientious in the matter. "I mean to call on Mrs. Hubbard myself while I am here," I told Lord Rodney. "From what you say, it sounds as if it would be better for me to wait and go tomorrow morning. By now she may have already begun drinking."

Lord Rodney said this was more than likely. "But you must be prepared to find her fuddled with drink no matter how early you call," he warned. "It is becoming a chronic condition, and I don't know where it will end. An asylum of some sort, perhaps. But one hesitates to take such a step when the poor woman has already had so much to endure."

It struck me that Lord Rodney was really the epitome of the conscientious landlord: almost too conscientious for his own good. "Was Dan Pyle's home environment as bad as George Hubbard's?" I asked.

Lord Rodney shook his head emphatically. "The Pyles aren't tenants of mine, but I *have* called on them about this matter, as I conceived to be my duty. I wouldn't at all consider them in the same class as the Hubbards. Mr. Pyle is employed as a dairyman and has the reputation of being a hard worker and an honest man. Mrs. Pyle's reputation is not quite so good, for I have heard some of the village women criticize her for allowing her children to run wild. But I know no real harm of the family."

"Didn't Dan indulge in the same kind of pranks as George?" I asked.

I knew from other accounts that he did, Dear Reader—and that "pranks" was a mild term for some of them. But I was curious to see whether Lord Rodney would minimize them, too.

"I believe he did," he said. "But they affected me only at secondhand. That is to say, my head gardener complained of both boys, and I recall the Vicar being rather upset about some prank they played last Whitsuntide. The General, too, had complained about them once or twice."

He spoke with seeming matter-of-factness, but I wondered if this might be a deliberate attempt to implicate his neighbours. "Are the Pyles as upset as Mrs. Hubbard about their son's disappearance?" was my next question.

"They are, but they don't show it the same way. Mr. Pyle is a silent kind of man who doesn't say much under any circumstances.

His wife, on the other hand, is all too voluble. I had a hard time following her digressions, but she seems inclined to attribute her son's disappearance to the malice of her neighbours."

I was interested to hear this, Dear Reader, for it coincided with the General's theory. I marked it down as a lead that might bear following up. "And what of Peter Dray? How are *his* parents taking his disappearance?"

Lord Rodney looked uncomfortable. "I fear their chief reaction has been one of relief," he said.

"Relief?" I exclaimed.

"I'm afraid so. Oh, it's natural enough under the circumstances. Mr. Dray is one of these big, bluff men who has no patience with weakness. And his wife is little better. She has seven children besides Peter and is currently expecting another. Peter, owing to his infirmities, demanded more of her than the others—and she was inclined to resent it."

"How sad," I said.

In fact it struck me as more than sad, Dear Reader: it seemed downright sinister. The General had not been wrong in saying there was ugliness beneath Ainsworth's Arcadian surface.

"At any rate, there were those who *did* treat the boy kindly," I said, as much to myself as Lord Rodney. "Though unfortunately it has recoiled on them since his disappearance."

He already knew about Ellen and agreed it was a great shame. "Though I hadn't heard it had gone so far as open harassment of the poor woman," he said. "Well, that makes another argument for calling in Scotland Yard. I shall send a note around to Sir Owen tonight, urging that it be done without delay."

He was so sincere, Dear Reader, that I felt almost ashamed of still suspecting him. But there remained a niggling doubt in my mind which his words had not quite assuaged. In some ways, in fact, my doubts were rather increased. Was it not a suspicious circumstance that the bloodhounds had traced Georgie's steps through Lord Rodney's own orchard and berry patches? And if he had himself proposed using them, who knows what misdirection he might have practiced to throw them off the track?

At that moment, I found myself missing Susan and Jenny and Inspector Harper. I wished they were all here to hear these people talk, or at least where I could tell them what had been said and get their opinions. Of course I meant to consult them when I returned home, but it wouldn't be the same.

While I was meditating on this, there was the sound of voices in the adjoining room. It was divided from the drawing room by a set of red velvet curtains, and I looked up just in time to see the curtains part, revealing a dramatic figure. A very tall, very thin gentleman with dark hair and eyes deeply shadowed stood regarding Lord Rodney and me with somber intensity. If you think of Mr. Poe's celebrated portrait, Dear Reader, you will have some idea of the effect.

"Mr. Alexis!" exclaimed Lord Rodney.

# CHAPTER TEN

M r. Alexis, having given Lord Rodney and me time to appreciate the picture he made in the doorway, came toward us across the drawing room. Not only did he look theatrical, he moved in a theatrical way, like a Shakespearean actor striding across the stage.

"I did not suppose you would be awake for another hour," said Lord Rodney in accents of surprise. "Otherwise I would have sent word that we were having tea." To me, he explained, "Mr. Alexis is a celebrated Trance Medium. As his work entails late hours and much psychic force, he is accustomed to spend afternoons resting quietly in his room."

Mr. Alexis smiled wanly. "Today I could not rest. Something told me my presence was required downstairs. This lady," he said, subjecting me to a deep, soulful stare. "She has perhaps been asking about me?"

"Oh, no," I assured him. "I was just talking with Lord Rodney."

In truth I was very glad to see Mr. Alexis, Dear Reader, but I felt no need to minister to his vanity by saying so. "May I offer you a cup of tea?" I added politely, indicating the tea-tray in front of me.

"Yes, thank you," he said, taking a seat beside Lord Rodney.

Up close, I could see that the dramatic shadowing around his eyes was artificial. I couldn't really fault him for that, Dear Reader. I use cosmetic aids myself to enhance my appearance—though as Letitia Blackwood I strive to look more natural than as Madame Fox, Spiritualist. But if I had no fault to find with Mr. Alexis's use of cosmetics, I still was inclined to fault him on general principles.

It's my opinion that men have no business being Mediums. We women have few enough occupations available to us as it is. Men get all the better ones, with a monopoly on the church, the law, and the military. I was making a decent living at Spiritualism nowadays, but for many years it had been an uphill battle with the outcome far from certain. On those grounds alone, I was inclined to resent Mr. Alexis for infringing on territory that properly belonged to me and my sisters.

"I don't know if you are a believer in Spiritualism, Miss Blackwood?" queried Lord Rodney. "Mr. Alexis has made a believer of most of us hereabouts. His powers are quite extraordinary."

Mr. Alexis smiled faintly and waved his hand in a deprecating manner, as though wafting away the compliment.

I told both men (sincerely) that I was very interested in Spiritualism. This caused Mr. Alexis to turn his soulful gaze upon me again.

"I thought so," he said. "As a Sensitive, I can generally tell."

I encouraged him to tell me more along these lines and listened to his response with a feeling that was half contempt and half an uneasy suspicion that I would have said pretty much the same things had our rôles been reversed. It was curious to find myself on the other side of the fence, so to speak.

I let him tell me all about sitting for the Czar of Russia and the late French Empress, then spoke with enthusiasm. "But this is wonderful," I said. "How fortunate that you should be in Ainsworth at the very time your powers are most needed!"

"Miss Blackwood is making inquiries about the boys who have disappeared," explained Lord Rodney.

He went on to tell Mr. Alexis all about the Society for the Prevention of Cruelty to Children and my supposed rôle in it. He had it all down perfectly, Dear Reader, after only one hearing. It was a remarkable feat of memory. I found myself more and more impressed by him.

"I have told her I shall throw my own weight behind her cause," continued Lord Rodney. "I plan to write Sir Owen Lecker tonight and ask him to call upon Scotland Yard without further delay.

"Unless you have any objection, Mr. Alexis?" I asked sweetly.

Mr. Alexis had been looking down at his teacup, but at these words the dark eyes beneath their shadowed lids very quickly turned toward me. There was a pause, and then he spoke. "Why should I have any objection?" he asked.

I opened my own eyes very wide. "Why, because you are privy to information that we have not. Indeed, given your wonderful powers, it seems surprising that you have not been able to shed light on the mystery before now."

He gave me a weary smile, Dear Reader. It was precisely the smile I myself would have given some skeptic who was making a nuisance of himself. "Unfortunately, Spiritual Communication is subject to rules of its own," he said. "I may ask questions of the Spirits, but they themselves decide whether to answer. So far, unfortunately, they have chosen to remain silent about this particular matter."

"How very strange," I said. "And how very disappointing. Have you any idea why they would refuse to speak?"

"No," he said shortly. "I don't."

Lord Rodney was looking guilty. "Perhaps I ought to have pursued the matter more diligently," he said. "My only acquaintance with Spiritualism previously was in the form of reading tea-leaves and similar parlour games, and of course it would never occur to one to apply *those* to serious matters. But it is different with you and your powers, Mr. Alexis. Perhaps we ought to broach the matter tonight?"

"Perhaps," said Mr. Alexis, contracting his brow. "But it may be that I shall be unable to sit tonight. I sense a disturbance in the Ether at present." He just glanced at me as he spoke these words, Dear Reader. "And of course missing my usual rest this afternoon does not bode well for a successful sitting, either."

Lord Rodney looked disappointed, and I expressed my own disappointment, too. It seemed I had gone too far in needling him and set him on his guard. I had no wish to do that, Dear Reader. Even if I did not care to expose him as a fraud, as the Major had suggested, I would still have liked to attend one of his sittings. It is always useful to see what the competition is getting up to.

To this end, I set myself to buttering him up. "I would *love* to be present at one of your sittings, Mr. Alexis. General Whitmore has told me so much about them. You were staying with him at Cincinnatus until recently, were you not?"

Mr. Alexis admitted that he was, Dear Reader. His manner was still discouraging, but I persevered. "The General is a remarkable old gentleman, is he not? For all that his health seems so frail, his mind is as keen as ever. Of course he is a thorough believer in Spiritualism. And more especially the Spiritualism that *you* practice, Mr. Alexis." I gave him a winning smile. "In fact, he urged me to consult you professionally in the matter of the missing boys. Now that I have seen you, and heard Lord Rodney's account of your powers, I have no hesitation about doing so. We must solve this mystery by whatever means necessary. Children's lives may depend on it."

Lord Rodney added his own urgings to mine: "I do wish you would, Mr. Alexis. It can do no harm to ask the Spirits, at any rate."

Mr. Alexis was looking troubled now, Dear Reader. Like all his expressions, it had a theatrical quality, but when he spoke his voice held a note of genuine emotion. "My dear Lord Rodney, I only wish that were true," he said. "But I have learnt through experience that there are forces it is better not to meddle with. In the matter of these disappearances, I *have* caught glimpses now and then of what might lie behind them. But they were glimpses of something very ugly—so ugly that I shrank from exploring further. I will do so if you ask it of me, but not willingly."

At this appeal, Lord Rodney appeared to hesitate, but I had no such scruples. "Oh, do it!" I urged him. "Do it for the children."

I think Mr. Alexis would still have liked to refuse, Dear Reader. But when Lord Rodney added his urgings to mine, he had no choice except to comply. "Very well," he said. "I will make the attempt. But not tonight," he added quickly. "Such an effort requires my Powers to be at their height. And that cannot be done without preparation."

It seemed pretty clear that he still distrusted me, Dear Reader. Delaying was merely another way of refusing, and a very good way, too, since I did not plan to stay in the neighbourhood more than another day.

I told him so quite frankly, since there seemed no point in dissembling. "Do please let me know if anything comes of your efforts, Mr. Alexis," I said. "And if I am able to return at some future time, I shall still hope to attend one of your sittings."

He promised that I might, accompanying his words with a soulful smile. Of course, his promise cost him nothing. He might use the same excuse indefinitely and so escape any future encounter in the same way.

It seemed he hadn't only profited financially from his sittings with the General, Dear Reader. He had also acquired a firm grasp of Fabian strategy.[5]

---

5 *I.e.*, that pursued by Roman General Quintus Fabius Maximus during the Second Punic War. He avoided open battle, but instead used a series of limited engagements and delaying tactics to negate the military superiority of his adversary.—*Ed.*

# CHAPTER ELEVEN

After taking leave of Lord Rodney and Mr. Alexis, I ordered William to drive me back to the Vicarage. My arrival there was timely, for the Douglases were just sitting down to dinner. I sat down, too, as soon as I had deposited the melon and bouquet in the scullery and washed my hands.

Of course I was not very hungry after taking afternoon tea twice in a single afternoon. But that did not matter, as the menu was scarcely appetizing. It consisted of beef boiled grey without being measurably tenderized, and a bread pudding to which the term "pudding" could be applied only by courtesy. Some essential ingredient appeared to have been omitted from its composition— sugar, at a guess.

As I partook sparingly of these viands, I reflected that Ellen was a much inferior cook to her sister. Then I reminded myself that she was presently doing all the household work, as well as labouring under conditions of emotional strain. Her best cooking might be much better than this. I hoped it might be, Dear Reader—for the Douglases' sake even more than my own.

I kept thinking of Susan during that dinner, wishing again that she was there for me to discuss the day's events with. To that end, there was a surprise awaiting me. When we retired to the parlour, Miss Douglas casually mentioned that Ellen's sister had come down from London to visit her.

"Her sister!" I exclaimed. "Here?"

"Yes," said Miss Douglas, looking at me rather curiously. "Her sister from London. You are acquainted with her, are you not?"

"Yes, I am," I said. "I must go and pay my respects."

━━┼┼━━

The two sisters were seated at the kitchen table, talking, when I came into the room. Or rather Susan was talking, and Ellen was looking down at her hands. They both looked up as I entered.

"Good evening, Mrs. Mason," I said, speaking to Ellen but looking at Susan with raised brows. "I understand you have a visitor."

Susan smiled rather grimly. "Yes, ma'am," she said. "My employer is out of London just now and gave me and the other servants a holiday. So I decided I'd come see how Ellen was doing."

I was very glad to see her, Dear Reader. Indeed, her presence seemed like a direct answer to a prayer.

I would have been even gladder if we might have dispensed with Ellen's company. As long as she was with us, we were obliged to keep up the pretence of being bare acquaintances.

Susan seemed to find it hampering, too. Eventually she suggested, in a self-conscious way, that she wished to visit her niece's grave in the churchyard before it grew quite dark.

"I'd like to see it, too," I said, rising to the cue.

Ellen might have accompanied us, but Susan discouraged this kindly but firmly. "You'd better set the bread for breakfast," she told her. "And if you'll start the water for the dinner dishes, I'll help you wash them when I come in."

The churchyard was an excellent place for a private conversation, Dear Reader. It was located on a hill with a clear view of the country all around. No eavesdropper could possibly steal up on us unawares. And of course, it made an appropriately Gothic setting for a case that seemed more and more to embody the conventions of the genre.

Before beginning our conversation, we paid our respects to the late Becky Mason. It had been long enough since the funeral for her headstone to be erected: a small stone tablet topped with the figure of a lamb and inscribed with the girl's name. I had brought along the roses the General had given me, and together Susan and I laid them on the grave. This ceremony complete, we withdrew to a nearby bench, where I described to Susan all I had learned that day during my various interviews.

"I hardly know whom to suspect," I said, at the conclusion of my report. "They all appear to have points against them."

Susan thought the General's *ménage* ranked a few points ahead of the rest. "All those foreigners," she explained. "It's likely enough one of them is a bad hat."

"But they've lived here in Ainsworth for years," I said. "If one of them were criminally minded, why did he wait until now to act?"

"Lunacy," suggested Susan.

"If it's lunacy, it might be anybody," I said. "English *or* foreign-born. In my opinion, the behaviour of the bloodhounds is worth considering. Were they deliberately decoyed out of the way? And was that done in the first instance so nobody would bother with the second and third? I got a little *frisson* down my spine when Lord Rodney told me about it."

Susan said that was hardly evidence. "At any rate, it seems likely the Inspector will be on the job soon enough. Or one of the other Scotland Yard men will be. And they'll find out the truth pretty quick, I don't doubt."

"*If* Lord Rodney does what he says," I agreed. "But I couldn't help wondering if his promise to act was just a feint. Otherwise, why wouldn't he have acted before now? And even if he does act now, it would be easy enough for him to word his suggestion so the local authorities ignore it. In fact, he might have been doing that all along."

Susan agreed this was possible. "If he was just wanting you to go away, he might do that," she said. "It sounds as though the Medium-man wanted you to go away, at any rate!"

"Yes," I agreed. "But that might have been simply because I cast aspersions on his powers. I'm afraid I let my impulses get the better of me there. It would have been wiser to play along and not show how skeptical I was. He was ready enough to be agreeable until he learned why I was there."

"*That's* suspicious, if you like," said Susan.

I paused to review the conversation in my mind. "It is, isn't it?" I said. "I hadn't quite made the connection until now, but you're right, Susan. It was when Lord Rodney told him I was making inquiries about the boys that he started to turn chilly."

We both thought about that for a while. "If it was him who took the boys, why would he want them?" asked Susan. "And what would he do with them?"

"Miss Douglas seems to think he is of the same persuasion as Lord Rodney," I said. "Which might well be the case, though I tend to think myself that his preferences might be more—ah—flexible. But that would give him a motive, though not what I'd consider a good one. Just because a man's tastes don't conform to the average doesn't mean he's a criminal monster. And even assuming he is, and that he makes a hobby of abducting and murdering boys, what would he do with them afterwards? Mr. Alexis is a stranger here. Disposing of the bodies would be twice as hard for him as for somebody who lived here and was familiar with the neighbourhood."

"You say he's been here a long time, though," said Susan.

"True," I said. "Over a year by the sound of it. And the boys didn't start disappearing until a few months ago. Yes, I suppose it might be possible. At any rate, I'd find that more believable than the idea that he sacrifices them to augment his psychic powers."

"It was the General who suggested that?"

"He didn't actually suggest it," I said, "but I thought that's what he was implying. Still, it's quite likely I mistook his meaning. Because later, he seemed to suggest it was a villager who was responsible—or more than one villager."

Susan said she thought *that* was hardly likely.

"I wouldn't be so sure," I said. "According to Lord Rodney, Peter Dray's parents seem actually relieved that he's disappeared. And though Georgie and Dan's families are upset enough, there are plenty of other people around who might be relieved that they disappeared, too."

Susan nodded soberly. "Put that way, it makes sense. More sense, really, than if you wanted to pin it on one of the local nobs. They might be annoyed at having a few apples and peaches pinched from their orchards, but it'd be the people who lived around the boys and had to rub elbows with them daily who really suffered."

I said I meant to call on the boys' families the next day. "It might be unnecessary if Scotland Yard is taking over the case, but I'd still like to see them while I'm here. Do you want to come with me?"

Susan said she would. "I can help Ellen with breakfast first, and some of the housework. And I'd like to get back in time to help her with dinner, too. God knows she could use some help in that department," she added with feeling. "Boiled beef needn't be as tough as shoe leather if it's cooked properly. And I couldn't eat a bite of the pudding."

I said it had made the cakes I had gotten at the General's seem quite appetizing by comparison. That made me recall I was still carrying a packet of the things in my pocket. Retrieving it, I offered Susan one. She took it and nibbled it meditatively while I ate the other.

"Not bad," she said. "The texture's odd, as you say, but the flavour's all right."

Once we had finished our cakes, we returned to the Vicarage, having agreed to meet on the morrow to visit Mrs. Hubbard, the Pyles, and the Drays.

⚊⚊

Mrs. Hubbard's cottage was our first stop. It wasn't yet noon, but her eyes were already glazed, and I could smell the alcohol on her breath. "Come in, come in," she said, gesturing largely toward the cottage interior.

I took one look—and one smell—and backed away. "It's a fine day," I said. "Why don't we sit on the doorstep?"

Even the doorstep was unwholesome, being adorned with dead leaves and streaks of what I sincerely hoped was mud. I spread out my handkerchief and sat on it, so as not to spoil my lavender voile. I had had it made new for the trip and did not care to sully it with Mrs. Hubbard's housekeeping, or lack thereof.

I explained to Mrs. Hubbard about the Society I was representing and my purpose in calling on her. But it wasn't clear she understood me. "Where's my boy? That's what I'd like to know. Where's Georgie?" she demanded, thrusting her face close to mine and enveloping me in a cloud of alcohol fumes.

"That is what we hope to find out," I said, drawing back as far as I could.

"He never did nobody any harm," she said, with an air of defiance. "Don't care what anybody says. He was a good boy."

"Of course he was," I said soothingly. "And I'd like you to tell me all about him, Mrs. Hubbard. We need information about his friends, and his pastimes, and what kind of boy he really was."

But I might as well have saved my breath, Dear Reader. If Mrs. Hubbard knew any of these things, she wasn't telling. She only reiterated stubbornly that her son was a good boy.

"What do you think has happened to him?" I asked instead. "Do you think he has run away?"

In a weak moment, Mrs. Hubbard admitted this might be possible. "He's done it before," she said. "Just for a lark. Got all the way to Portsmouth once, and then came back." Then, with a return to belligerence, she added, "But where is he, then? Where's Georgie? That's what *I* want to know."

I glanced at Susan in a meaning way. She nodded, and while Mrs. Hubbard continued to bewail her son's disappearance, she quietly got up and slipped inside the cottage. A short time later she reappeared on the doorstep, her nose wrinkled expressively. She gave me a short nod, then sat back down on the other side of Mrs. Hubbard.

"Is there anyone whom you suspect might have played a rôle in your son's disappearance?" I asked.

Mrs. Hubbard said she didn't know, she was sure. "He was a good boy," she repeated, dissolving into tears.

As I was sitting on my handkerchief, I couldn't very well loan it to her. I contented myself with patting her arm, a part of her that looked comparatively clean. "Don't despair," I said. "I have spoken with Lord Rodney, and he is throwing his weight behind our cause. The local authorities will be compelled to call in Scotland Yard, and then perhaps we will get answers."

"Scotland Yard," she said, rearing back and showing the whites of her eyes. "What do they think he's done?" With increasing agitation, she added, "Lord Rodney didn't care if Georgie took some of his fruit now and then. He told me so himself. And as for Georgie breaking his window with his catapult—that was just a mistake. It's all a mistake, I tell you."

"Very likely," I said, looking eloquently at Susan.

As soon as possible, the two of use made our excuses to Mrs. Hubbard, though that was a mere formality. She had lapsed into silence and sat staring out at the weed-filled cottage yard, seeming hardly to notice our leaving.

"Well," I said, as we walked away, "what a beautiful thing is a mother's love."

Susan grimaced. "It's enough to turn your stomach," she said. "So's her house. No thanks for making *me* go inside rather than you," she added sourly.

I told her it had been a heroic act, for which I would eternally honour her. "Did you find anything suggestive?"

Susan shrugged. "Some of his clothes are still there. That'd seem to show he hadn't run away, though maybe we shouldn't refine too much on it. A boy that age might not think to take extra clothes. But . . . .." She paused, looking at me out of the corner of her eye.

"But what?" I asked.

"His penknife's still there. *And* his catapult."

"The one he broke Lord Rodney's window with," I said. "Yes, you wouldn't think he'd leave that behind, would you? Or his knife, either."

I mused a little as we went along together. "Lord Rodney didn't mention the broken window when I was there yesterday," I said. "I wonder if that means anything."

Susan laughed shortly. "He probably just didn't have time to list everything the boy had done in the way of damage! A regular limb of Satan, by all accounts." In an altered tone, she added, "Mrs. Hubbard certainly seemed to take against the notion of calling in Scotland Yard, didn't she? For all she's so eager to get her son back?"

"Yes, that's suggestive, too. Well, make a note of it, and let's see what the Pyles have to say."

# CHAPTER TWELVE

The Pyle cottage was markedly better than the Hubbards', Dear Reader, inside and out. Their yard was thriftily planted with rows of pole beans and vegetable marrows, and when Mrs. Pyle invited Susan and me inside, we found ourselves in a room that was admirably clean, though dim and sparsely furnished.

The family had just finished dinner, which they took midday in the country style. Mr. Pyle, a burly man with a shy, downcast manner, gave us a quick nod of greeting and then retreated to a seat beside the fireplace. A couple of small boys, evidently Dan's younger brothers, stood staring at us with round eyes. They seemed disposed to hang about and listen, but their mother shooed them outside, whereupon they dispersed with shrieks into their neighbour's yard.

"It's criminal," Mrs. Pyle told us. "The police had ought to have found Dan by now, and the other boys, too. I can't think what's stopping them." She was small and stout with prominent pale-green eyes like gooseberries. A single tear ran down her cheek as she spoke, which she wiped impatiently away with a corner of her apron. "They made out as how Dan must have run away, but you'll never make me believe that. Not without a word to his mother all this time."

Thinking of Georgie's knife and catapult, I asked her if any of her son's belongings had vanished with him. "Oh, aye," she said, clearly missing the significance of the question. "His hoop's gone, for one thing."

Her husband cleared his throat. "Thought I saw Jem and Bill playing with that hoop today," he remarked. "Outside in the yard."

Mrs. Pyle said it was no matter. "For if his hoop's there, *he's* gone," she stated. "Gone since Midsummer, and not a word have we had from the police. Criminal, that's what it is."

"Do you have any idea what might have happened to him?"

Mr. Pyle threw his wife a look that seemed to have a warning in it. If so, she did not heed it. "So I do," she said at once. "I don't like to think he's come to harm, but if he has, I can tell you there's them hereabouts that wished him ill." She jerked her head toward the window. "Old Mrs. Seward across the way with her flowers, for one. Made a regular fuss if the boys so much as set foot in her yard. Children are children, that's what *I* say. You can't blame 'em for wanting to run about and explore."

I said that by all accounts, Dan had been a very adventurous boy. Mrs. Pyle agreed that he was remarkably high-spirited. "But not vicious," she added quickly. "The way some people talk, you'd think he was a regular bad boy like Georgie Hubbard. Now *he* was a vicious one if you like."

"Did the two boys often play together?"

Mrs. Pyle looked uncomfortable. "Now and again, ma'am. But I didn't like it, and I beg you'll believe I didn't encourage it. If Dan *did* find himself in a bit of trouble (as it might be once in a while), it was only because Georgie led him into it."

I asked what kind of trouble Georgie had led him into and was entertained with the same accounts of garden and orchard raids

I had gotten from everyone else. "Lord Rodney and the General didn't make too much of it, but some of the others did. Mr. Ferry at Greengages Farm, *he* said they ought to be horse-whipped."

Mr. Pyle observed that he himself had been whipped for stealing apples as a boy, which made his wife ask irritably what that had to do with anything. To me, she added, "If you can make the police do anything, ma'am, I'm sure Giles and I'd be very grateful. It's terrible worrisome, having our boy gone missing. We'd like him back, and whoever took him punished."

Susan and I agreed that the Pyles did not seem so delusional as Mrs. Hubbard. "Mrs. Pyle is certainly inclined to gloss over her son's misdeeds," I said, "but no more than a mother's natural partiality might account for. And of the two boys, it does sound as though Georgie was the ringleader."

Susan said you often saw that kind of thing with boys. "Egging each other on to misbehave," she said. "And the more of 'em you get together, the worse trouble they generally get into."

"But Peter Dray doesn't seem to have been a part of their group," I said. "It's queer, isn't it? His being so different from the others, yet disappearing just the same way."

After the superior amenities of the Pyles' cottage, the Drays' represented a downward turn. It was surrounded by an expanse of bare earth, devoid of weeds, flowers, and vegetables alike. Looking at the half-dozen ill-kempt children chasing each other round and round in a game involving a ball, and at the hens pecking underfoot, I thought I could guess how it had gotten that way.

The ball came careening past my foot as Susan and I approached the cottage doorstep. A girl with tangled dark curls came to retrieve it, surveying us with interest as she did so. "My mum's not here," she informed us. "She's gone across to the grocer's."

"Will she be back soon?" I asked.

The girl shrugged. "Dunno," she said, and went back to her game. Susan and I conferred together on the doorstep, uncertain whether to remain on the chance Mrs. Dray might soon return from her errand. Fortunately, while we were trying to decide, Mrs. Dray *did* return and put an end to our uncertainty.

I knew at once it must be she, for she was pregnant, Dear Reader—very nearly as pregnant as Mrs. Clarke. Apart from that similarity, however, no two women could have afforded a more shocking contrast. Mrs. Clarke, despite her increasing size, always contrived to look neat and well-dressed, and of course she had a maid to help care for her and a husband who catered to her every whim. The overall picture she presented was of a much-loved woman glowing with health and fecundity.

Mrs. Dray, on the other hand, looked worn and weary and at least a couple of decades older. She had hardly a tooth left in her head, and her greying hair looked thin beneath her battered straw hat. She moved with a slow, shuffling step to where Susan and I stood on the doorstep and paused, like a broken-down horse that finds its stable door barred against it.

I explained to her why we were there. She listened, but with an air of distraction, as though I was merely one more thing to endure in a day that already held too many.

There was good reason for her distraction, for the children had gathered around her and were clamouring for her attention. She scooped up a toddler and hitched him onto her hip, slapped in an absent-minded way at an older boy who was likewise begging to be picked up, and frowned at the dark-haired girl with the ball. "Leave that, Abby, do," she said, "and mind your brother while I talk to these ladies." Turning back to Susan and me, she said, "I don't know that I understand why you're here. What d'ye want from me?"

"We are seeking information," I said patiently. "About Peter, your son."

"Pete's gone off," she said at once.

"Yes, I know," I said. "We are hoping to find out how and where. Do you have any idea where he might be?"

She shook her head with an air of finality. "He's gone off," she stated again.

Abby, the dark-haired girl, had been listening to our conversation. "Pete's simple," she told us. "I'm younger than he is, but I can read better than he can, and run better, too. He's lame."

"So I have heard," I said. She looked like an intelligent child, Dear Reader, and certainly she appeared more interested in her brother's fate than her mother did. I transferred my attention to her. "Have you any idea where your brother might have gone?"

The girl gave us a look that held an element of calculation. "Some folks think Mrs. Mason took him," she stated. "Mrs. Mason what works for Vicar and his sister."

"She's an old maid," added one of the other girls, who had also been listening to this conversation. "Vicar's sister, that is, not Mrs. Mason."

"Mrs. Mason's a widow woman," agreed Abby. "She had a little girl, but she died. Now folks say she's gone nutty and started stealing other folks' children."

Not daring to look at Susan, I said we had heard the rumour about Mrs. Mason, and that it was as unkind as it was untrue. "That's why we are here. We want to find out what really happened. Was your brother accustomed to wander about the village alone?"

I let my gaze drift to Mrs. Dray as I asked this question. Rather defensively, she said there wasn't any harm in Pete, and she hadn't seen any reason why he mightn't go where he pleased. "It's not like the lad could go far, lame as he was."

"Would he have gone off with someone? A stranger, perhaps? If they offered him sweets, or something of the sort?"

Mrs. Dray merely stared at me dully, but Abby said at once that he would. "Pete's simple," she explained. "He'd do anything people told him to. And he liked sweets. *All* of us like sweets," she added, with a suggestive air.

Susan and I remained a while longer, asking questions, but we didn't get much more information. Mrs. Dray seemed hardly to know her son, and to have no interest in his activities outside the cottage. Certainly she showed little interest in getting him back.

"Do tell us if you can think of any more information that might help," I said. "You may get in touch with me through the Vicar."

I didn't have much hope that anything would come of it, Dear Reader. But as Susan and I were walking away, Abby came running after us. "Ma'am," she said urgently. "Ma'am. What you said back there?"

"Yes?" I said, turning to look at her.

She glanced back at her mother, then spoke again, lowering her voice. "I saw him," she told us. "I saw him talking to Pete."

Susan and I exchanged startled glances. "Who?" I asked. "Whom did you see?"

"The man," she explained. "The man who gave him sweets."

Susan said, "What man?" at the same moment I asked, "You saw him give your brother sweets?" We both paused, while Abby looked from one to the other of us. It was I who spoke next. "Do you know who he was?" I asked. "The man you saw?"

She hesitated, looking again from one to the other of us. It was clear she was deciding whether to tell us what we wanted to hear, or what she actually knew.

In the end, she decided on the truth. "No," she said, shaking her dark head. "I don't know who it was."

"Had you ever seen him before?"

Again the hesitation, with a flash of calculation in her eyes. "I *might* have," she said. "I might have seen him before."

"But you don't know who he was? Or whether he was someone who lives here in the village?"

"No," she said, and she spoke with so much regret that I felt sure that here, at least, she was speaking the truth.

"And did you actually see this man give your brother sweets?" I asked.

Again there was hesitation, then capitulation, as the truth-telling faction won out. "No," she said. "But he *might* have done."

"Can you tell us what the man looked like?" asked Susan.

Abby was maddeningly indefinite on this point, Dear Reader. It seemed the man was neither extraordinarily large nor small; that she had not observed the colour of his hair; that she was unsure whether he had been dressed like a gentleman or a work-man; that she could not, in fact, swear to any single identifying feature. "I didn't see him but for a minute," she said regretfully. "We were playing on the green, and it was my turn at bat. And when I came back round, Pete was gone and so was the man. But I didn't think anything about it—not then. It was only when you said that about the sweets, that I saw how it might have been."

"In any case, it's important information," I said. "And I am glad to have it." I hesitated a moment, looking down at her. It seemed quite possible she might be the only one in the village who had seen Pete's abductor (if she really had). Although her testimony amounted to little, it still might be enough to put her in danger.

In the end, I decided a word of warning was in order. "You must be very careful," I told her. "It would be better if you didn't say anything about this to your friends or family. I myself will tell the police what you have told me, and they may want to ask you some questions about the man you saw. But for now, please don't tell anyone else. Whoever that man was, he took your brother away," I went on, squatting down to look her directly in the eye. "If he knew you had seen him, he might want to take you away, too."

She nodded, looking solemn. "I won't tell," she said.

"Not even if someone offers you sweets?" asked Susan pointedly.

She hesitated, then shook her head vigourously. "No," she said. "I won't."

"That's right," I agreed. "Much safer to buy your own sweets."

To that end, I bestowed a sixpence upon her. As Susan and I left, we could hear her behind us, marshalling her siblings into formation for a trip to the local sweetshop.

⚊◄⊢ ⊣►⚊

"Hard to know if the girl really saw anything," observed Susan, as we retraced our steps toward the Vicarage. "I wouldn't give sixpence for her evidence, myself."

"It's not much," I agreed, "but it's something. For if she's telling the truth, the man she saw can't have been any of the General's foreign servants. She would know them by sight—it sounds as though the whole village does. And they are very noticeable in any case. Likewise, it probably wasn't Mr. Alexis. He's very noticeable, too."

"Narrows it down some," agreed Susan. "But for all we know, it might have been somebody who's not even from around here. After all, if you were wanting to steal children, it'd be a deal safer not to do it in your own neighbourhood."

I told her this was a depressing thought. "It would mean all our work was for nothing," I said. "And I'm not sure it wasn't for nothing anyway. After all, what have we learned today? It's not as though any of these people were very forthcoming."

Susan opined that we might have learned more if we had had more time. "It's not to be expected that folks of that sort will open their hearts to people they've just met," she said.

"Probably not," I agreed. "It takes a gradual approach. Or better yet, someone who already knows them."

"*And* somebody of their own class," said Susan. "I don't doubt Felicity could do it easy as winking."

Felicity was the chief of my agents in London, Dear Reader. Our relationship was a profitable one, stretching back for many years. She provided me with information about my clients, present and potential; I paid her and asked no questions about how she obtained the information. Her rates were quite reasonable, considering. I might have thought of employing her in the present case, but as I told Susan, it was rather outside her usual sphere of operations.

"Even if I could make it worth her while to come down from London, I doubt she'd be willing to consider it," I said. "But possibly she could farm out the work to someone local." We had done this in other cases with satisfactory results,[6] though there was, as Susan and I agreed, no one like Felicity herself. She has a gift for drawing confidences out of people, and the working classes are her specialty. I felt myself at a disadvantage there. People of Lord Rodney and the General's sort were much more my own area of specialty.

"It couldn't hurt to ask," I decided. "I'll do it once I am back in London."

"When will that be?" asked Susan.

"Well, I am promised to return to the Clarkes in Hampshire tomorrow. But I expect I will spend just a few more days with them. The worst of the hot weather is past now, and they are probably thinking about returning to London themselves."

Susan said that in that case, she would spend another day or two with her sister and then return to London. "I can give her a hand with the housework, if nothing else," she said. "Seeing that's she's short-handed."

I remarked that if Felicity knew a suitable agent, installing her as a maid at the Vicarage would be an excellent cover. "But it may not be necessary," I added hopefully. "Scotland Yard will be taking over soon, and then the mystery may be cleared up without any further trouble on our part."

---

6 See *All Hallows' Eve*

# CHAPTER THIRTEEN

I ended up returning to London sooner than I expected, Dear Reader. When I arrived at the Clarkes' country house the following day, I found that Mr. and Mrs. Clarke were already preparing for their own return to London.

"I have been having cramps now and then," explained Mrs. Clarke. "Not proper labour pains, but still they make me nervous." Even in the short time I had been gone, she seemed to have grown larger. "If you don't mind, I would prefer to return to Town immediately."

I assured her I did not mind at all, Dear Reader. As a result, within twenty-four hours I was back at the Temple being welcomed home by Jenny, with Sam hovering in the background smiling his own shy welcome.

"Susan's not here," Jenny informed me. "She's visiting her sister in Dorset."

"Yes, I know," I said. "I met her when I was down in Ainsworth. She'll be back tomorrow, I think."

Jenny and I had supper together that evening in our usual style. As we ate, I acquainted her with my activities in Dorset.

Jenny has not Susan's acumen, but she makes an excellent audience. She listened eagerly as I described the Vicar and his sister; the General's exotic household; Lord Rodney's grand establishment; Mr. Alexis the Spiritualist; and my interviews with the families of the missing boys.

"It's a strange business," she observed. "I must say, I don't like the sound of that Alexis fellow. I reckon he's a fraud, don't you, ma'am?"

I told her that in my opinion, there was no doubt about it. "I can't say I've any objection to his defrauding Lord Rodney, who's a rich man and thus fair game. But I do feel badly that he has been bleeding General Whitmore so freely. From what the Major said, the poor old man can't really afford it. And I don't like to see people defrauded who can't afford it. Especially when they are flattering enough to make me a proposal of marriage after less than an hour's acquaintance!"

Jenny chuckled. "That's a turn-up, that is," she said. "I doubt the Inspector will appreciate the competition."

After making this statement, she watched me expectantly to see how I would respond. As the Inspector had noted, the exact status of our relationship was evidently of interest to her and the rest of my household. I did not rise to the bait, however, saying merely that I looked forward to acquainting him with the case.

"Well, you won't do it tonight," she said, producing a sealed note. "He's been called down to a case in Exeter. Left this for you before he went."

I was disappointed, Dear Reader—disappointed for more reasons than one. I had hoped to see him that night for the same reasons any devoted wife might wish to see her husband (for we were still newly married, after all). But I had also wanted to acquaint him with my experiences in Ainsworth. I had been counting on him personally undertaking the investigation. If he was away working on a case in Exeter, it seemed likely that it would fall rather to one of his colleagues at the Yard.

On reading the note, however, I found that he was expecting to return on the morrow. "So both he and Susan will be here with any luck," I said. "And I'll be glad to see them both."

"What will you do in the meantime?" asked Jenny. "Have you scheduled any sittings for tomorrow?"

"No," I said. "As I came back early, I shall take tomorrow as a holiday. I have some business in the East End, and while I am there, I mean to call on Felicity."

<hr />

I have it on good authority, Dear Reader, that finding Felicity can be difficult—even dangerous—for people by whom she doesn't wish to be found. Fortunately, I was one of the privileged few, a friend as well as a client. I knew her habits, and better yet, I knew her especial lair, The Calico Cat.

The Cat is a tea-shop (though I would not like to guess what else might be sold there). It is an unprepossessing place with a low-timbered ceiling and uneven floors and an atmosphere so dark as to verge upon the murky. I stood blinking for a moment until my eyes adjusted to the gloom. Normally, one is pretty certain of finding Felicity taking tea and cakes beside the fire around five o'clock in the afternoon, but today looked like being an exception. Her usual table was vacant.

It was a disappointment, Dear Reader, but we all must bear some disappointment in life. As I turned to go, a man in rough working garb touched my sleeve. "Hist," he said softly. "Not there—here. Follow me."

I obeyed him, Dear Reader, albeit with a certain trepidation. One hears stories about Felicity's associates. The man might be anything from a pickpocket to a confidence-man to a full-fledged assassin.

As it turned out, he wasn't a man at all: he was Felicity. I laughed aloud at the revelation and was promptly hushed into silence. "Quiet," she hissed, glancing about in alarm. "You're here by yourself, Seraphina?" When I nodded, she added, "You didn't see anyone hanging about outside, by any chance? When you came in just now?"

I assured her I had seen no policemen outside. She gave a contemptuous sniff. "It's not the *police* I'm worried about," she said. "It's a partner of mine—a *former* partner, as I should say. We've had a falling-out, and he's kicking up a bit of a fuss."

We sat down together at a table some way removed from her usual one, but from which we could watch both it and the door. It gave me a chance to admire her disguise. Really, it was quite masterly, Dear Reader. The face beneath the man's hat was round and ruddy, for Felicity had not only rouged her cheeks, but padded them somehow. Her chin was fringed round with what I would have sworn was a genuine beard. Her legs were encased in corduroy pantaloons, and the chest beneath the calico shirt had been padded to give her the shape of a portly male rather than a matronly female.

"I seem to have come at a bad time," I observed. "Would it be better for me to leave?"

Felicity said that as long as I was there, I might as well stay and have some tea. "I've got the situation in hand—I think," she said, glancing around uneasily once more. "After next week, everything should be bob. But in the meantime, I'm obliged to play least-in-sight. You're lucky you caught me, Seraphina. I only came in today because I had some business that couldn't be managed by anyone else."

On the whole, it wasn't the most comfortable situation in which to take tea, Dear Reader. As I nibbled at buttered scones and sipped Bohea, I had the uneasy feeling that violence might erupt around me at any moment. Given that the employees of the Cat probably felt the same way, I was surprised to find it didn't make any difference in the refreshments or the quality of the service. The Cat serves a very fine tea: as good as one can get anywhere in London. It is only one of the many deceptive qualities about the place.

The tea seemed to calm Felicity, who became much more her usual genial self under its influence. "What brings you here, Seraphina?" she inquired.

My problems seemed pretty minor compared to hers, but I went ahead and told her about them. "It's not really my affair, of course," I said at the conclusion of my tale. "But you know Susan has worked for me a long time. Since it's her sister, I feel bound to help if I can."

Felicity nodded gravely. "We women have to stick together," she said (a statement that contrasted amusingly with her appearance, Dear Reader).

"That's why I came today," I said. "There's an opening for a maidservant at the Vicarage. I thought if we could install somebody there, they might succeed in ferreting out more facts than I could manage during the short time I was there."

"Dorset," said Felicity meditatively. "I wonder."

"Do you know anybody in the area?"

"No," said Felicity. "But I've an idea."

"And that is—?"

"I'll go myself," she said.

Although I am not disposed to look a gift horse in the mouth, Dear Reader, I could not help pointing out the difficulties with this proposition. "It wouldn't be just a matter of dusting and making beds," I warned. "They want someone to do the heavy housework—scrubbing floors and so forth."

Felicity explained that she did not intend to do the work herself. "I'll take Sally for that. One of my girls, and between you and me, one who's got more hair than wit. But that needn't matter, as I'll be there with her."

"How will you explain your presence?" I wondered.

"Oh, I'll be Sally's old auntie or granny who she's obliged to look after. You say it's a big place, and they're desperate for help. I reckon they won't make any bones about taking two instead of one, especially since I'll come without paying."

Of course she meant that *I* would be paying *her* salary, Dear Reader. But I had no issue with that. And in fact, she proved willing to work for less than her usual rate on this occasion. "For your offer comes in very good time, Seraphina, I don't mind saying. Indeed, I'm much obliged to you." She smiled with a hint of glee. "Nobody'll look for me down in Dorset. And in a week or so, when things have blown over, I can come back to Town and nobody the wiser."

Having reached this arrangement, I was fairly eager to quit the Cat, whose atmosphere was resembling more and more a ship sailing into stormy weather with the crew striking the sails around us and battening down the hatches. Still, I did not neglect to ask if I might pay my respects to the teashop's eponymous cat. Some people think calico cats are lucky, Dear Reader. It may be a superstition, but I had followed it on previous occasions, and my luck had held then. Given the perilous nature of the present occasion, I felt I needed all the luck I could get.

This feeling was not ameliorated by finding the cat cowering beneath a chair. "She won't come out," explained Felicity. "Hasn't hardly put her nose outside for the best part of a week. Knows what's in the wind as well as any of us, I don't doubt. Very smart creatures, cats."

The cat did consent to be petted by me, after a little coaxing. This was cheering, but was counterbalanced by Felicity's parting instructions.

"When you go out, make sure to put up your veil so they can see your face," she said. "And take off your shawl so they can get a look at your figure. You're skinnier than me, so I reckon you'll be all right."

⇒⊰ ⊱⇐

I *was* all right, Dear Reader, but I don't mind confessing that I did not draw an easy breath till I was back at the Temple. Once there, however, all my worries were relieved, and for the best of possible reasons: Inspector Harper was there to greet me.

"It's a continual source of amazement to me that nowadays I actually *welcome* the presence of a policeman in my home," I remarked, as we exchanged greetings in an appropriately conjugal fashion. "But so it is, astonishingly enough."

He agreed it was astonishing. After a few more minutes, it occurred to me to wonder where the servants were. "Susan is arriving at Waterloo by a late train," he explained. "So I suggested that Jenny and Sam could have dinner in a public house and then meet her at the station. It seemed to me a good arrangement."

It seemed good to me, too, Dear Reader. We enjoyed a very pleasant dinner *à deux*. It consisted of nothing more than bread and cheese and cold ham, but better a dinner of herbs, &c.[7] In any case, there was champagne to wash it down. I am very fond of champagne, and the occasion seemed a cause for celebration.

As we ate, he told me a little about his case in Exeter. Most of our conversation, however, apart from the purely personal, revolved around the Ainsworth situation. I was overjoyed to hear that Scotland Yard had indeed been called in, and that he was personally overseeing the case.

---

7 "Better is a dinner of herbs where love is, than a stalled ox and hatred therewith." *Proverbs* XV, 17. Madame Fox might have gone on to draw a comparison between stalled ox and boiled beef.—*Ed.*

"Yes, indeed," he said. "You've stirred up quite a hornets' nest down there, seemingly." He surveyed me with a quizzical expression. "I'd be interested to hear how it came about."

I told him everything, Dear Reader. That is, I told him everything eventually, though I could not help teasing him a little in the process. When I first described the General and his marriage proposal, for instance, I somehow failed to mention his age and debility, so that the Inspector received the impression that it was a younger, more virile man who had proposed to me.

"Now I wish more than ever that I had gone with you," he said, looking at me sternly. "Don't tell me you encouraged the fellow!"

"I don't think it would matter very much if I had," I said. "Seeing that he's about ninety and at death's door. But it's as well for you to know you have competition, Tom, just to keep you on your toes."

He grinned at that and remarked that I kept him pretty well on his toes anyway.

Having had my fun, I went on to describe the other people I had met in Ainsworth. He took an occasional note as I spoke, observing that it would save him time to have a grasp of the *dramatis personae*. "Though I gather my appearance will be just a formality, more or less," he said. "Assuming I'm reading the signs aright."

"Whatever do you mean?" I exclaimed.

"I mean that, reading between the lines, I'd guess the local force already has a good idea who's responsible."

"You mean that they've solved the case? But then why would they call in Scotland Yard?"

He smiled patiently. "Probably because the culprit's somebody important with a lot of influence. Or at least someone with ties to somebody with influence. We see that a lot, Seraphina. The local officials don't want the onus of making the arrest themselves, so they palm it off on the Yard."

After recovering from my astonishment, I began evaluating the possibilities. "Lord Rodney," I said. "Or the General—or the Major. Or possibly the Vicar. It's got to be a man, anyway, if Abby Dray's evidence is worth anything."

The Inspector remarked with feeling that children's evidence was always an unknown quantity. "Let's hope they have more than that to go on," he said. "But I'd guess that they have. As I said, it sounds as though the investigation is pretty much over apart from the matter of making the actual arrest."

"I can hardly believe it," I marveled. "The police actually *know* who did it and why. *I* don't. Really, I am tempted to come down with you and see for myself how it plays out."

"Wanting to be in at the kill, are you?" he inquired sardonically.

"I wouldn't put it quite like that, Tom, but—yes, I would like to be there. And there is no compelling reason why I may not be," I said, mentally reviewing my schedule. "If it's just a matter of your going down to make an arrest and then coming straight back, I can accompany you perfectly well. I wouldn't consider it if you were planning to make a lengthy investigation, but this is different. Indeed, it might be considered a matter of duty"

"For the children," he suggested, grinning. I had, of course, told him about my conversation with Mr. Alexis.

"Yes, exactly that," I said with decision. "I shall do it for the children."

# CHAPTER FOURTEEN

B efore the Inspector and I left the next morning, I sat down with Susan and told her the latest developments. We were both full of conjecture about whom the police were going to arrest, but agreed it could not be Ellen.

"They wouldn't bother to call in Scotland Yard if it was just a matter of arresting the Vicar's housekeeper," was Susan's cynical summing-up. "It's got to be somebody with money, or influence, or both."

Obviously, the Inspector and I could not travel as a married couple. But we took tickets on the same train and shared a compartment on the way down. I reminded him he must remember to call me Letitia Blackwood, and he observed that he was getting tired of deception and false names, and how much easier it would be if I could just call myself Mrs. Thomas Harper. At length, we reached an agreement—that is to say, I prevailed—and for the rest of the journey we talked about the case.

"I suppose it couldn't possibly be Mr. Alexis?" I suggested. "He's on close terms with the General and Lord Rodney, and perhaps other influential people as well. But it's not as though there's any real relation between them. No, I don't see them sticking up for him, if he were proved to have committed a serious crime."

The Inspector nodded. "And it sounds as though this is a very serious crime," he said. "They'd hardly call in the Yard if it were anything less than murder."

"Murder," I repeated. "So that means the boys are dead—or at least one of them is. Georgie Hubbard for choice," I added, with an attempt at humour.

In truth, I wasn't feeling very humourous, Dear Reader. Earlier, the business had seemed a kind of intellectual puzzle in which I might entertain myself in a harmless, even beneficial fashion. But now it looked like being a tragedy that would cut one or more people very deeply.

"I wouldn't want *your* job," I observed aloud.

"Most people wouldn't," he said. "Some days I don't myself."

I told him that I was always available for wifely support. "Although we'll have to be discreet about it. I suppose it wouldn't do for us both to stay at the Hound and Huntsman. I'd better see if they'll put me up at the Vicarage again."

As it seemed likely the Inspector's business would keep him overnight, he had brought a few necessities with him in a Gladstone bag, and I had brought my own traveling-bag as before. When we arrived at Ainsworth, I proceeded on foot to the Vicarage, trying not to look too wistfully over my shoulder. The Inspector had been met on the platform by a contingent of serious-looking men including a couple of constables, a uniformed police sergeant, and a small man in country tweeds who was evidently some local official—probably Sir Owen Lecker. I would have loved to have stayed and been part of the discussion, but doubted whether I would have been welcome.

At any rate, I was welcomed with open arms at the Vicarage. Gossip was rife in the village about the coming arrest, and Miss

Douglas was all a-twitter at the prospect. "The case is in the hands of Scotland Yard," she told me. "They are sending down one of their best men. He is supposed to be arriving today."

I explained that he had actually been on the same train with me. "A very gentlemanly-looking individual," I pronounced solemnly. "And he seemed quite intelligent and well-spoken, for a policeman. I exchanged a few words with him during the journey, as we are here on the same business."

"And a very bad business, too," said the Vicar, who had come into the room as I was speaking. "Sir Owen, our local J.P., just sent me round a note. And if half what he hints at is true—well, I can only pray it isn't."

Miss Douglas immediately demanded to see the note, Dear Reader. I wanted to see it, too, but he wouldn't show it to us. "The matter is not a fit one for women," he said firmly.

That was maddening enough, but the delay that followed was more maddening still. The afternoon dragged on with nothing for Miss Douglas and me to do but wait for news from some less discreet source. Every so often, a parishioner would arrive with what purported to be the latest bulletin.

These visits followed a pattern. The Vicar would invariably attempt to calm speculation in the same ineffectual way he had done before; the woman (they were all women) would then turn to Miss Douglas and ask what *she* thought; and the whole situation would then be threshed over in spite of the Vicar's protests.

In ordinary circumstances, the presence of a stranger would probably have dampened this discussion. But it was such an exciting situation that I was drawn into the group despite my outsider status. In any case, as Miss Douglas noted, I had a legitimate connection with the business.

"What do *you* think, Miss Blackwood?" asked one of the women, when everybody else had had their say. "Is there any truth in the story that Lord Rodney himself is going to be arrested?"

I said I didn't know. "*I* heard it was one of the General's servants," said one sharp-faced old biddy. "The big negro." She did not actually use the word "negro," Dear Reader, but rather a ruder word that I was taught no lady would ever allow to sully her lips.

"That's what I heard, too," agreed another. "That he belongs to one of those African tribes that are *cannibals*. And that he killed those boys and *ate* them."

This produced pleasurable shudders all around. The Vicar expostulated at some length about the evils of gossip. The women listened patiently, then resumed their discussion as before.

Around tea-time, an incident occurred to relieve the monotony. Ellen appeared in the doorway, looking a little flustered. "There's a girl here, ma'am," she said, addressing Miss Douglas. "Come about the position."

"Position?" repeated Miss Douglas vaguely. "What position is that, Mrs. Mason?"

"Maggie's old position, ma'am. As maidservant."

"Oh! Is that so?" said Miss Douglas. Her attention was divided just then, as one of the other women had begun a lurid story, *sotto voce*, about a child murder in Yorkshire. "Do her references appear to be in order?"

"Yes, she's got very good references, ma'am."

"Then let's have her. Tell her she can have Maggie's old room and the same wages."

"Very good, ma'am," said Ellen. "Only there's one thing I need to ask you about. She's got an old aunt who she needs to look after while she's here, and she was wondering if her aunt could stay here at the Vicarage with her? Or if not, if you know somewhere cheap she could board."

"These women," said one of the lady parishioners in a commiserating voice. "It's always something, isn't it? So difficult to get good help nowadays."

"She says her aunt doesn't want any wages, ma'am," continued Ellen. "Only just her board. And that she'll come at half-wages herself to pay for it."

"Oh! Well, that sounds all right, Mrs. Mason. Indeed, it sounds very good. We've got plenty of room, certainly." Miss Douglas looked around her rather ruefully. The Vicarage was one of those big barracks of a place built during an era when labour was cheap. There was probably room for a dozen servants—and work for them, too, if they could be had.

Ellen bowed acknowledgement. "Very good, ma'am," she said, and departed. I saw two of the parish women look after her with appraising expressions.

"I suppose it's not *her*, then," said one of them.

"Hardly could be, if the police haven't come around by now," agreed the other.

They both sounded disappointed.

As soon as there was a lull in the conversation, I excused myself and drifted off toward the kitchen. Sally, an ingenuous-looking girl with blonde curls and freckles, was peeling potatoes while Ellen dressed a chicken. A huddled figure, wrapped in a shawl, was sitting by the fire. I went over and whispered in its ear.

"I'm afraid you've come rather late to the party," I said. "It seems it's all over but the arrest."

"Ah, well," said Felicity philosophically. "As long as it's not *me* they're arresting."

She could afford to be philosophical, Dear Reader. *She* wasn't paying for services that were no longer needed. But there is never any use crying over spilt milk. I chalked it up on the side of goodwill and told her I hoped she would have a pleasant holiday. "With plenty of peace and quiet, and no need for beards," I added.

"I could use some of that," agreed Felicity, stretching out her feet to the fire.

—◆—

Back in the parlour, the ladies were getting restless. It was past six o'clock, and still no news had come of any arrest. One by one, they were obliged to excuse themselves and go off to see about their separate dinners.

Eventually, the Douglases and I sat down to dinner ourselves. It was a better dinner than last time—roast chicken, potatoes, and vegetable soup—but even so, it wasn't a patch on Susan's cooking.

Conversation was scanty during the meal. I myself was formulating a daring strategy. I reckoned I had sat long enough in the Vicarage parlour waiting for news. I didn't intend to spend the whole evening there. Although I had hoped the Inspector might send me a note, or perhaps even come himself to let me know what was happening, thus far he had been unaccountably silent. That seemed to indicate there had been a hitch somewhere. I thought I would go find out for myself.

Miss Douglas obviously felt the same way, for she mentioned that she might just run over to Cincinnatus after dinner to have a word with the General. "I would like his advice about our parsnips," she said, in an innocent but unconvincing voice. "His seem to grow so much better than ours do."

Her brother looked at her sternly. "Don't meddle, Celia," he said. "I doubt not they have trouble enough at Cincinnatus right now. There's no need for you to go mixing yourself up in it."

I pricked up my ears at this, Dear Reader. It sounded as though Cincinnatus was indeed the locus of the business. Immediately I felt I ought to have guessed as much. That strange *ménage*, so ripe with sinister possibilities—how could it be otherwise?

As I was speculating about this piece of information, the doorbell rang. Both Miss Douglas and I looked up alertly. The Vicar pretended to be busy dissecting a nectarine, but I could tell he was listening, too. We could all hear Ellen open the door and hold a low-voiced colloquy with whoever was outside.

Presently she appeared in the doorway with a note in her hand. Miss Douglas looked as though she would have liked to snatch it away from her, and the Vicar actually reached out a hand to take it, but she shook her head. "It's for Miss Blackwood," she said.

I accepted the note rather self-consciously, Dear Reader. Normally one does not open and read private letters in front of others. I paused, looking at my host and hostess.

"*Do* go ahead and read it," urged Miss Douglas.

Nothing loath, I broke open the seal. From the handwriting, I knew immediately it wasn't from the Inspector. In fact, it proved to be from Major Phelps-Whitmore, though this fact took a little puzzling out. The Major's handwriting was very poor, the characters tiny and closely packed together. He was also a very poor speller. Even after lengthy scrutiny, I could only be sure of a word here and there among the thicket of agitated letters.

"*Terrible business—General hard-hit—seemed to take his fancy*," I managed to translate after much puzzling. "*Would be greatly obliged if you would be so kind.*"

"What is it?" asked Miss Douglas eagerly.

"Major Phelps-Whitmore is asking me to come over to Cincinnatus—I think."

"Now?" demanded the Vicar.

I shook my head uncertainly. "Perhaps I'd better have a word with the servant who brought the note. Did he wait?" I asked Ellen.

"Yes, ma'am," she said. "I think he's expecting you to go with him."

"Very well, then," I said, getting up from the table. "I'll go."

"*Do* let us know if you need anything," urged Miss Douglas. "Or if there's *any* way we can be of help. Tell the Major I'd be glad to come *myself*, if I would be of any use."

"Cecilia," said her brother sternly.

"I'm just *offering*, Julian. There's no harm in that."

She had been very kind to me, Dear Reader, and very generous about sharing information. I felt the least I could do was to reciprocate. "I'll send you word as soon as I know anything myself," I promised her, and went off to fetch my hat and shawl.

# CHAPTER FIFTEEN

The servant waiting at the door was Phillipe. Together we set off toward Cincinnatus.

It was growing dark, with only a faint glow of sunset still visible in the west. I tried not to be nervous in Phillipe's company, but I was, Dear Reader—just a little. It wasn't the silly gossip about his being a cannibal; that I set aside easily enough. But in fact I had forgotten the sheer presence of the man: his height and build, and the splendid way his gold-and-red livery set off his own particular style of masculine beauty.

Eventually, feeling he might take silence for disapproval, I forced myself to make conversation. "I could not wholly understand the Major's note," I said. "But it sounds as though there is trouble at Cincinnatus."

"Yes, madam," said Phillipe, a note of sorrow in his deep voice.

"I am very sorry to hear it. I gather it has to do with this business of the missing boys?"

"Yes, madam," he said again. This time, there was a different note in his voice: a restraint that hinted at anger or resentment.

"Are the police there now?" I asked.

"Yes, madam," he said. "They have been there for some time. I believe the arrest may have taken place by now."

I nerved myself to ask the question. "Whom are they arresting, Phillipe?"

At these words he glanced at me, Dear Reader. Night had fallen completely by now, and given that his skin was so dark, I could see little except his eyes. "Joseph Shaddock, madam."

It was not the answer I had expected. "Joseph Shaddock!" I exclaimed. "But who is that? I don't think I have ever heard the name before." As Phillipe did not answer, I asked again, "Who is Joseph Shaddock? Does he work for the General?"

"Yes, madam," said Phillippe. "He is a member of the gardening staff."

"And they think he was responsible for the boys' disappearances?"

Phillipe said he believed this was the case. He spoke with extreme deliberation, Dear Reader, hesitating over every word. It might have been the natural hesitation of a foreigner searching for words in an unfamiliar tongue, but I thought it was more likely the caution any intelligent person would use when negotiating a verbal minefield.

I didn't ask any more questions, being too busy rolling this new information around in my mind. Phillipe was silent, too. When we reached Cincinnatus, he ushered me into the Spartan parlour, where I found the General, the Major, and the Little Fellow.

All three of them rose as I entered the room. "This is good of you, ma'am," said the Major with feeling. "I take it as a great favour, I do assure you."

"What's this, what's this?" asked the General, surveying me with surprise. "Miss Blackwood?"

"Heard she was at the Vicarage," explained the Major. "Scotland Yard fella mentioned it when he was here earlier. Thought we could do with some company just now, to take our minds off this whole dirty business."

"Ah," said the General, looking nonplussed. "Well, Miss Blackwood is certainly welcome, although I wish with all my soul we were entertaining her in happier circumstances."

The Little Fellow said nothing, but smiled shyly at me from beside his father. I smiled back, glad to have this evidence of friendly feeling, for between you and me, Dear Reader, the General's greeting had been a bit chilly. In general, a lady expects more warmth from her would-be bridegroom.

He seemed to feel this himself, for his next utterance was more in his old courtly style. "Come over and sit beside me, Miss Blackwood," he said, patting the chair beside him. "I'll ring for tea, or something stronger, if you like. We could all use a pick-me-up, I daresay. This business has been a shock, I can tell you: a very great shock. I wouldn't have thought it of one of my own men."

Clearly the news *had* shocked him, Dear Reader. The frailty I had noted at our first meeting was intensified, along with the unhealthy pallor of his skin. Even his voice was affected, for there was a quaver in it as he added, "I never thought to be mixed up in a murder case. When that Scotland Yard fellow showed up at my door, you could have knocked me over with a feather."

I asked—casually, I hope—if the Scotland Yard fellow were still on the premises. The General made the noise that is usually written "harrumph." "He'll be back soon, no doubt," he said. "Once he's got his papers in order."

"There's been some trouble about the warrant," explained the Major. From the look he cast at his father-in-law, it was pretty clear where the trouble had originated.

The General said firmly that he could never abide slip-shod work on the part of his subordinates, and that the Scotland Yard *wallahs* shouldn't either. "Regulations are regulations," he stated. "You've got to dot the I's and cross the T's, or you're nowhere."

He then summoned Phillipe with a pull of the bell. Once again, Phillipe appeared in the doorway with magical promptitude. "Drinks," ordered the General. "And shake a leg, will you, Phillipe?"

Phillipe did shake a leg. In fact, he reappeared so suddenly and noiselessly with the refreshments that he made me jump. It was uncanny that such a large man should move so silently. But it was yet another qualification that would make him ideal for my business.

I watched his hands deftly arranging the tray in front of us, and the way he waited on the company. It was hardly necessary for the General or Major to give him any order. He responded to the needs of the company with a promptitude that was more like clairvoyance. At one point he paused to look at me, and I realized I was staring at him with naked longing in my eyes. I took care to be less obvious after that.

As well as a plateful of the gelatinous cakes, there were a couple of decanters and a soda-siphon on the tray. The General and the Major both took undiluted whiskey, and after some ladylike demurring, I accepted a brandy-and-soda. The Little Fellow was allowed a half-glass of soda but was more interested in decimating the cakes. I took one before they had quite disappeared. They seemed to improve on acquaintance.

The doorbell rang. Both the General and Major looked up at the sound and sat listening in silence as Phillipe went to answer it. But instead of the police, the callers proved to be Lord Rodney and Mr. Alexis.

"I hope this is not an intrusion," said Lord Rodney as he entered the parlour. "In the ordinary way, I know callers at such a time would hardly be welcome. But my dear General, I feel I bear a degree of responsibility in this matter. I wanted to express my regrets to you and your family, and to assure you that I intend to use whatever influence I have to smooth over this whole lamentable affair."

"And I, too, wish to tender my regrets," said Mr. Alexis. His dark eyes were aglow with feeling, Dear Reader—I would not like to say how sincere a feeling, but the effect was very picturesque. His dress, too, was picturesque, consisting of a suit of unrelieved black worn with a sweeping cloak lined in scarlet satin. "After the hospitality I have enjoyed in this house, I felt the least I could do was to express how sorry I am that the shadow of trouble should ever rest upon it. Although not, I am happy to learn, in a way that personally involves any of *you*, my dear friends."

I thought he was laying it on a little strong, but it seemed to go down all right. I noted jealously that the General's greeting to Mr. Alexis was much warmer than the one he had given me. "Glad to see you, Mr. Alexis," he said, getting up to shake his hand. "You're always very welcome here." With growing animation, he added, "Once this business is wrapped up, we'll have to have a sitting in our old style, eh? Might help take the taste out of our mouths."

"But my dear General, I should be delighted!" said Mr. Alexis, opening his eyes very wide.

The Major brusquely broke in on this exchange to offer him and Lord Rodney drinks. They both accepted, and in the pause that followed the doorbell rang again. This time, there was no mistaking it for anything but the arrival of the police. I recognized the Inspector's voice, upraised in official accents. His words were followed a moment later by the tramp of heavy footsteps in the corridor.

The men of our party were already on their feet when Inspector Harper came into the room. It was easy for me, who knew him well, to tell he was out of temper. His lips were drawn into a thin line, and—since he had removed his hat on entering—I could see that his hair was disheveled as though he had been driving his fingers through it in frustration.

The sight of me sitting there with a glass in my hand, tête-à-tête with the General, did not seem to improve his mood. He threw me an "*Et tu, Brute?*" look, and thereafter addressed himself exclusively to the General. "If you will be so good as to inspect the warrant again, sir, I believe you will find that all is in order now," he said, laying a good deal of emphasis on the words "again" and "now."

The General glanced it over, then returned it with a nod. "Yes, quite in order," he said. "You'll understand that as a property owner, I must insist that the legal formalities are observed."

The Inspector said he understood this. He said it very shortly, Dear Reader. "If we are ready now?" he added, addressing someone behind him. "I would like to finish this business tonight if possible. Always assuming the fellow hasn't already caught wind of our intentions and made good his escape."

A uniformed police sergeant, who had been lurking behind in the corridor, came forward to reassure him. "Should be all right, sir," he said brightly. "I've had a couple of men keeping an eye on his cottage all day. From the road," he added, with a hasty look at the General. "He hasn't stirred a step, I'll take my oath."

"Let's hope so," said the Inspector. With a nod to his men, he turned and left, accompanied once again by a clatter of boots.

The General made as if to follow them, but the Major intervened. "Sir, you shouldn't," he said. "I'll go see that fair play's done if you really think one of us should be present."

"I do think it," said the General. He seemed to deliberate, then sat down on the sofa again. "Very well, Major," he said. "Tell Shaddock I shall see that he's properly defended. Even if he proves to be guilty of this abominable crime, I suppose I owe him that much. A clever fellow, with a real genius for gardening," he told me, with a shake of his head. "I'll have a hard time replacing him."

A memory suddenly rose in my mind: an aproned man standing silently alongside the hedge, watching my departure. "Was Shaddock the man who was clipping the hedge when I was here before?" I asked.

The General said he was. The Major, with energy, added that he was a scoundrel if even half what the police suspected was true.

This inspired the Little Fellow to speak for the first time since my arrival. "Why is Shaddock a scoundrel, sir?" he asked. "What's he done?"

It was clear that the Major had forgotten his son's presence. He looked at him with dismay. "Never mind, lad," he said at last, in a tone of would-be reassurance. "It's nothing you need addle your brains about." With a theatrical look at his watch, he added, "Good God, look at the time! You ought to be in bed. Go find Sandeep and tell him so."

The Little Fellow, with daring, said he didn't want to go to bed. "I want to go with you, sir," he said. "I want to see what happens."

The Major turned on him violently. "You'll go to bed now," he said, "*now.*"

The alteration in his manner was shocking, Dear Reader. I knew, of course, that he had been an officer in the army; that he must have given many orders in his time; and that he must have given them in a way that ensured they were promptly obeyed. But I had fallen into the habit of seeing him as a gentle bumbling presence like a large, amiable dog. Now it was as though the dog had turned and bared his teeth.

The Little Fellow made no further demur. He got up quietly and left the room. Lord Rodney and Mr. Alexis exchanged glances. "Do you mind if *I* accompany you, Major?" asked Lord Rodney. "I likewise have an interest in seeing that fair play is done—if you've no objection."

It was amusing to hear him speak so timidly, Dear Reader. He was a rich, titled gentleman who could probably buy up the Major a thousand times over. But after the latter's display of temper, I didn't blame him for his timidity.

The Major said brusquely that he had no objection and departed forthwith on his errand. Lord Rodney and Mr. Alexis trailed after him at a respectful distance. I would have liked to go, too, but of course there was no hope of their allowing a woman to join their party. Besides, I judged I had been brought there to keep the General company and, if possible, to prevent him from distressing himself.

To this end I applied myself, Dear Reader, but it was no easy task. The old man seemed restless and not much interested in anything I had to say. At one point, he went over to the window and pulled up the blind to look outside. It was now completely dark. Dim shapes of trees were visible against the starlit sky, but nothing else. Or so I thought until I joined him at the window. There were moving lights among the trees, winking in and out of sight. I supposed they must be lanterns carried by the police.

"Is Shaddock's cottage in that direction?" I asked.

"Yes," said the General. "It's about a quarter mile from here if you take the path through the woods."

The moving lights looked like will-o'-the-wisps, Dear Reader—not that I have ever seen a will-o'-the-wisp, but that was the comparison that occurred to me. The General, however, said they put him in mind of one of Hannibal's tactics during the Second Punic War. "At Mount Callicula, he had his men tie torches to the horns of a herd of cattle and drive them up the mountain. The Roman garrison guarding the pass saw lights moving all around 'em, supposed they were being outflanked, and abandoned their position. So Hannibal was able to get his whole column through the pass without any trouble. A very clever fellow, Hannibal."[8]

"Very clever indeed," I agreed. As this seemed a safe subject, I encouraged the General to sit down and tell me more about it. But he had barely embarked on an account of the Carthaginian general's campaigns when the door of the parlour was flung open, revealing the Major in a state of breathless excitement.

---

8 See Livy 113—*Ed.*

"My dear Major, whatever's the matter?" exclaimed the General, rising to his feet.

The Major swallowed hard, then pulled himself to attention. "He's dead, sir," he told the General. "Shaddock's dead!"

# CHAPTER SIXTEEN

The Major was not a very coherent witness, Dear Reader. From what he said, the General and I could only gather that Joseph Shaddock had escaped the Law's grasp just as the Inspector had feared—but that he had chosen a very drastic and permanent way of doing so. It wasn't until Lord Rodney and Mr. Alexis arrived that we could obtain the details.

"He *hanged* himself," Lord Rodney informed us in a hushed voice. "Right there in his cottage from one of the beams. He was dead when the police arrived. Apparently, he has been dead some hours."

"A terrible thing," observed Mr. Alexis. He looked shaken, Dear Reader, but also (I thought) rather pleased with himself. The cause of his pleasure emerged with Lord Rodney's next words.

"The most remarkable thing about it, to my mind, is that Mr. Alexis had predicted just such a development! You are, of course, familiar with the Tarot deck?" We all nodded, at which Lord Rodney continued: "Mr. Alexis is in the habit of laying out the cards each day at my request. 'The Hanged Man' has appeared repeatedly during our 'spreads' this past week."

Everyone looked respectfully at Mr. Alexis, Dear Reader—everyone but me. I didn't think his prediction demonstrated any great percipience. Murder is a capital crime, meaning there was pretty sure to be a hanging in it somewhere if only the police did their job. Besides, I have some acquaintance with the Tarot, enough to know that the images on the cards don't translate literally to their meanings. As nearly as I could recall, "The Hanged Man" signified something like a sacrifice rather than an actual hanged man.

To say this would have appeared mean-spirited, however, so I refrained. The Major wasn't so reticent. "Seems to me that if you knew this was going to happen, you might have said so beforehand, Alexis," he said sharply. "It's easy to be wise after the fact."

With a wave of his hand, Mr. Alexis said that interpreting portents was always an uncertain business. Lord Rodney, who seemed to have recovered from his earlier diffidence, was more direct. "My dear Major, we could all wish this had turned out differently," he said. "But I hardly think there is any reason to reproach Mr. Alexis. Indeed, I am not sure that Shaddock's taking this way out may not have been for the best. It saves the necessity of a trial and thus averts a great deal of painful publicity which would have rebounded upon you and the General—most unjustly, I need hardly say. But it is an unfortunate fact that the press in this country tars with a broad brush."

The others, by and large, seemed to partake of these sentiments, Dear Reader. But the Inspector was of a very different opinion when at last I managed to exchange a few words with him later that evening.

"It's a damnable business," he said. "Damnable! This never should have happened. And it wouldn't have happened if the warrant had been executed properly in the first place. I can't tell you whom I'm angrier with—the local magistrate, that old ass of a pettifogging general, or with myself. Between us, we gave Shaddock ample time to make away with himself. And in the process, a lot of the evidence went with him."

"Does it matter so much?" I asked. "Surely suicide must be considered a confession of guilt."

"You'd think so," said the Inspector. "But I'd be happier if the fellow had left something behind in writing to that effect."

"He didn't leave a note?"

"Not a scrap of one."

"Do you think it *wasn't* suicide, then?"

Reluctantly, he shook his head. "No, I wouldn't go as far as that. I examined the scene thoroughly—a case of shutting the barn door after the horse was stolen, perhaps, but at least I determined that there wasn't any sign of foul play. Before he died, Shaddock had not only locked both doors on the inside but barred them. All his windows were shut and fastened as well. And the fastenings weren't the flimsy catches you find on modern houses, either—the kind any clever thief can open from outside with a knife-blade. They were serious and substantial pieces of ironmongery. I'd take my oath that no one got into the cottage that way, or out of it, either. As for there being no note—well, not all suicides leave notes, Seraphina. It's possible this fellow was one who didn't. Especially since there's evidence to show he couldn't read or write."

"Oh," I said, digesting this.

"But you can see what an unsatisfactory situation it is. I'll always blame myself that I wasn't able to effect the arrest in a timelier fashion. Though I'm damned if I know what more I could have done."

I told him he ought not to blame himself. "There was gossip all over the village well in advance of your arrival, Tom. Most of it seemed to centre around Cincinnatus. Shaddock must have got wind of it along with everybody else and decided to cheat the hangman. And that might well have happened even if the warrant had been properly executed in the first place. Do they know exactly when he killed himself?'

"It seems pretty clear it was sometime this afternoon," said the Inspector, looking a little comforted by my words. "The doctor will probably be able to narrow it down based on the stomach contents and so forth." His expression became thoughtful. "It does appear he'd got word we were coming to arrest him. Suicide doesn't seem to have been his original plan, however. He had a bag half-packed, there by the door, as though he originally thought of doing a bunk. He must have meant to run, then discovered the place was being watched by the local force. Knowing there wasn't any other way out, he lost his nerve and hanged himself."

I told him that Lord Rodney & Company were inclined to look upon Shaddock's suicide as a fortunate outcome that spared them much ill publicity. He nodded, looking grim once more. "Yes, I imagine they are. It was mighty convenient for *them*, his taking that way out. So convenient that I keep wondering if it was wholly coincidental."

"But you said you had no doubt he committed suicide?"

"No," he said. "But I'll always wonder what he could have told us if we'd got to him while he was still alive. As it is, we aren't even sure yet that he was the one who abducted those boys. Although if our suspicions are correct, there'll be evidence to prove that, at least—once we've had opportunity to look for it."

It was easy to guess what kind of evidence he meant, Dear Reader. Given that Shaddock was a gardener, it was also easy to guess where it was likely to be. "You'll wait for daylight to make a proper search, I suppose?" I asked.

"Yes," he said. "We want to meet with the other gardening staff and get an idea of likely places to search. Given that the whole bloody place is a garden, it would take a long time to dig everywhere the ground's been disturbed. And your precious General wouldn't thank us for *that*, I'll wager."

I told the Inspector he wasn't *my* General. "I've decided to break the engagement, Tom. As far as I can tell, he's more enamoured of Mr. Alexis than of me. Mr. Alexis predicted the suicide, by the way," I added, and went on to tell him about "The Hanged Man."

He was inclined to look on the circumstance much as I had done, Dear Reader. "You Spiritualists," he said, "you'll take credit for anything if it casts you in a favourable light." He added one or two remarks in this vein and was smiling when Phillipe came into the room carrying a note on a salver.

"I have a message for Miss Blackwood," he said, tendering it to me. I noted that he was regarding both the Inspector and me with a certain curiosity. Possibly we looked a little too confidential for chance-met acquaintances.

As soon as he had gone, I opened the note. "It's from Miss Douglas at the Vicarage," I said. "Poor thing, she is perishing with curiosity. I had promised to let her know the news as soon as I found out. In all the excitement, I haven't had a minute to sit down and write her, but I'll do it right now."

The Inspector, however, said I might as well go and tell her in person. "There's nothing else likely to happen tonight," he said. "As you say, we'll have to wait until daylight to make a proper search of the grounds."

Fixing him with a skeptical gaze, I inquired whether he wasn't just saying that to get me out of the way. "Because I know you men like to keep all the fun to yourselves," I added.

"You have an odd idea of fun if you think I'm having any at present," he retorted. "For my part, I'm going to return to the Hound and Huntsman, write up my report, and get an hour or two of sleep—if I can. You could help me by carrying a message to the Vicar. Since Shaddock's dead, there'll have to be arrangements made for a funeral once the inquest is done. Probably more than one funeral, if we find what we're looking for tomorrow," he added grimly.

That sobered me a bit, Dear Reader. I promised to give the Douglases an account of the evening's events, and we went our separate ways, taking a restrained leave of each other for the benefit of the servants. Once again, however, I thought Phillipe regarded us with a certain curiosity. That is the devil of having intelligent servants, Dear Reader. One cannot prevent them from drawing intelligent conclusions.

⇌ ⇋

Miss Douglas received my news with a thin veneer of Christian sorrow that overlay a deep well of avid speculation. "Joseph Shaddock," she repeated. "*Shaddock*. Yes, of course: old Ben Shaddock's son. Ben was the General's head gardener for years and years, Miss Blackwood. He only died last spring. Joe must have stepped into his shoes—or at least followed in his footsteps."

The Vicar was frowning, his eyes unfocused in an effort at recollection. "I don't seem to recall the family," he said.

"You wouldn't, Julian," said Miss Douglas. "They weren't churchgoers." She cast a meaning look in my direction. "They didn't attend church *or* chapel, Miss Blackwood. Whatever you may say of the Methodists, they do at least encourage temperance and decent living."

The Vicar, attempting to quell this line of discussion, said that one ought not to speak ill of the dead. Miss Douglas retorted that one could hardly do anything else in the case of the Shaddocks. "Though certainly none of us imagined anything as bad as *this*," she said. "Dead by his own hand, and suspected of having made away with those unfortunate children, too. I wonder what gave the police the idea he was guilty in the first place?"

I had no information to give on this subject, unfortunately. The Inspector and I had spoken too briefly for me to obtain all the details. "I am sure we will learn more tomorrow," I said. "I must go over to Cincinnatus early in any case. If Inspector Harper is there, I will ask him about it."

Both Douglases assumed that the Major had invited me once again to keep his father-in-law company on the morrow. But in fact that wasn't the case, Dear Reader. I was simply inviting myself— and Cincinnatus was not my real goal. I wanted rather to look at Joseph Shaddock's cottage. Fearing that the local police might prevent me if they knew my intention beforehand, I thought it better to simply show up and brazen my way in, if I could. If I couldn't, I still might be able to coax the Inspector into letting me look at it later on.

In the event, Dear Reader, I got more than I bargained for.

I left the Vicarage early and made my way along the lane, which allowed me to reach the cottage without coming in view of Cincinnatus. Once I could see the cottage roof through the trees, I stepped onto a footpath that seemed to lead in the right direction.

There was no sound to give me any warning, Dear Reader. Rounding a turn in the path, I came upon what looked, at first glance, like a scene of activity. At second glance, however, it appeared more like a frozen tableau. The Inspector was there, his back to me, bending down as though examining something on the ground. Two uniformed constables stood nearby, shovels over their shoulders and perspiration trickling down their faces. There were two or three other men as well, all standing still as stones. That was the thing that impressed me most, Dear Reader: the absolute immobility of the whole group.

I must have made some sound, inadvertently, for the Inspector turned to look at me. He did not appear pleased by my appearance. In fact, his expression was singularly grim. I noted this in passing before my eyes moved on to the thing he had been examining.

A garden urn stood there, earth-stained and green with moss. Two similar urns stood behind it at a little distance. There was a series of holes nearby, surrounded by heaps of upturned earth. They were not large holes or large heaps, Dear Reader. Each contained no more soil than might easily be accommodated in a bushel basket. The first thought that crossed my mind was that someone had been planting little trees.

I did not understand my mistake until one of the men slowly and reverently removed his hat. Another made a choking sound and turned away.

Even then I did not understand. Like the dirt-heaps, the urns were not large. They were no bigger than the one that held the potted palm in my own Sitting Room. I looked at the Inspector for enlightenment. He came quickly forward, taking me by the arm and steering me firmly away from the clearing.

"You shouldn't be here, Seraphina," he hissed.

I reminded him that he needed to call me Miss Blackwood. He let out an oath, and I noticed then (what I should have noticed before) that he was looking very upset indeed. "What's wrong, Tom?" I asked, modulating my tone to a gentler one.

"Those urns," he said. "You saw those urns?"

"Yes, of course," I said. "What are they?"

He made a gesture eloquent of despair. "The missing boys," he said. "All that's left of them, I fear."

I stopped to stare at him. "But how could that be?" I asked.

As I spoke, a series of odd, disconnected images flashed through my mind: a fœtus curled in its mother's womb, Shelley's heart pressed between the pages of a book—and then, more appositely, his funeral pyre. "Ashes?" I whispered. "They were *burned?*"

He nodded, his face grim. "It appears so," he said. "And then the ashes were put in urns and buried. I've never seen anything like it—not in all my years on the force."

# CHAPTER SEVENTEEN

I am not the sort of woman who swoons at every little thing, Dear Reader. But the Inspector's words made me feel as if I needed to sit down for a while—preferably in company with a brandy-and-soda.

When I expressed this desire aloud, he said he felt the same way. "But I've got to go back and finish this beastly business, worse luck," he said, glancing over his shoulder. "Shaddock's cottage is just a little further on. Why don't you go and sit there, out of the sun? We're finished investigating the place, so it ought to be all right."

In this way, I got to see the cottage after all, Dear Reader.

It was a squalid place, closer to the Hubbard than the Pyle model in terms of housekeeping, and almost as Spartan as the General's in terms of furnishings. Evidently Shaddock, too, had suffered from the lack of a woman's touch. But it was clear he had no objection to women themselves. There were a lot of lurid portraits of actresses (one calls them actresses as a convention, Dear Reader) pinned to the cottage's dingy distempered walls.

Although his décor was wanting in taste as well as cleanliness, Shaddock had some possessions of surprising quality. There was a shotgun with an engraved barrel leaning in the corner next to the unmade bed, and a fine eight-day clock stood on the mantelpiece. It sweetly chimed the quarters as I prowled about, examining the rooms' contents. I could not help glancing up at the rafters now and then, but the police had taken away the apparatus of suicide, and there was no sign to show exactly where he had met his end.

There was, however, ample evidence to support the Inspector's theory that suicide wasn't his original intention. An open valise with some clothing hastily tumbled inside lay discarded near the kitchen door. It was an unwholesome place, that kitchen, Dear Reader. The sink held a mass of dirty dishes littered with bits of uneaten food, which the flies had found before me and were merrily colonizing. I also found a flask of what appeared to be spirits. Even had I been more in need of stimulant than I was, however, I wouldn't have eaten or drunk anything in that house. This was particularly true because, when I peered deeper into the same cupboard, I discovered a small bottle bearing an apothecary's label, on which I at length deciphered the words "chloral hydrate."

"Well," I said aloud. "*That* seems suggestive."

I had used chloral hydrate myself, Dear Reader, at an earlier period of my life. When one is forced to make one's way in the world as a woman alone, one may occasionally find one's self in company with someone (usually male) whom it is desirable to reduce (temporarily) to a more tractable state. It seemed likely that Shaddock had used the stuff the same way, which was a cheering thought. Whatever had happened to the boys, they likely hadn't been awake to feel it.

Still, I found myself suddenly repulsed by my surroundings. I had an overwhelming desire to get outside in the fresh air, away from the buzzing flies and unanswered questions.

Once outside, it occurred to me that I might as well go back to the Vicarage.

And once I was *en route* to the Vicarage, I realized that as long as I was going, I might just as well pack my bag and return to London. The Inspector might be obliged to stay a day or two longer to finish up his business here, but I wasn't under any similar obligation. What with one thing and another, the beauty of the countryside had been spoiled for me.

⋙⋘

Eager as I was to shake the dust of Ainsworth from my feet, my leave-taking had to be delayed some hours. As soon as I entered the Vicarage, both Douglases came out of their respective rooms to meet me, eager to know if the police had made any progress toward finding the boys. So it fell to me to break the news.

Both of them were shocked by my report, Dear Reader. All Miss Douglas's gossipy cheer fell away from her, leaving her stricken-looking and subdued. "It seems quite impossible," she said, then added, with apparent irrelevance, "He was such a dear little baby."

As for the Vicar, he bowed his head sorrowfully and said, "Alas, it is as we feared. One hopes their souls may be at rest, poor children. But their families will be hard-hit by this news. I must call upon them at once." It was a perfectly correct response for a clergyman, Dear Reader, but something about it struck me as less sincere than his sister's.

I warned the Vicar that he ought to wait to hear from the police before calling on the boys' families. "They have only just unearthed the—*ah*—remains. A doctor will need to examine them. And there may be other tests required before identification is certain. It may even be that the police wish to keep the discovery secret for a time." Frankly, Dear Reader, I doubted that they *could* keep it secret, seeing the way gossip flew around this place. But until I knew for certain, I felt I ought to add this caveat.

Fortunately, the issue wasn't left in doubt for very long. While we were still discussing it, Ellen came into the parlour to announce the arrival of Lord Rodney and Mr. Alexis.

The greetings on all sides were properly subdued. Lord Rodney appeared on the verge of tears, and even Mr. Alexis seemed more genuinely grieved than he had earlier. When he spoke, however, it was to give voice to his usual Spiritualistic cant.

"It is a comfort to reflect that the transition to the Spirit Realm is wholly painless," he told us solemnly. "And it is a comfort likewise to know those unfortunate children are now evolved into much higher and happier beings than we ourselves."

The Vicar looked mildly resentful—it was, I supposed, a trespass on his own rôle of Spiritual Comforter. Lord Rodney, however, said it was all very true. "Though I am not evolved enough myself to feel anything but stricken to the heart," he added sadly. "One feels so helpless—so hopeless—at the revelation of such evil. What a terrible crime has been committed in our midst! And it is a crime with no possibility of remedy or restitution."

The Vicar, trying to add his own mite of Spiritual comfort, said that at least something might be done for the boys' families. "Yes, that is so," agreed Lord Rodney. "I would be happy to do anything—anything that might be of use."

They drew together to discuss the matter. Miss Douglas excused herself to go see about tea, and I was left *tête-à-tête* with Mr. Alexis.

"You spoke very eloquently just now about the Spirit Realm," I told him. "It would indeed be a comfort to believe our dead are not really lost to us—that they might even be able to communicate from the Other Side."

I had hoped this might draw him out, but he only looked at me suspiciously. "Indeed it *is* a comfort," he said. "Yet one must remember that just as Earthly children quickly adapt to new surroundings, so Youthful Spirits quickly embrace their new Celestial existence. That is to say, they still love their Earthly friends and families—love them more than ever and with a deeper, purer love. But I have found that few retain much memory of their lives on Earth. And curious as it may seem, none of them ever seem willing to dwell upon the circumstances of their death. Dying, to them, is but a passage to a better existence."

I agreed that this did seem curious, Dear Reader. Privately, I felt "suspicious" was a better word. Mr. Alexis was evidently warning me off from any attempt to pursue the investigation via Spiritualism. Of course I had no such intention (knowing well enough the futility of it), but my interest was aroused by his behaviour. Was it possible he had something to hide, even beyond the fact that he was a charlatan? I set about allaying his suspicions with a view to finding out.

"I am sure it is all just as you say, Mr. Alexis," I said warmly. "And I, for one, can see little point in dwelling on such an unpleasant subject. Especially in the present case. We know who the culprit is, beyond doubt. His guilt has been established, and he is now gone beyond Earthly punishment. It has been a sad business, but it is over."

Mr. Alexis agreed to this with an enthusiasm that I once again found suspicious. "Yes," he said, "and the sooner we put it behind us, the better. As a Spiritualist, I often find myself impatient with the earthly conventions of mourning. To weep over the dead husk of the body, while the winged Soul is fluttering joyfully in our midst, seems to me the height of folly." In a segue I found rather insulting, he added, "I suppose you will soon be returning to London, Miss Blackwood?"

I admitted that I would be. "I am only sorry I was unable to attend one of your sittings while I was here," I added, gazing at him soulfully. "I have been so much interested by all I have heard of them."

"The opportunities have not been favourable," he said, with a shake of his head.

I agreed that they had not. "But I could wish it were otherwise, Mr. Alexis. Spiritualism is an interest of mine. Although I wouldn't admit it to Miss Douglas," I added, lowering my voice.

"I have reason to know she is a skeptic," he said, with another shake of his head. "It is a pity that Christians are so often narrow-minded on the subject. For what is Spiritualism but living proof of the doctrine of the Soul's immortality?"

I enthusiastically seconded this idea, which caused him to move a step closer to me, both literally and figuratively. "I could tell immediately on meeting you that *you* are a Spiritual woman, Miss Blackwood. Oh, yes, I could," he added, as I feigned a look half awed and half disbelieving. "You have a very distinct violet aura. It would not surprise me if you had psychic abilities yourself."

Straight-faced, I said that one or two people had suggested as much. "Together with some of my friends, I have experimented with automatic writing," I told him, "and with—what do you call it?—table-turning? We have had some strange and even suggestive results. But I cannot say that anything of moment has happened. Nothing that would prove beyond doubt that the Dead can speak."

He gazed at me with his artificially shadowed eyes. "For myself, I have no doubt," he said. "And I would welcome a chance to assuage your doubts as well. If only you were staying on in the neighbourhood! I am sure Lord Rodney would invite you to one of our sittings at the Priory if he knew of your interest. But I doubt he will be hosting anything resembling a party for some time to come."

We both looked at Lord Rodney. He was talking to the Vicar with tears running freely down his face. "No," I said regretfully. "Of course one cannot wonder at it. His feelings are very much to his credit."

Mr. Alexis agreed that they were, and on that note we parted.

By this time, Miss Douglas had returned with the tea-tray. She set about serving her brother and Lord Rodney. It occurred to me to wonder if she had broken the news to Ellen. Once again, I drifted off to the kitchen.

# CHAPTER EIGHTEEN

In the kitchen, I found Ellen seated at the kitchen table weeping into a dishtowel. Sally and Felicity stood on either side of her, wearing matching expressions of concern. Felicity, noticing me, made a significant grimace accompanied by a shrug. In reply, I nodded toward the scullery. Leaving Sally to minister to Ellen alone, Felicity accompanied me into the scullery and shut the door.

"I take it that Miss Douglas told Ellen the bad news," I said.

"That she did," agreed Felicity. "And might have done it better, if you ask *me*. But there, the poor lady was pretty upset herself, and no wonder. Hardly surprising if she blurted it out sudden-like." With a glance back toward the kitchen, she added, "Still, I'm afraid it's come as a nasty shock to our friend Ellen. Seeing that one of those boys was by way of being a pet of hers."

"I was afraid of that," I said. "What a damnable turn of events. She is still grieving her daughter's death, and this isn't going to help matters."

Felicity agreed it was an unfortunate turn of events. "But I suppose she had to be told sometime. It would be bound to come as a shock, however it was told." Lowering her voice to a whisper, she asked, "Is it true what Miss D said? About those boys being burned alive?"

I was happy to set the record straight, Dear Reader—or at least to cast a reasonable doubt on this ghastly idea. "The presumption is that they were drugged first," I said. "And they might well have already been dead by the time the bodies were burned. The cause of death hasn't been established."

Felicity, in a relieved tone, said that wasn't quite as nasty as Miss Douglas had led them to believe. "But nasty enough, all the same," she added. "If this is the way people go on in the country, then give me London any day!"

I said I felt the same way. "I wish more than ever we could get Ellen away from here. I am sure being in this neighbourhood only encourages her to dwell on the loss of her daughter. And now there is this business of the Dray boy, too. You might try if you can convince her, Felicity. I think the Douglases would encourage her to go, sorry though they would be to lose her services as a housekeeper."

Felicity said that in her experience, employers weren't usually so understanding. "They must be wanting to get rid of her anyway," she suggested cynically.

"I don't think so," I said. "I took them for genuinely good people. But feel free to draw your own conclusions. You'll have a chance to get to know them better than I have!"

Felicity agreed that she would. "And I'll do what I can with Ellen," she promised. "At the very least, I can lend her a sympathetic ear and let her tell me her troubles."

"That'll do as much good as anything, I should think," I said. "Though a little brandy might not come amiss, either. Especially now, while the wound is still raw."

Felicity said she and Sally were making do with the Vicar's sherry for now. "But I was planning to step around to the public house later, for something stronger."

I gave her a half-crown for the purpose, Dear Reader. It seemed the humanitarian thing to do.

＝⇥ ⇤＝

As I was getting ready to go back to the parlour, there was a scratching at the kitchen door. Ellen didn't hear it, but Sally did, and went to see who it was. She returned a moment later, followed by Major Phelps-Whitmore.

The Major came sidling into the kitchen like a large dog trying to slip unobtrusively into a room he had been forbidden to enter. He was dressed in an unaccustomedly formal manner: tailcoat and trousers along with a silk top-hat which he swept from his head on entering and then did not seem to know what to do with. "Didn't mean to intrude," he said, glancing apologetically from one to the other of us. "I came round to see the Vicar, but he's busy, it seems."

At this point, his eye fell on Ellen. She was still sitting at the table clutching the dishtowel, her face wet with tears. "Oh, I say," he said, sounding extremely shocked. "I *do* beg your pardon, ma'am. I didn't mean to intrude."

Here Ellen shook her head and murmured something inaudible. The gist of it seemed to be that he wasn't intruding, for his face cleared and he came a step nearer. "I do beg your pardon," he said again. "I came to speak to the Vicar about this business. You know what business I mean, I daresay. This matter of the boys being—er—found."

He looked with concern at Ellen, who had dissolved into tears at these words. Felicity took it upon herself to explain the cause of her distress, while Sally relieved him of his hat, brought a chair for him to sit in, and set about making tea for the whole party. As a maid she seemed quite competent, Dear Reader, whatever Felicity might think of her intellectual qualities.

The Major was full of sympathy on hearing that Ellen had just learned of the death of her protégé. "Hard lines, that," he said, shaking his head. "I'm not surprised you're unhappy about it. I'm pretty cut-up about it myself. Mean to say, I've got a Little Fellow of my own, and just the thought of something like that happening to him—Lord, it's enough to unman me completely. I wouldn't have had this happen to poor little Pete, not for the world. Nor to the others, either," he added as an afterthought.

Ellen made no reply to this but to weep harder. The Major, looking more troubled than ever, begged her not to distress herself. "I shouldn't have spoken of it," he said. "Always was a clumsy fellow. Here I am putting my foot in it every chance I get and making matters worse instead of mending them."

Ellen pulled herself together enough to reassure him. "It's not that, sir," she said, wiping her eyes. "Don't think of it, I beg you. Only I can't help being sad and sorry."

"Of course not," said the Major. "Of course not." He hitched his chair a little nearer hers. "Stands to reason you'd feel that way. A shocking business, upon my word. Wouldn't have believed Shaddock was capable of such a thing. But there doesn't seem to be any doubt about it, unfortunately. Rather a black mark on Cincinnatus, having this kind of thing tied to one of our men."

The tea was ready at this point, and Sally served us very neatly and efficiently. I accepted a cup myself, Dear Reader. I can always drink tea.

The Major, after saying again how sorry he was, made allusion to Ellen's earlier trouble. "Now we know Shaddock was at the bottom of it, I trust you won't have any more bother on *that* score," he told her. "Only bright spot in the business, as far as I can see. A great shame that a lady like you should be troubled by a lot of village Yahoos."

Ellen said listlessly that it was no matter. I sat drinking my tea, watching them both with interest. I had noticed in our earlier conversation that the Major seemed to have something of a partiality for Ellen. Now here he was, actually in her kitchen, calling her a lady once again and evincing (to my eyes) unmistakable symptoms of admiration. There was no surprise in that, as far as it went. The two of them clearly came from the same social stratum, if you set aside the Major's artificial elevation via marriage. And Ellen was an attractive woman, if you could see beyond the reddened nose and swollen eyes. Most men can't, Dear Reader. I thought it counted strongly in the Major's favour that he could.

With the idea of helping matters along, I said how kind it was of him to come and offer his sympathies. He assured me it was nothing, looking all the while at Ellen as he spoke. "Had to come anyway, to speak to the Vicar," he explained. "As he was busy, I thought I'd pop in and see how Mrs. Mason was bearing up."

"Well enough, sir," she said, mopping her eyes. "I'm sure it's very kind of you." In a more formal voice, she added, "Shall I go see if Reverend Douglas is free?"

"No, don't trouble," he said, getting to his feet.

"It's no trouble, sir," she insisted, getting to her feet likewise. "I mustn't shirk my job."

While they were arguing about it, Sally adroitly slipped out and returned presently to say that Reverend Douglas was still closeted with the gentlemen. "Gentlemen," repeated the Major in a scathing voice. "*One* of 'em might be a gentleman. But the other— pah! Nothing but a scoundrel to *my* way of thinking. I'd as soon stay here till he's gone, if it's all the same to you."

We all assured him he was welcome to stay, and the efficient Sally poured him another cup of tea. To distract Ellen from her sorrow (as well as to indulge a rather malicious curiosity), I encouraged the Major to expand upon the subject of Mr. Alexis. "The General still seems to have a great regard for him," I remarked.

"Yes, unfortunately," said the Major gloomily. "Wish it were otherwise. Sooner or later Lord Rodney'll get tired of having him at the Priory, and then ten to one but he'll be back battening on us."

"Perhaps the General will not care to have him," I said. "Especially after the—er—recent events."

I did not wish to be more explicit, out of concern for Ellen's feelings. The Major, however, seemed to understand. He shook his head. "It's true this business has hit him pretty hard. But he's a wonderful hale old fellow, is the General. I daresay you thought he looked bad yesterday, ma'am, when you were at Cincinnatus, but I wouldn't count him out just yet. There's been more than once we've thought he was down for good, but he's always come charging back."

I expressed gratification at this idea, whereupon the Major gave me a shrewd look. "If you're staying in the neighbourhood, I daresay he'd be glad to see you, Miss Blackwood. We'd *all* be glad to see you. You'd be doing him a kindness, keeping his thoughts from dwelling on this business of Shaddock."

"And on Mr. Alexis as well?" I suggested.

He grinned, looking a little shame-faced. "It *did* cross my mind," he admitted. "Kill two birds with one stone, what?"

I thought this was interesting, Dear Reader. It seemed to show that his dislike for Mr. Alexis outweighed his own self-interest. As far as he knew, I was a single woman, and if I were to become the General's wife, the old man might well leave some of his property to me. He might even leave *all* of it to me. That would cut out the Major and his son even more effectually than if Mr. Alexis was allowed to pursue a more gradual process of financial bloodletting.

Rather apologetically, I explained I was going back to London on the afternoon train. "Pity," said the Major, and sounded as though he meant it. "You'd said something before, about knowing some of the tricks those Spiritualists use to get their fancy effects."

I didn't dare meet Felicity's eye. "I know a few of them, certainly," I said.

"So if you got a chance to attend one of Mr. Alexis's séances, you might be able to tell how he's bamboozling the General?"

"I might," I said guardedly.

"If you could wean him away from that fellow, I'd be no end grateful."

"Unfortunately, I don't think the opportunity will arise," I said. "But I would have no objection to trying, if it could be arranged."

To that end I gave him my address in London and told him he might write me if an opportunity *did* arise. Of course it was not the address of the Temple I gave him, Dear Reader. It was rather an accommodation address, one of many I use for professional purposes. Recognizing it, Felicity winked at me.

"I'll see if I can't wangle it," said the Major, putting the address carefully away in his coat pocket. "Shouldn't be hard to get you invited to one of the fellow's sittings. Likes an audience, he does, and the bigger, the better."

"If the sitting is held at the Priory, I could not think of coming without a direct invitation from Lord Rodney," I warned him. "That might present a problem."

The Major, however, did not think it would be any problem. "Lord Rodney and I get on all right," he said. "And he's a generous fellow, whatever else you might say about him. He'll be glad to have you as his guest, I don't doubt."

I doubted myself it would be so easy, Dear Reader, but I was willing to let the matter rest on these terms. I wasn't in such a hurry to return to Ainsworth that I felt any anxiety about the outcome one way or another.

# CHAPTER NINETEEN

A few hours later, I was at Ainsworth's little rail-station with bag in hand, watching a distant plume of smoke that signaled my train's approach. I had hoped to leave by an earlier train, but there proved to be only the one, and a slow one at that.

It was a sufficient indictment of the country, in my opinion—even without madmen who ran about slaughtering children and incinerating their corpses.

As the train approached, I felt a touch on my shoulder. Turning, I found Inspector Harper standing by my side. He, too, was in traveling garb and carrying his Gladstone bag.

"I thought you were staying on," I exclaimed. "Didn't you get my note, Tom? You must have done, I should think."

I had earlier sent a note to the Hound and Huntsman to let him know I was returning to London that day. I had not expected that he would return with me, however. Indeed, I had carefully refrained from implying that he should. A policeman's job often requires him to stay on a case for days on end, sometimes without any advance warning and occasionally without any sleep. In my opinion, that was a hard enough lot for a man without his wife making it any harder.

"Yes, I got your note," he said. "As my work here seems done, I thought I might as well accompany you."

I eyed him speculatively. There was a bitterness in his voice that hinted at interesting revelations to come. I could hardly pursue them on an open platform, however. Fortunately, the train arrived a few minutes later, and we were able to find an empty compartment. I might have burst otherwise, with pent-up curiosity.

⇥ ⇤

"I supposed you would stay on another day or two in Ainsworth," I told him, once we had taken our seats and disposed of our bags. "To tie up any loose ends in the case."

"I can see how you might have supposed that," he returned. "*Anyone* might have supposed that."

The bitterness in his voice was more pronounced than ever, Dear Reader. Ordinarily, I would have offered him a drink at this point. Deprived of this means of comfort, I made do with patting his hand. "What has happened, Tom?" I asked. "Surely you're not abandoning the case?" It seemed unlikely, Dear Reader, yet I could interpret his words in no other way.

He gave a laugh of the sort commonly described as hollow. "Perforce," he said. "Having been summoned down to do the dirty work for the local police, I am now sent away like a house-maid whose work didn't suit."

"Can they do that?"

"It appears that they can. And in fact, they have done so. The criminal is dead; his victims have been found and identified; and thus there is no further need for the poor Scotland Yard expert."

I shook my head. "There must be more to it than that," I said. "Otherwise you wouldn't feel so badly about it. In general, you are only too glad to see a case wrapped up even if the credit doesn't fall to you."

"There's little enough credit in *this* case," he said, with a bitter emphasis.

"Well, tell me about it, then. I only know the bare bones of it—if you'll pardon the expression."

He said he would be glad to flesh out those bare bones but warned me that the information wasn't for public consumption. "It is the expressed wish of Lord Rodney & Company—to use your own expression, Seraphina—that the matter be hushed up insofar as it may be."

I assured him he might rely on my discretion, whereupon he launched into his story. "You know I came down here to make an arrest," he said. "But that was all I knew myself until I got here and saw the actual evidence."

"And there was evidence that Shaddock was the guilty party?"

"Yes, and it was very suggestive evidence, as far as it went."

"Then I wonder the local police didn't make the arrest themselves."

"As for that, it was just as I had supposed, Seraphina. There were people of money and influence involved in the case, and they wouldn't have credited either the evidence the police had found or the direction in which it led. Not without making a lot of fuss, anyway. The witnesses were all quite humble people, and one of them was actually a criminal himself, which further complicated matters."

"What kind of a criminal?" I asked with interest.

"A poacher. He'd been caught snaring rabbits in Lord Rodney's woods last winter. He got off with a light sentence only because Lord Rodney himself argued for leniency. Which leniency was rewarded as it usually is," he added with a policeman's cynicism. "The man was back in Lord Rodney's woods a few months ago when he saw Shaddock in company with a boy of nine or ten.

Judging by the date, and from the description the man gave us, we think it must have been Dan Pyle."

"I can see how that testimony would pose some problems," I agreed. "Did it appear Shaddock was abducting Dan against his will?"

"No, our witness said they seemed to be on perfectly good terms. They were walking side by side and talking in a friendly manner. And though he didn't see the two of them actually enter Shaddock's cottage, they were headed in that direction."

"Suspicious," I observed.

"Very suspicious," agreed the Inspector. "Especially since it appears to be the last time Dan was seen alive. Our witness didn't make anything of it at the time, which was natural enough, for there wasn't much hue and cry over the first two disappearances. Most people thought the boys had simply run away. It wasn't until Peter Dray disappeared that our witness came forward. And even then he waited a few weeks to do it. One can understand his reluctance, of course."

"Of course," I agreed. "He was risking a second prosecution for poaching. I wonder if Lord Rodney will be lenient again?"

"As far as I can see, he's declaring a general amnesty all around," said the Inspector bitterly. "Everything is to be laid to Shaddock's account—the state of the government, too, I shouldn't wonder, along with the latest drop in the Funds. It's enough to make me wonder whether something more than simple beneficence is motivating him."

I looked at him with interest. "You think Lord Rodney may have been involved somehow?"

The Inspector hesitated before answering this question. "No," he said at last, "no, I wouldn't go as far as that. Not, at least, without more evidence than we've got. But I'm positive there's more to this business than meets the eye. For one thing, the disappearance of those boys seems to have coincided with Shaddock's coming into a lot of money. And nobody's been able to give me a satisfactory explanation of where that money came from."

"Ah," I said. "I noticed he had some rather expensive possessions for a gardener. A clock fit for a bishop's parlour, and a shotgun of the sort I'd more readily associate with a landed gentleman."

"Yes, those caught my eye as well. But there's more evidence than that, Seraphina—and more damning evidence, too. You remember the clearing where we dug up those urns?"

I did remember it, Dear Reader, with the utmost vividness. I said so, whereupon the Inspector explained that two of the under-gardeners at Cincinnatus had directed the police to that location. "They, along with the poacher, were our main witnesses against Shaddock. They had witnessed a lot of little things which, added together, made them suspect he might have played a rôle in the boys' disappearances."

"Again, not witnesses that would rate very highly with the local authorities," I noted.

"No, and their testimony would weigh all the less because Shaddock, as head gardener, was their immediate superior. What's more, he had made himself very unpopular in that capacity—throwing his weight around and being altogether a bit of a bully. That's why they, like our poacher, were slow to come forward with their evidence. It's also why, when they *did* come forward, they preferred to deal directly with the police rather than going to the General. As they explained it to us, if they had told *him* what they thought, he would likely have put it down to jealousy and resentment. That, at least, was the reason they gave."

"It seems understandable enough," I said. "Knowing the General's character, I can't say I blame them. Very well, then. They directed you to that clearing?"

"They did. And once we'd raked away the leaves and twigs and so forth, it was obvious somebody had been digging there.

Although I had my doubts at the outset, simply because the disturbance was so small. I have some experience in these matters, unfortunately." He ran a hand through his hair. "Even children's graves would require a larger amount of excavation than we found there, or so I thought. It wasn't until we found the urns and investigated their contents that it all made sense."

Here he gave his head a little shake, as though shaking away a disturbing mental image. I patted his hand again. "A very nasty business," I observed.

"Yes, it is," he agreed. "But urns weren't all we found."

"No?"

"No. It turned out there were *four* burials, not just three. It's a fortunate thing we caught that. Indeed, I might have overlooked it if left to myself. But one of the local constables is a sharp lad, and he spotted another place where the soil appeared to be disturbed a little distance from the others."

"So there was a *fourth* set of remains?" I exclaimed.

"No, not remains," he said. "What we found was a wooden box. And when we opened it, it was full of money."

"*Money?*" I repeated. After a moment, I nodded. "Yes, that does seem highly suspicious, Tom. How much money was there?"

"Nearly a hundred pounds. Being a good policeman, I naturally inquired of the General what Shaddock's pay might be. It turns out he received sixty pounds per annum, exclusive of the use of his cottage."

"Which wouldn't account for his possessing such a sum," I said, "in addition to fancy shotguns and clocks and so forth. Unless—could he have got it from his father? I understood from Miss Douglas that his father was head gardener at Cincinnatus before him. Both the job and the cottage passed to him on his elder's demise. Possibly there was an inheritance as well that would account for the difference?"

"I inquired about that, too, Seraphina. His father left nothing but debts. No, I think we can accept, provisionally, that Shaddock had some other source of income besides his pay. We can't be sure it was connected with the boys, but it does seem indicated. His affluence seems to have more or less coincided with their disappearances. And he buried his private earnings near their graves."

We both contemplated this problem for a moment or two. "I wonder why he burned the bodies before burying them," I said.

"The usual reason would be to disguise the identity of the victims," said the Inspector. "Alternately, it might be to disguise the cause of death. That seems the likeliest reason in this case, since the identity of the victims was already known."

"But why go to so much bother? Murder is murder no matter how you commit it, and the penalty is the same. It seems like a lot of extra risk and trouble for nothing."

"It *was* risky," agreed the Inspector. "In fact, that's one of the things that aroused the suspicions of our gardener witnesses. Shaddock appears to have used the General's patent heating system as his crematory."

"Good God," I said. After a moment, I added, "I expect the General regarded that as little less than sacrilege."

"He did," agreed the Inspector, smiling slightly. "I must say, I took a certain satisfaction from the circumstance!"

I thought this information over. "It's a curious thing," I said, "but Miss Douglas actually suggested the bodies might have been burned during our first conversation. Only she supposed Lord Rodney's bonfires were used for the purpose."

"That *is* curious," he agreed. "The more so because those bonfires seem to have served as a kind of red herring. The nights George Hubbard and Dan Pyle disappeared coincided with village festivals, and so most of the staff at Cincinnatus were given permission to attend them. And that included the gardening staff. And while they were cavorting around bonfires in the village, Shaddock was free to conduct his own activities at Cincinnatus in relative safety. But that wasn't the case with Peter Dray."

"He always seems to be the exception," I observed.

"So it seems. But in fact, the exception in this case was purely accidental. You'll recall he disappeared on the thirty-first of July."

"Yes?"

"Well, I made a few inquiries, and it turns out there was a bonfire party planned for that night, too. A kind of harvest festival, it was meant to be. But it ended up being cancelled owing to rain. That same night, the under-gardeners noticed a smell coming from the hothouse furnace that didn't seem like coal burning."

I shuddered. "How horrible," I said. "And how perfectly inexplicable. Why would he take such a risk?" I thought about it a while longer. "He clearly had a powerful reason for burning those bodies. If it wasn't to hide the cause of death, then it must have been to conceal the boys' identities, as you say. Even if he didn't succeed in doing so."

The Inspector shook his head. "No, he didn't succeed in doing so. Coal fires burn pretty hot, but though the General's system uses coal as fuel, it wasn't designed as a crematorium."

"I suppose not," I said. "Though I wouldn't know exactly where the difference lies."

"Size, for one thing," said the Inspector, "and temperature for another. It takes a very hot fire to reduce human remains to ashes. And even then, there are usually bone fragments that are identifiable as such, unless an effort is made to grind or crush them afterwards. Shaddock doesn't seem to have done that. In fact, a lot of the smaller bones were completely intact." After a brief pause, he added, "The skulls were intact, too, more or less."

"Oh," was all I could think to say.

"As a result, we were able to identify all three sets of remains with some certainty." He paused again, eyeing me with concern. "I'm not being too explicit, am I?"

I said that he was not, whereupon he went on: "George Hubbard had an unusually prognathous jaw—underslung, that is, like a bulldog's. You must have noticed his mother does, too. That, along with a clubbing of the fingers which seems to have been the result of some childhood illness, was sufficient to identify *him*. Dan Pyle had lost his front teeth in an accident a while back, not to mention having healed fractures in both arms and legs. That served to identify *him*. As for Peter Dray, the pelvic bones of the third set of remains weren't wholly intact, but there was enough to show a deformity in the right hip and thigh, which was consistent with the lameness that afflicted him."

His voice had grown steadily grimmer throughout this catalogue. I could think of nothing better to do than pat his hand again. "I'm so sorry, Tom," I said. "I can only imagine how ghastly that must have been."

"Ghastly enough," he agreed.

There was a pause, and then I nerved myself to ask the question that troubled me most. "Was there anything to show the cause of death?"

He shook his head. "No, the fire was hot enough for *that* purpose. If there was any evidence, it was all burned away." He smote his thigh in a sudden passion. "But they must have been dead before they were burned. They must have been! Only think of the risk if they weren't. It would have been madness to proceed otherwise. That's what I keep telling myself, anyway."

There was a note in his voice that was close to anguish. I looked at him with concern. "Of course," I said. "I'm sure they must have been dead, or drugged at the very least. Probably with chloral hydrate."

"Chloral hydrate?" he repeated. It struck me he was looking at me rather oddly, Dear Reader.

"Yes," I said. "You no doubt observed that Shaddock had a bottle of the stuff in his cupboard. I assumed that's what he used it for. Didn't you?"

As I spoke, he was slowly turning his head from side to side in apparent disagreement. "But there wasn't any chloral hydrate in his cupboard," he said. "Not in his cupboard or anywhere else. I went through everything in that cottage very thoroughly indeed on the night he hanged himself."

"Are you sure?" I demanded.

He nodded grimly. "I'd take my oath on it."

# CHAPTER TWENTY

The Inspector made me tell him all about finding the chloral hydrate in Shaddock's cupboard. Then he made me tell it all over again. Finally, he sat back and stared at me.

"I don't know what it means," he said, "but it proves what I've been saying all along. There's more to this than meets the eye."

"There must be," I agreed. "I can't imagine why someone put a bottle of chloral in Shaddock's cottage *after* the police had searched it. What would be the point? And who could have done it?"

The Inspector suggested, logically enough, that it must have been someone who wanted to convey the idea that Shaddock had drugged the boys. I agreed that this seemed logical. "But I'd say it also must have been someone who didn't realize the police had already searched the cottage."

"Not necessarily," said the Inspector. "You're assuming it was done for our benefit, Seraphina. But that needn't have been the case. It might rather have been intended for some outside person, as a kind of misdirection." He sat up in sudden excitement. "Or it might simply have been a way of getting rid of evidence that would have implicated somebody else if it had been found in his or her possession. By Jove, I believe that must be it! It only goes to prove my theory that Shaddock wasn't working alone."

He was quite excited about this in the beginning, Dear Reader, but by the time the train had carried us forward another league or two, he had begun to subside into gloom once more. "Unfortunately, it's only a theory," he said. "I can't prove that any-one else was involved."

"Doesn't the chloral prove it?" I asked.

"No, because I didn't find it myself. All I've got is hearsay evi-dence. Not that I'm doubting your word, Seraphina," he added, at my affronted expression. "I'm sure the stuff was there just as you say. But unfortunately, the case is now closed. And it would take more than an unaccounted-for bottle of chloral hydrate to open it again."

"But don't you think the fact the bottle was there proves the boys were drugged before they were killed? Perhaps even given a fatal dose to facilitate whatever came after? As you say, it would have been a great risk otherwise."

I wanted badly to believe this, Dear Reader. Even more, I wanted *him* to believe it. Policemen see a lot of brutality in their jobs. Their only comfort can be in apprehending the brutes responsible and bringing them to justice. In this case, where it looked as though justice would be thwarted, I wanted to soften the apparent brutality as much as I could.

I think he understood what I was doing, for he reached out to pat *my* hand. "Yes, Seraphina," he said. "I can think of no rea-son why the chloral would have been introduced in that highly meretricious way if it hadn't played *some* rôle in the business. As a false trail, it wouldn't lead anywhere—unless it was to the local apothecary, perhaps."

"Are you going to investigate him?"

He laughed, and I was pleased to note that though it was a rueful laugh, it wasn't actually bitter. "I haven't any excuse, unfortunately. That would probably be my first act if I were still on the case. I'd try to determine where the stuff came from and who bought it. And that, in turn, ought to provide some clue about who put it in Shaddock's cottage. But as I said, the matter is now officially closed."

"But it could be reopened again, if more evidence were found?"

He was smiling now but also shaking his head. "It's always diverting to see you so warm in the cause of justice," he said. "What a highly specialized conscience you've got, Seraphina! Allowing you to run with the hares *and* hunt with the hounds."

I pointed out that as a Fox, I was well-qualified to do both. "It depends on what game the hounds are pursuing," I explained. "Sometimes my sympathies are with the prey, in which case I prefer to stand aside. But there are other chases in which I can join with enthusiasm, and this appears to be one of them. I don't approve of children being murdered. Not even public menaces like Georgie Hubbard."

The Inspector had sobered at these words. "I'd be glad to know that murder was the worst of it," he said. "All that money Shaddock had is very troubling. Boys like that wouldn't be of much value, ordinarily. At least not for anything apart from purposes I don't like to think of."

"You are speaking of immoral purposes, I suppose," I said, matter-of-factly. One knows such things go on, Dear Reader. Girls and women are more commonly the victims, but males of any age are not exempt.

I went on to consider the matter as dispassionately as I could. "I suppose there would be money in it," I said. "But it could only come from men with rather *specialized* tastes. And it seems unlikely that there could be many of them in a small village like Ainsworth."

The Inspector did not say anything, but I could guess the direction of his thoughts. "You are thinking of Lord Rodney," I said accusingly.

"Perhaps I am," he returned. "It's obvious, isn't it? All that money had to come from somewhere. And Lord Rodney is the richest man in the county. As for having what you call specialized tastes, well, I heard plenty from the local force about the parties he's given in the past there at the Priory. It sounds pretty much the same thing as what we're talking about."

I could see what he meant, Dear Reader, yet to my mind there was a crucial difference. "Did the local force suggest he was in the habit of abducting his party guests and forcibly detaining them at the Priory?" I demanded. "Because unless he was, I don't see that it's the same thing at all."

"If they were doing what has been suggested, it's a crime whether or not they *were* forcibly detained," said the Inspector doggedly.

"The Law may see that as a crime, but to my mind it's distinct from the crime you are investigating," I said. "You must see the difference yourself, Tom. In such matters, it makes a great difference whether or not a man is a willing participant. Even leaving his age out of the question!"

He admitted this, Dear Reader, but said he thought the matter might not be as clear-cut as that. "There might have been willing *and* unwilling participants," he said. "Though I'd rather not think of it."

"Nor would I," I said. "Especially as I don't believe it's true. I *like* Lord Rodney."

"I like him, too," said the Inspector. "But unless you can offer me an alternative theory, it seems to me he's our most likely suspect."

I told him I had no alternative theory, but added that if I were looking for suspects I would focus my attention on Mr. Alexis. "There's something definitely shady about that man." I said.

He looked me over with a half-smile. "You're not letting professional jealousies affect your judgment, I hope?" he asked.

"It's possible," I admitted, "but I don't think so." I then gave him the gist of my conversation with Mr. Alexis that afternoon. I stressed how relieved he had seemed at Shaddock's death and how firm in his assertions that the matter was now closed and had better be put behind us.

The Inspector conceded that this was suspicious. "Perhaps he did play some rôle in the business. Though as he's a guest at the Priory, I'd still tend to think Lord Rodney must be at the bottom of it."

"He was a guest at Cincinnatus until a few weeks ago. You might as well suggest the General was at the bottom of it," I returned.

He regarded me evenly. "I wouldn't rule it out, Seraphina," he said. "Shaddock was in the General's employ. That in itself would be a suspicious circumstance. And there's no getting over the fact that he was damned obstructive in the matter of the warrant. But I can't see any motive there—not unless he's of the same persuasion as Lord Rodney and has managed to hide it all this time."

I pretended to be affronted: "Are you saying his admiration for me was only a blind?" I exclaimed. "And here I had put it all down to my charm and beauty!" More seriously, I added, "Indeed, one could hardly blame a man for trying to hide it, if he *were* of that persuasion. Considering that you police see it as a crime."

The Inspector said it wasn't the police who saw it that way, it was the Law, whose dictates the police merely enforced. I said that was quibbling, but in any case, I doubted the General had an unnatural interest in boys. "He doesn't even seem much interested in his grandson as a grandson," I said, "let alone having a more—er—esoteric interest."

The Inspector, in trenchant language, gave it as his opinion that the General was an old egotist with no interest in anything but himself.

"And gardening," I suggested.

"And gardening," he agreed. With a touch of mordant humour, he added, "I've heard wood ashes are good for the garden. Possibly there's some virtue in human ashes, too?"

"It would be an original motive for murder."

"Not a very likely one, however." With an air of shaking himself free of recollection, he added, "I don't know why I'm wasting time theorizing this way. It's not as though anything can come of it. The case is closed."

"*I* know why you're doing it," I said. "Because a good hound doesn't like abandoning the chase when the scent is still running high."

He smiled at this, a little sadly. "If the hound's master calls him off the chase, he hasn't much choice in the matter. And that's what's happened here, Seraphina. Indeed, I may as well give it up sooner as later."

And for the rest of the journey, Dear Reader, he refused to talk any more about it. Outwardly I let the subject go, but inwardly I was meditating measures I might take myself. As the Law's servant, he was obliged to answer to a master's dictates, but I wasn't. That's the thing about Foxes. We are answerable to no one but ourselves.

# CHAPTER TWENTY-ONE

Once I was back at the Temple, life speedily resumed its normal course. I took up my work with an enthusiasm that was all the greater for my holiday in Dorset, and so did the rest of my staff.

Susan was still concerned about Ellen, naturally enough. I had described to her the scene that had ensued when she had learned of Pete's death. But we had frequent encouraging bulletins from Felicity. She reported that Ellen's spirits were steadily improving; that she was no longer being harassed by the villagers; and that a few of the better sort had even come to apologize personally for their former suspicions.

I thought I recognized Felicity's hand in this. For a woman of her abilities, managing a village full of people would be child's play. If the City ever becomes enlightened enough to elect a woman mayor, Dear Reader, she would be the first woman I would think of. Though it might represent a conflict of interest, given the usual sort of business she transacts there.

At any rate, it was a comfort to have her in Ainsworth, oversee-ing Ellen's recovery. From occasional remarks she let drop, I gath-ered the Major was doing his bit to help, too. Apparently, he had even proposed taking Ellen to some sort of village festival that was coming off in a few weeks, though so far Ellen had resisted the idea.

There was an attraction in the idea of these two lonely people coming together, Dear Reader. She was a woman bereft of hus-band and child, while he was struggling to raise a son without a mother's care. Still, there are worse things than being alone, as I observed to Susan. "In storybooks, marriage is represented as a woman's best and happiest state, but in real life it very often brings its own problems."

"I wouldn't know," she retorted. "Would *you?*"

I thought it better not to let myself be drawn into a personal discussion. "The Major seems a decent sort," I went on, "but appearances can be deceptive. And love affairs are chancy, even under the best of circumstances. Much better to let them sort it out on their own."

Susan concurred with me there, Dear Reader. "No business of ours," she agreed. "I'll be glad enough simply to see Ellen recover her usual tone of mind."

With some curiosity, I asked what her usual tone of mind was like. Susan drew her brows together and demanded to know what I meant by asking such a question. I groped for a way to put it diplomatically. "What I mean is . . . without wishing to disparage your sister in any way, Susan, she does seem to be quite *different* from you. Not as—ah—*quick*, perhaps. And much less decisive and—er—*determined.*"

Susan's lips twitched. "Less stubborn, you mean," she said. "And quite right, too. Ellen and I are as different as chalk and cheese. I expect it comes of my being the elder. That, and the fact our mother hadn't any more idea how to raise children than the

King of Prussia.[9] One way or another, I ended up being more of a mother to her than a sister."

I apologized for alluding to such a personal subject, but Susan said she didn't mind. "Ellen's turned out a good, decent woman. It's no fault of hers that things have gone badly for her these last few years. I only hope she's seen the worst of it now."

"I think she has," I said. "I think things will improve for her from now on. For her, and for you, too, I hope."

"Me?" said Susan dismissively. "*I'm* all right. You needn't worry any more about *me*."

And in fact it appeared that I needn't, Dear Reader. From this point on, Susan discharged her duties with her usual brisk efficiency and a reassuring air of normality.

That was very satisfactory. Even if I had accomplished nothing else in Ainsworth, I could plume myself on that—though of course Felicity and the Inspector had done the actual work.

As far as the Inspector was concerned, I found the situation less satisfactory. That is to say, our private relations were satisfactory enough, but professionally, I could tell the Ainsworth business was still weighing on him. "Were your superiors content to accept that Shaddock was working alone?" I asked him the night after our return, when we were lying together in bed. "Or do they share your opinion that he must have had an accomplice?"

He sighed. "As the local authorities seem satisfied, they're quite content to let sleeping dogs lie. So you may as well do the same, Seraphina." He kissed me with a finality that would have told me the discussion was at an end, even had he not added, rather pointedly, "I'm sure you've got plenty of your own business to keep you busy."

---

9 Susan may be thinking here of Friedrich Wilhelm I. He did succeed in raising most of his children to adulthood, but his methods have not generally been admired. —*Ed.*

He was right about that, Dear Reader. With September approaching, and the weather as nearly ideal as London ever gets, my clients were flocking back into Town. Soon there was more demand for sittings than I had evenings to schedule them.

Normally I try to be even-handed in distributing my favours, but just now I chose to give precedence to Mrs. Clarke. She was still not delivered of her baby, and once again she seemed to have grown larger even in the few days I had been absent from Town. Privately, Susan, Jenny, and I all speculated about the size of the coming infant.

"Twelve pounds if it's an ounce," said Jenny with authority. "My sister Emma was near as big with *her* first, and that's what *he* weighed."

"In that case," I said, "I pity poor Mrs. Clarke! Indeed, I can't think why any woman would choose to endure such an ordeal."

"She mightn't make much of it," said Jenny matter-of-factly. "Emma didn't. She was back to work within the week."

That would have been reassuring, Dear Reader, except that I gathered Jenny's sister was much like her: a woman whose dimensions were scaled up from the average by a factor of about fifty percent. That wasn't at all the case with Drusilla Clarke. Still, I am assured by those who know about such things that a woman's external size has no apparent correlation with ease of labour. So I put my misgivings aside and sought to make our sittings as reassuring as possible.

To that end, I found my time in Ainsworth had accomplished another and unexpected benefit. Before, I had yawned a little at evenings spent dwelling amid Light and Beauty and Understanding, but now I found I welcomed them. They made a pleasant change from tragedy, brutality, and unsolved mystery.

◄╫ ╫►

About two weeks after my return, I unfolded the morning newspapers to find that a wave of crime had swept over London.

As it happened, I already knew this from private sources. The Inspector had been routed out of bed in the small hours by an urgent message from his superiors at the Yard, and I had heard the fire-engines clattering by several times during what remained of the night.

The newspapers reported that a gin palace in Holborn had burnt to the ground. So had an opium den near the shipyards and a gaming hell in Soho. To cap matters off, the police had recovered a couple of bodies from the River which appeared to have got there in other than accidental ways.

As I was poring over these newspaper accounts, Susan brought in the morning post. Among the various bills, circulars, and missives I found a note from Felicity:

> *Well My Dear, I am back in Town and you will be glad to hear that Little Business which was giving me trouble before has now been settled to my own <u>COMPLETE SATISFACTION</u>.*

The last two words were not only capitalized but underlined three times.

> *You will find me at the Old Shop same as ever & very glad to see my Friends of which you are One Dear & No Mistake.*
> *Yours, F*
>
> *P.S. Come drink Tea with me, I can tell you the latest News of our Friends in Dorset.*

It struck me as quite a coincidence that Felicity should have arrived back in London just as the city erupted into violence. Or rather, it struck me as no coincidence at all, in light of the business settlement she had hinted at in her note. At any rate, I was glad to hear it *was* settled, and settled satisfactorily from her point of view. I filed it away as one of those things I probably shouldn't mention to the Inspector.

That afternoon, I put on my hat, ordered out the carriage, and had Sam drive me to the Calico Cat. On entering the shop, I was pleased to see that here, too, normalcy had been restored. Attendants bustled to and fro with platters of muffins, scones, and teacakes; patrons gossiped, ate, and drank at little tables scattered around the rooms; and the eponymous cat purred from her usual place by the fire.

As for Felicity, she was purring, too. Gone were the beard and man's attire and the air of anxiety that had gone with them. She looked very sleek and self-satisfied as she sat before the fire, resplendent in a dress of crimson brocade trimmed with a fine display of old lace.

"You look magnificent," I told her. "No lying low for *you*, I see. A very sound strategy. As long as you act normally and go about your ordinary business, ten to one the police will never guess you were involved."

"Don't know what you mean, dear," she said, but she was grinning. "Besides, it's as I told you before. It's not the *police* I'm worried about."

I felt obliged to mention that bodies in the river were likely to bring the police into the matter willy-nilly. Felicity waved this aside as irrelevant, however. "Those bodies," she said. "I hadn't anything to do with *them*. Not directly, anyway." She smiled wickedly. "*That* was just a case of rogues falling out. And you can tell your Inspector so, with my compliments. Remember how I told you I'd had a bit of a disagreement with my former business partner?"

I told her I remembered. "Er—that wouldn't now be your *late* business partner, would it?"

"So it would," she agreed, with a look of indescribable mischief. "The bastard wanted to take another fellow into the business instead of me. Well, I couldn't be having *that*, of course, but with both of 'em against me, it wasn't so easy, just at first, to get the upper hand. Finally, it occurred to me that if they were busy fighting each other, they'd be too busy to bother me anymore. So I just waited till the time was right and then gave 'em the impression that the one was double-crossing the other. And what should happen but they ended up doing for each other!" She laughed aloud at the recollection. "Even *I* didn't expect anything as good as that. But I was happy enough to have it happen, you can bet!"

I don't suppose Felicity ever heard about Cadmus and the dragon's teeth, Dear Reader, but she appeared to have replicated his strategy very successfully. When it comes to warfare, she could probably teach Hannibal a thing or two. The only matter left unexplained, to my mind, was how the bodies had come to be in the river. It was a circumstance that did not seem to fit the explanation she had given me. Felicity, however, assured me that that had merely been a matter of tidying up after the business was over and done with.

"Very well," I said. "I will pass the word on to the Inspector. And it might be as well to let him assume those fires were all part of the same business, don't you think?"

Felicity pointed out very logically that they *were* part of the same business, if you looked at it the right way. I agreed that they were, and from there our conversation passed to other matters. "It's very good to have you back in Town," I told her. "But I daresay our friends in Dorset were sorry to lose you. Did Sally come back, too?"

"No, she wanted to stay on down there," said Felicity, with a disparaging look. "Between you and me, I think she's picked up a beau in the village and don't want to risk losing him. Poor taste if you ask *me*. Far better she should bring him back to Town and let me find him a proper job of work here. If she'd been one of my better girls, I'd have said as much, but being as it's Sally, I gave her my blessing. Housework and village life is about all she's fit for, when all's said and done."

I said she did at least seem quite fit for that, and that they seemed pleased with her work at the Vicarage. Felicity agreed with me. "Though I don't think they'd have any trouble getting another girl now the trouble is cleared up. The old trouble, that is." She paused, regarding me with an air of hesitation.

"What is it?" I asked, disturbed by her manner.

She let out her breath in a gusty sigh. "I hate to say it, but it looks to me as though there might be trouble of a different sort brewing," she said. "There at the Vicarage."

Naturally I demanded to know what sort of trouble she meant. She rubbed her thumb and forefinger together in an expressive way. "The sort that troubles most of us from time to time," she said. "Money, that is."

"Money?" I repeated. "Ellen has money troubles?"

"No, not her. It's the master I mean. The Vicar, Mr. Douglas."

"The *Vicar* is in financial difficulties?"

"So I gathered," said Felicity. "Heard him and his sister talking about it t'other night." She dropped one eyelid, significantly. "They thought they were alone, but I just happened to be passing by the parlour and heard them arguing. Through the keyhole." Again she dropped her eyelid, with a knowing smile.

I could not fault her methods, Dear Reader. Indeed, Miss Douglas herself would have approved them. "Go on," I said. "What did you hear?"

"It sounds as if the Vicar's run himself into debt. And in consequence, they're obliged to make economies there at the Vicarage. He was talking about selling their horse and carriage and letting their outside man go. That doesn't bode well for Ellen, does it? Next thing you know, they'll be thinking they can get by with a maid-of-all-work and let *her* go."

I stared down into my tea-cup, considering what this might mean. "So the Vicar is in debt?" I said. "I wonder how that happened. From what I saw, neither he nor his sister appear to live in an extravagant way."

"No," said Felicity, "but there's no doubt that he's wasted the ready one way or another. His sister was scolding him for it something dreadful—going on and on about what a disgrace it was. She seemed pretty upset."

"I wonder," I said. "Could he possibly have had something to do with those boys' murders? I wouldn't have thought so, but it's suggestive that he suddenly finds himself with too little money, while Shaddock died having too much."

As Felicity appeared interested, I told her about the valuables the police had found at Shaddock's cottage, and the Inspector's theory that he was getting money from some unexplained source. As not uncommonly happens, Felicity knew more about it than either of us.

"Started back in the spring," she said with authority. "All of a sudden he was flush with money, and nobody knew where it was coming from. Caused a bit of talk, naturally. Next thing you know, he's broken off his engagement to his sweetheart. She was the daughter of the local smith and had a bit of money of her own, which is why a lot of folks thought he took up with her in the first place. He was one of those men who'd marry a midden for muck, as the saying goes. So when he threw her over and took up with a fancy woman in the next town, that caused talk, too. But nobody thought to connect it with this business of the boys until after he was dead."

"And no one has any idea where the money came from?"

"Oh, they've *plenty* of ideas," said Felicity with emphasis. "But none that struck me as very likely. Mean to say, there's those that would have it he was a resurrection man. Selling corpses to the medical schools and making them to order when there weren't enough to hand. But that's not likely, is it, dear? No money in corpses nowadays."

"They get them from prisons nowadays, I believe," I said absently. I was considering this idea, Dear Reader, and finding I shared Felicity's opinion. I simply could not envision quiet Ainsworth as the centre of a Byzantine plot wherein medical students paid for freshly-made corpses, dissected them, and then returned them as ashes to cover their work.

"I don't think so," I said regretfully. "Even Burke and Hare[10] didn't get rich at the resurrection business, and *they* practiced on a wholesale basis. Any other ideas?"

"The General's black manservant is a cannibal," said Felicity promptly. "He paid Shaddock to slaughter the boys and then he ate 'em."

"Incinerating the bones afterwards to hide the evidence," I said, nodding. "Yes, I've heard that theory, but to my mind, it's even less likely than the other. For one thing, Phillipe is a good deal more civilized than most of the people in Ainsworth. For another, I doubt he makes enough money at his job to afford human flesh, if it comes as dear as what Shaddock appears to have charged for it."

Felicity observed leniently that she'd taken it for nothing more than silly talk herself. "But it does seem queer, Shaddock having all that money. I'd guess your Inspector is in the right of it and there was somebody behind him in the business, pulling strings."

Felicity had long ago assigned me proprietary rights in the Inspector, Dear Reader, so I did not cavil at her terminology. "He is inclined to suspect Lord Rodney," I said, "as having the best means and motive."

Felicity shook her head. "There's not many would agree with him," she said. "A very well-liked gentleman, is Lord Rodney. Miss Douglas did jib at him, to be sure," she added thoughtfully. "But seeing as she's a spinster, and he's a man who hasn't a lot of use for women, I put it down to that."

---

10 The most famous resurrection men in history and guilty of making corpses to order in the manner described by Felicity.—Ed.

"It would chafe her more than ever now," I said, "if she and her brother are really in financial difficulties. Lord Rodney is a rich man, and marrying a rich man is one of the few ways a woman can better her condition."

"Speaking of marrying," said Felicity, "if the Major has his way, our friend Ellen's likely to make an appearance at the altar one of these days."

"It's serious, then?" I asked. "I thought he seemed to admire her, but she didn't appear to be encouraging him."

Felicity said that in her opinion, the Major wasn't playing his cards right. "Instead of mooning around trying to pay her compliments, he should talk about how that boy of his needs a mother, and what a hard time he's having raising him alone. As soft a heart as she's got, she'd never be able to resist him."

"For my part," I said, "I think the better of the Major, that he should refrain from such blatantly manipulative tactics. Especially since the poor woman has already been twice bereft of children she loved. It would be hitting her in a weak point. And though it's true the Little Fellow hasn't a mother, there are plenty of people at Cincinnatus to care for him besides the Major. The General's servants all dote on him; that's clear enough."

Felicity put her head to one side. "But Shaddock was one of the General's servants, too, wasn't he?" she asked.

"Yes, to be sure," I acknowledged. "That does rather weaken my case, doesn't it? But it didn't appear he personally had much to do with the Little Fellow. And nor did any of the other gardening staff."

"Just as well, I'd say!" said Felicity.

"Yes, indeed," I agreed with a shudder. "A child murderer right there on the estate. It doesn't bear thinking about. That might be what motivated the Major to think about marrying again in the first place, quite as much as his admiration for Ellen."

# CHAPTER TWENTY-TWO

S am was waiting with the carriage when I came out of the tea-shop. As I settled myself inside, he handed me a sheaf of papers.

"Thought I might as well drop by the accommodation shop and fetch your mail while I was in this part of town," he explained. "Saves making a trip later."

I praised his enterprise in the warmest of terms and then turned my attention to the papers. As he manœuvred his way through traffic, I glanced through them one by one. They were the usual mixture: bulletins from servants giving information about their masters and mistresses; notes from hairdressers and bath attendants; a letter or two addressed to my various alter egos.

One of these last caught my attention, for it seemed to have been redirected from its original destination. The first address had been scored through, with another written above it in a different handwriting. Looking at it closely, I thought I could see why. The original was all but illegible and appeared indeed to be addressed to some personage named "Mua Blodcurl" rather than

"Miss Blackwood." Looking at it more closely yet, I recognized the Major's tiny, cramped handwriting. "Ah!" I said.

The contents proved as hard to decipher as the address. I had not half puzzled them out by the time we reached home. To assist me, I rang for Susan and then, after a moment's thought, Jenny as well. Jenny had come rather lately to the written word, but it struck me that this might give her an advantage in the present instance. She would, I thought, be more familiar than Susan and I with the pitfalls besetting an inexperienced scribe.

Working together, we were able to puzzle out most of the message. "It sounds as though the General is still hankering after Mr. Alexis's Spiritual charms," I said. "And the Major wants me to come down there and unmask him as a fraud."

"Are you going to?" asked Susan.

"Not without an invitation from Lord Rodney," I said. "My position would be invidious enough even as an invited guest. True Believers don't thank you when you show them their idols have feet of clay. And Lord Rodney appears to be as much a True Believer as the General. I am willing to do it as a favour because I like the Major and because I feel sorry for the old man—"

"And because you dislike Mr. Alexis," suggested Susan with a half-smile. "Don't tell me it's all philanthropy, for I won't believe it."

I said it was philanthropy enough, considering I would be obliged to pay my train fare to Ainsworth and back. "As you know, I do a certain amount of *pro bono* work, and this would appear to be a worthy cause. But I won't move without a direct invitation from Lord Rodney. I thought I made the Major understand that."

"I think you did," said Jenny, looking up from the letter. "He says that Lord Rodney is writing you—let me see—yes, 'under separate cover.' That's what he says right here."

I got up and went to look at the other letters Sam had given me. Surely enough, there was a heavy cream-coloured envelope addressed to "Miss Blackwood" in an elegant hand. Breaking the seal, I found it was indeed an invitation to a party at the Priory.

"There can't be many women who have had *that* honour," I said, perusing the invitation. "'The pleasure of your company is requested at a weekend house party, culminating in a sitting Saturday evening with the celebrated Mr. Alexis, Spiritualist and Trance Medium.'"

Susan observed that I would feel pretty funny as a woman alone in that household. "I would if I were, but I won't be," I said. "Lord Rodney writes that he has invited his sister as well, to preside over the gathering. So it's all very proper and according to Hoyle."

"Very well," said Susan, "I'll reschedule your sittings for that Friday and Saturday. Will you be home on the Sunday?"

"Probably I will be, if the sitting is Saturday evening," I said. "In fact, if everything goes well, I may be obliged to leave Saturday night! But we'll cross that bridge when we come to it."

⇥ ⇤

The Inspector's reaction was much less matter-of-fact. "You're going down to Ainsworth again," he said, regarding me with narrowed eyes. "To unmask this Spiritualist fellow, as you say. What on earth do you hope to accomplish by that?"

"Just that," I said. "Isn't it enough, Tom? I will be doing a good deed for the Major and General—and, indirectly, for the Little Fellow. Keeping the old man from squandering his inheritance on Spiritualistic charlatans," I added piously.

The Inspector said he could see how that might be a refreshing change for me. "But are you sure there isn't more to it than that?" he asked. "The Spirits haven't, for example, given you any new information that might bear on those child murders?"

"As to that," I said, "they did drop a word in my ear the other day." I told him what Felicity had told me about the Vicar's money troubles, although—as the Inspector had no idea of her rôle in the business—I let him assume my information had come from Ellen.

He thought about it, his expression sharp with concentration. "The Vicar," he said. "It doesn't seem likely, but as you say, it's suggestive. He and Lord Rodney *were* as thick as inkle-weavers now that I think about it. Perhaps the same motive would do for both."

I objected to this, saying it was natural the Vicar and Lord Rodney should collaborate on parish business. "You keep trying to bring Lord Rodney into it," I said, "and I'm convinced he's as innocent as a lamb. Only look at how Mr. Alexis has deceived him."

"And you intend to destroy his faith," he returned. "Don't you suppose he might resent that? Mr. Alexis certainly will."

I said I counted on Major Phelps-Whitmore to protect me. "But I don't see Lord Rodney being violent in any case. In fact, I'd say he's about the least violent person I've ever met."

"Not if he's at the bottom of *this* business."

I clicked my tongue. "I'm sure he isn't. Anyway, you can't have it both ways, Tom. It's the Vicar who's short of funds. If Lord Rodney were paying the piper—or paying Shaddock—Reverend Douglas wouldn't have to."

"You don't know that," he returned. "We're only guessing at this point. Both of them could be in it, or someone else entirely. Means, motive—the whole business is still a complete mystery."

"Perhaps I can pick up another clue, then," I said, "while I am in Ainsworth."

In a troubled voice, he said he didn't like my going there. "I feel certain there's someone in Ainsworth who's a murderer morally, if not in actual fact. If you go looking for clues, you might inspire him to murder *you*. I'd rather not have that happen—not for all the clues there ever were."

"There now!" I said. "You ought to have begun with that argument, Tom, and let well enough alone. If you had, you might find me more tractable."

Smiling grimly, he advised me to tell it to the Marines. "I don't expect you to be tractable," he said, "God knows! But I do hope you'll take care while you're in Ainsworth. If you stumble across something you can't manage alone, be sure to send for me. I'll be glad to come down at a moment's notice, night or day."

I looked at him closely. There was a seriousness in his tone that was unexpected. "That sounds as though you thought I might solve the case," I said. "Can it be?"

He ran a hand through his hair. "It did occur to me," he admitted. "Though I don't see how. But I suppose men may be allowed to have their intuitions the same as women."

"You'll be setting up as a Spiritualist yourself next," I said, at which he snorted.

"I wouldn't dare," he said, "seeing how you treat the competition!" With curiosity, he added, "Exactly what do you mean to do to Mr. Alexis, if I may ask?"

"It depends on the circumstances," I said. "I don't know exactly how he works, or how the séance room will be arranged. But I rather gathered that complete darkness is essential for his purposes."

"And in that case?" prompted the Inspector.

"In that case," I said, "I intend to shine a little light in the darkness."

# CHAPTER TWENTY-THREE

I had never stayed anywhere as luxurious as the Priory, Dear Reader. It was a delightful experience—or would have been, if I had been there as an ordinary guest. Knowing I was there to disrupt my host's featured entertainment, I could not help feeling a little uncomfortable. Not enough to wholly outweigh the pleasure of being served breakfast in bed (a most luxurious goose-down bed, and a most delectable breakfast), or drinking tea from Catherine the Great's own tea service. But I was prey to an occasional twinge of conscience when I reflected that if my plans came off, I would be making a poor return for Lord Rodney's hospitality.

On my arrival, I had been welcomed by him and his sister Lady Theresa, a large woman with dark hair and strong features who treated her brother with good-humoured condescension. "*You* may prefer to steep yourself in the occult, Rodney," she told him, as we drank our tea together on Friday afternoon. "But I am more orthodox in my ways—or more eclectic, anyway. If I am to attend a Spiritualistic séance tomorrow evening, then I must balance it with decent Christian Evensong tonight. Is your Vicar any good?"

"Yes, very good, Tess," said Lord Rodney, smiling. "And I assure you I don't steep myself in the occult to the exclusion of everything else. Indeed, I frequently attend Christian services myself. I don't regard them as incompatible with Spiritualism."

Lady Theresa said talking paid no toll. "You may prove it by accompanying me to Evensong tonight," she told him. Turning to me, she added courteously, "Do you care to come with us, Miss Blackwood?"

On consideration, I said I would. As I wasn't staying at the Vicarage this trip, I hadn't had any chance to see Reverend Douglas, and I was curious to do so in light of Felicity's revelations. If he was in financial difficulties, then it seemed at least possible they might have some connection with Shaddock's unexplained riches. I thought I would like an opportunity to reconsider him with this in mind.

I am not a great churchgoer, Dear Reader, but I found the evening's service enjoyable—beautiful, even. The sun, low in the west, illuminated with dazzling effect a stained-glass window depicting the sacrifice of Isaac. The boy was depicted gazing up at his father Abraham, who stood over him with knife in hand. An angel, wearing a sternly admonitory expression, was halting the parental blade while indicating a ram which the Lord had supplied as a substitute. It was a glorious thing, Dear Reader, but I thought it must be painful viewing for the parents of the murdered boys, who had received no such eleventh-hour angelic intervention.

The liturgy, too, had its moments of relevance. The opening prayer, for instance, spoke of darkness and light being the same in the eyes of the Lord, and of making the night the same as the day. I found this very amusing, considering it was more or less what I was planning to achieve tomorrow night.

The Old Testament reading was less amusing, but no less relevant. It was one of those passages from Jeremiah denouncing the Israelites for worshipping false gods. "'And they have built the high places of Tophet,'" intoned Reverend Douglas, "'to burn their sons and their daughters in the fire; which I commanded them not, neither came it into my heart. Therefore, behold, the days come, saith the Lord, that it shall no more be called Tophet, but the valley of slaughter: for they shall bury in Tophet until there be no place.'"

I wasn't the only one struck by these words, Dear Reader. I saw several members of the congregation exchange startled glances. As for Lord Rodney, he gave a little shudder and bowed his head. His sister kindly put her arm around his shoulders.

I wondered if Reverend Douglas had chosen that passage deliberately, or if it were merely some scriptural lottery that had brought it forward on that particular night. I wasn't familiar enough with church liturgy to know. Reverend Douglas himself seemed unaware that his words had caused any consternation. He went through the service with calm self-possession, his golden head bright against the dark wood of the church's interior. Looking at him, one might have fancied him an angel like the one on the church window, or at least a minor prophet. I noticed several young ladies who seemed very struck by his appearance. If Jeremiah had been that good-looking, Dear Reader, he might have had an easier time convincing the Israelites of the error of their ways.

<hr />

The next day was Saturday. As the whole day was centred around the séance that evening, the schedule was arranged for the convenience of Mr. Alexis. Lord Rodney explained that it was the Spiritualist's custom to take a light meal at mid-day and then eat nothing until after the sitting. "But there will be a cold collation in the dining room at seven o'clock. for those who want it," he told us. "And Mr. Alexis will be reading the cards in the library after luncheon, for any guests who might be interested."

I *was* interested, Dear Reader. In any case, I had some hours to get in before I was called to action, and Tarot cards seemed as good a way to pass the time as any. So I went along to the library with the others and watched Mr. Alexis lay out the cards. The deck was the standard *tarot divinatoire,* brightly coloured with strange archaic images. He used a very simple spread: three cards only, drawn by the questioner and laid in a line across the table. They were supposed to symbolize the past, the present, and the future.

The first card I drew was "The Hanged Man."

I looked at the card, then at Mr. Alexis, just in time to catch him exchanging significant looks with Lord Rodney. *"Le Pendu,'"* he said, "'The Hanged Man.' Yes."

"What does it mean?" I asked.

For answer, he merely told me to draw another card.

This time it was the Seven of Swords, depicting a man carrying off an armful of weaponry with an expression of deep cunning.

"What does *that* mean?" I asked.

With another glance at Lord Rodney, Mr. Alexis said its interpretation depended on the other cards in the spread. "Draw another," he invited.

This time it was "Death."

I looked at the card, depicting a grinning skeleton on horseback beneath the word *"Mort."* "Well," I said, as lightly as I could, "it appears my future may be in some doubt."

Mr. Alexis assured me this was a superficial reading of a by-no-means negative card. "'Death' in this case need not signify death," he explained, "but rather change, rebirth, and re-invention. I would interpret the whole—" he indicated my three cards with a sweep of his hand, "—as an emerging from a period of confusion and deception. A period in which you have, perhaps, been insufficiently esteemed or regarded." As he gathered up the cards from the table, he added with an encouraging smile, "Now you will be entering into a better and more spiritual existence."

On the whole, I wasn't as reassured as I might have been, Dear Reader.

⇒⊱ ⊰⇐

I whiled away the rest of the afternoon with tea and conversation. When seven o'clock came, I had no appetite for Lord Rodney's cold collation, but I went along to the dining room anyway and picked at salad and chicken with Lady Theresa to help pass the time. It was a great relief when the clock struck nine, and it was time to take my place at the séance table with the other guests.

We were eight in number, counting Mr. Alexis. Besides myself, Lord Rodney, and his sister, the party included the Major and the General from Cincinnatus and an elderly couple whom Lord Rodney introduced as the Hartfords. "They, too, are Spiritual enthusiasts," he told us.

The séance room was a parlour opening off the main drawing room. I had explored it beforehand, Dear Reader, with an eye to my own purposes. It was pretty much as I would have arranged it if I had been the presiding Medium. There was a round central table, large but not heavy, which was covered with a dark cloth. Eight chairs had been placed around the table, spaced so as to leave a goodly distance between them. The windows were curtained with a pale, thin set of inner draperies hanging beneath a heavier set of dark red velvet. Only the inner curtains had been drawn, but as we were approaching the new moon, there wasn't much light from outside to exclude anyway.

Inside, there was even less light. No fire burned in the hearth, and only a single, shaded candle flickered in a low stand in the centre of the table. This provided a very inadequate illumination, and there wasn't provision for any more because this room, like the rest of the Priory, had never been equipped with gas fixtures. I had asked Lord Rodney about this earlier, and he had told me, with an apologetic smile, that he found gaslight unaesthetic. I couldn't help suspecting this might be one reason why Mr. Alexis found the Priory such a congenial place for his sittings.

The eight of us took our places around the table. It was obvious where Mr. Alexis would sit: he had his own special chair, larger and more ornate than the others. It stood with its back to the curtained windows. Lord Rodney directed me to a seat almost opposite, between the Major and the General. He himself sat at Mr. Alexis's left hand, while the General sat at his right. These were clearly the prime seats, reserved for Mr. Alexis's favoured patrons.

I smiled at the Major as I sat down beside him. He smiled back with a boyish air that put me strongly in mind of his son. "Glad to have you back in Ainsworth, Miss Blackwood," he said. "Here for the show with the rest of us, I see."

He accompanied these words with a broad wink. I fervently hoped neither Mr. Alexis nor the General had seen it. Looking toward them, I was relieved to see they were speaking together— or rather the General was addressing a low-toned harangue to Mr. Alexis, who looked as though he were an unwilling listener. "Yes, yes," he said, when at last the General paused for breath. "Of course we will try, my dear sir. But you know such things are not wholly within my control, nor Sister Angelique's."

I thought the General looked displeased by this statement, Dear Reader. But catching my eye at that moment, he turned to me, smiling and bowing in his courtliest manner. "Miss Blackwood," he said, "I've just been telling Mr. Alexis how I hope he'll give us a good showing tonight."

I said I had no doubt that he would. Privately, I thought it was likely to be a memorable showing if my strategy proved successful. I only hoped the General's health would not result in a last-minute cancellation of the whole affair. He was looking frailer than ever, and the waxen pallor of his complexion was very pronounced. With concern, I asked him if he were quite well.

"Yes, very well," he assured me. "I'll admit I've been a bit off-colour lately, but Mr. Alexis is better than a dozen doctors. Well, I mean to say: when a man can communicate with Hippocrates himself, you can be sure you're in the right hands!"

"Does Mr. Alexis practice psychic healing, then?" I asked with interest. It was the first I had heard of it, Dear Reader.

The General said no, it wasn't a matter of psychic healing so much as simply having access to expert advice. "Sister Angelique can put you in touch with anybody, alive or dead," he explained. "Some of those old classical fellows are worth a dozen of your modern leeches."

Sister Angelique was, it appeared, the name of Mr. Alexis's Spirit Control. In life she had been a fourteenth-century French nun who had been walled up alive for some trifling offense in the most approved fashion of the day. Now she played the rôle of Spiritual go-between, fetching Souls from the Other Side to communicate with the séance-goers.

I had supposed Mr. Alexis would begin by extinguishing the candle and having us join hands. But for the first part of the sitting, he did neither. Instead, he simply went into a trance, allowing his head to drop back and his eyes to close. His artificially shadowed lids looked very dark and dramatic in the dim light. "*Voila*, I am here," he announced presently. "Here from— 'ow do you say?—ze Ozzer Side. Zis is *Soeur* Angelique."

The effect of this announcement, spoken in a high falsetto voice, was quite ludicrous. I wanted to laugh, but since no one else did, I bit my lip and kept my face as straight as possible.

Immediately after Sister Angelique's announcement, the table began to rock. I looked narrowly at Mr. Alexis's hands. He had them folded together in front of him—at least that was how it appeared from where I sat, but the light was so dim and he was situated at such a distance from me that I couldn't be sure. Scrutinizing his hands, however, I thought one or both of them were probably dummies: false Spirit Hands to hide the fact that his real hands were busy rocking the table from beneath.

The candle was still burning in the centre of the table. With feigned alarm, I pointed this out to the others. "The table is moving up and down so violently that I am afraid the candle is going to slide off!"

Mr. and Mrs. Hartford looked at the candle with apprehension. Lord Rodney merely chuckled, however, and so did the General. "You'd think so, wouldn't you?" he told me. "But just you watch. No matter how high the table tilts, the candle won't move. Quite miraculous, really."

At these words, the table gave a particularly energetic tilt. And the candle *did* move, Dear Reader. Not only did it move, it slid right off the table into Mrs. Hartford's lap.

She let out a shriek and leaped to her feet. Her husband sprang to his feet to assist her. So did Lord Rodney. It was quite an amusing scene, Dear Reader. The candle had fortunately failed to ignite her dress, but one corner of the tablecloth caught fire and was badly charred by the time they got it put out. And then, of course, once it *was* put out, there was no light at all in the room. Lord Rodney had to stumble around in the dark to find the candle, fetch it out, and re-light it.

Under cover of the darkness, I smiled to myself. Having inspected the room beforehand, I had detected the fine thread tied to the base of the candlestick that ran across the table to Mr. Alexis's place. By keeping hold of this thread, he could tilt the table as much as he pleased without the candle sliding off. Or rather he could have, before I interfered with his arrangements. As I had feared he might notice if I removed it altogether, I had merely severed the thread close to the candlestick's base.

It took a little while for the party to recover from this incident. But eventually we were all seated at the table again, with the candle burning in its centre. Mr. Alexis, looking ruffled, slipped into a second trance, and eventually Sister Angelique indicated she was once more in our midst. "Hands off ze table and all join together," she instructed.

It appeared we were done with table tilting for the time being, Dear Reader. We all joined hands—all except Mr. Alexis, who kept his hands folded on the table as before. Presently other hands appeared, ghostly white in the near-darkness. They would slide briefly onto the table beside Mr. Alexis, or wave gaily in the air above him. Others manifested themselves as little taps and touches on our legs.

It was nicely done, but not at all mysterious, Dear Reader—not to me, at least. Some of the hands were his own; some were Spirit Hands attached to telescoping rods that allowed him to wave them in the air or prod people under the table. I might have joined in the fun, for I had a Spirit Hand of my own in my pocket. He wasn't the only one who thought it might be useful to have an extra hand available tonight. Not knowing the exact order of events to come, however, I wasn't yet sure I would need this particular piece of equipment.

The hands having finished their display, Sister Angelique got down to business. We had a succession of Spirits seeking to communicate with people in the room. One, a gentleman described as "*Très gentil*—dark and rather melancholy," Mrs. Hartford tentatively identified as her late father. Another, in connection with whom Sister Angelique persistently invoked the letter "B," went unclaimed.

I suspected this was meant for me, Dear Reader. Mr. Alexis would naturally assume a woman of my age would have a few Dear Departed Ones, and as my name was supposed to be Blackwood, the letter "B" would seem a sure-fire winner. I took great pleasure in frustrating him.

For the General, there was "a man *militaire*, of ze ancient times—a man grim and fearsome of aspect."

"Hannibal," said the General at once. "It's Hannibal, by Jove." He seemed quite excited.

Sister Angelique, however, said it was *not* Hannibal. "Zis is not a bearded man," she said, "no, he is enemy to your Hannibal. The great Scipio Africanus, hero of Rome." Here Sister Angelique's falsetto lowered to a booming bass: "*Ave,* my dear General!"

If the hero of Rome had really been there, he must have been disappointed by his reception. The General wasted no time in small-talk but addressed himself to Sister Angelique. "Can't you get Hannibal?" he asked.

"No," squeaked Mr. Alexis in Sister Angelique's voice, "no, he is not here. Zese men, zey are enemies.[11] He will not come."

"Not at all?"

"Not zis evening, at any rate. We will try again another time."

The General sank back in his chair, every line of his face expressing bitter disappointment. "Would rather have had Hannibal," he muttered. "But never mind, never mind."

The incident seemed to cast a pall on the proceedings. At any rate, it prompted Mr. Alexis to hurry on to the next act in his show. "I am leaving you now," announced Sister Angelique. "Zere is another spirit who wishes to occupy ze body." At these words, Mr. Alexis stirred and, without opening his eyes, addressed us in his ordinary voice. "I feel the presence of another Spirit," he said. "This Spirit requests that you put out the lights."

I reckoned we were approaching the climax now, Dear Reader. As Lord Rodney got up to extinguish the candle, I threw a

---

11 Sister Angelique may or may not be correct here. Plutarch describes a rapprochement between the two men, late in life, in which they praised each other's military prowess. —*Ed.*

meaning look at the Major. As soon as the room was completely dark, I pulled my hand away from his.

Under cover of the darkness, I then drew from my right boot-top a small oblong package. This I held very carefully in my hand, ignoring Mr. Alexis's injunction that we keep our hands joined together as before.

With the candle extinguished, the room seemed at first pitch black. Once my eyes had adjusted, however, I could distinguish dim grey rectangles where the room's unshaded windows glowed faintly in the darkness. They were directly behind by Mr. Alexis, so that his figure could be seen silhouetted against their feeble light. "There is a Spirit," he said. "It is possessing me . . . filling me . . . controlling me. And now it is *lifting* me."

Staring into the darkness, I could see that Mr. Alexis's figure did seem to bulk a little higher against the grey of the windows. It was difficult to be sure, however, since the room was so nearly dark. "I am rising," he announced in a euphoric voice. "Rising . . . rising . . . rising off the ground."

"I see it," announced Mrs. Hartford in an awed voice. "Look, there against the window! He *is* rising."

There was no doubt that the dark shape now bulked higher against the grey window. "Rising," repeated Mr. Alexis, his voice languid. "Rising higher and higher. My feet are quite in the air now. Feel!" he demanded suddenly. "Lord Rodney—General Whitmore—feel how I am risen."

"I can feel it," affirmed Lord Rodney from his place at the head of the table. "His boots are on a level with my shoulder!"

The General, sitting to the left of me, withdrew his hand from mine to make his own examination. "I can feel it, too," he reported. "He's floating, all right. Can hardly keep hold of his foot, he's risen so high."

I judged it the perfect moment, Dear Reader. Quickly I turned the little bundle in my hand upside down, then tossed it onto the table.

A blue-white light illuminated the room like a flash of lightning. Unlike lightning, however, it did not vanish as quickly as it came. It lingered long enough for us all to see Mr. Alexis, not floating at all, but simply standing behind the chair he had formerly occupied.

There was an expression of shock on his face. And in his hands were a pair of boots. One was held over Lord Rodney's shoulder, and one over the General's, and both men were gripping them for all they were worth.

# CHAPTER TWENTY-FOUR

Although I have no actual experience with Pandemonium, Dear Reader, the scene that ensued in Lord Rodney's parlour must have closely resembled it.

Lord Rodney and the General, seeing what they were holding, immediately relinquished their hold on Mr. Alexis's boots with twin looks of revulsion. Lord Rodney got to his feet and stalked into the next room to fetch candles. Once the parlour was illuminated, he resumed his seat at the table with the grim air of a judge about to preside over an unsavoury inquiry. If gaslight had been available, I felt sure he would have used it, with a complete disregard for aesthetics.

Mr. Alexis, meanwhile, had dissolved into hysterics. As you may know, Dear Reader, the word "hysterics" derives from the Greek word for uterus, *hystera*, based on the idea (endemic among medical men) that hysterical behaviour stems from a disorder of this organ—and meaning likewise that it must therefore be restricted to the female sex. If those selfsame medical men had seen Mr. Alexis on that occasion, they might have reconsidered. He wept and wailed, thrashed around on the floor, and deported himself like a madman.

Mrs. Hartford also wept, but more quietly. Her husband hovered over her with smelling salts in hand and a look of concern on his face. "She is very delicate," he told the rest of us reproachfully. "This sort of thing is very bad for her."

The Major, by contrast, took the whole incident as a joke. He roared with laughter until tears ran down his face. Every time he seemed about to master himself, he would look at Mr. Alexis and start laughing again. "Caught in the act!" he kept saying. "Done up brown, by God!"

I thought Lady Theresa shared his enjoyment, Dear Reader. Out of consideration for her brother, she did not manifest it quite so openly as the Major, but when Mr. Alexis's hysterics showed no sign of abating, she fetched a pitcher of water from the kitchen and poured it solicitously over his head. This left him gasping, but somewhat calmer.

It also left dark streaks on his face where the eye-black had run.

As for me, I might have enjoyed the whole business more had I not been so concerned about the General. The old man sat trembling in his chair, his shoulders bowed and his head hung low. His colour was very bad. "What does this mean?" he kept saying over and over. "What does this mean?"

"I would like to know what this means also," said Lord Rodney, glaring at Mr. Alexis with a fiercely militant expression. It was as though he and the General had exchanged rôles.

Lady Theresa threw him a look of sisterly condescension. "Don't get on your high horse, Rodney," she said. "It's perfectly obvious what it means. Mr. Alexis has been making monkeys of us all, and now the tables are turned. There's no need to go spelling it out any more than that. I'd say the poor man has suffered humiliation enough for one evening."

Mr. Alexis grasped at this speech as the closest thing to sympathy he was likely to get. "I would like to go to my room now," he said, with an assumption of bravado. "This has been a most distressing incident. Although I am not altogether sure *what* has taken place . . . some mischievous Spirit playing tricks, I fear. But even so, you should not have awakened me while I was in a trance. That is a very dangerous thing to do. It might easily have been fatal."

"No loss if it were," said the Major audibly.

Lord Rodney made a gesture of repudiation that would have done credit to Mrs. Siddons. "Go," he said. "Go and pack your bags. I'll expect you out of the house by morning."

Mr. Alexis went, Dear Reader. I reflected once again how deceptive appearances could be. From the gentleness of his manners, I would have supposed Lord Rodney would have been more forgiving and perhaps even seized on Mr. Alexis's excuse that he was the victim of a mischievous spirit. But he was clearly having none of it. I thought his being such a connoisseur might explain it. He would probably have reacted the same way if he found out his tea service had belonged to some commoner rather than Catherine the Great.

⇥⇤

With Mr. Alexis's departure, the party quickly broke up. Lord Rodney, after gazing into space for a moment, stalked out of the room without saying a word to anyone. After a glance at the rest of us, his sister followed him. The Hartfords then signified their desire to go to their rooms. No one made any objection.

By this time, the Major had regained control of himself. He leaned over to look at the packet I had tossed on the table. "What *was* that thing?" he asked, reaching out a hand to pick it up.

I cautioned him against handling it. "It's something like a lucifer match, similar in composition but made on a larger scale,"

I said. Using the fire tongs, I picked the thing up to show him before disposing of it in the fireplace. "The paper case originally contained a piece of phosphorous, and in one end was a glass tube holding a few drops of vitriol. There's a buffer that kept the two chemicals separate. When they combine, they make a very bright light—as you saw."

"Dashed clever," said the Major approvingly. "Lit the place up like a Guy Fawkes's firework. With Mr. Alexis being the Guy, of course." He let out another guffaw of laughter.

"Don't," I said, gesturing toward the General.

For the first time, the Major seemed to notice his father-in-law's state. "Sir!" he exclaimed. "Are you feeling unwell?" He went over and thumped the General on the back in a manner I thought more well-intentioned than prudent. "You mustn't let it get you down, sir," he urged. "That fellow being a charlatan, I mean. It's like the fakirs doing the rope trick in India. Anybody might have been taken in."

The General lifted his head to look at him, then at me. His face wore a haunted expression. "*Was* he a charlatan?" he whispered. "Was he?"

"I'm afraid he was," I said, as gently as I could. "There seems to be no doubt of it."

The General let his head drop down again. "I don't believe it," he said.

At these words, the Major looked quite crest-fallen, Dear Reader. For my own part, however, I wasn't surprised. True Believers take a lot of convincing—or unconvincing, as the case may be. I felt there was a chance the General might eventually accept the truth if he were given time to digest the evidence on his own. My concern was lest he might die before he had time to do it. His colour was still very bad, and I didn't like the way he was breathing.

"We ought to get him home," I told the Major. "And perhaps he ought to have brandy first or some other restorative."

"Home," agreed the General in a faint voice. "I want to go home."

⛌

The Major and I, helped by the General's coachman, managed to get the General out to his carriage with a minimum of jostling and discomfort. I decided to go to Cincinnatus along with them, on the chance I might be useful. In truth, I was feeling a little guilty, Dear Reader. I had wanted to cure the General of his delusions, but I had not anticipated that the treatment might kill him.

As we drove away from the Priory, I caught a glimpse of a man standing in the archway leading to the coach-house. Probably he was merely some stable functionary, but something in his appearance made me wonder if he might not be Mr. Alexis. Like the Spiritualist, this man was tall with an angular figure. He seemed to be gazing after our carriage as we drove away. But I caught no more than a glimpse of him, and a groan from the General made me forget everything else as I sought to make him comfortable.

At Cincinnatus, our arrival caused a great flurry. "Blankets!" roared the Major, as he carried the General into the house and deposited him on the sofa. "Hot water! Brandy! Stir yourselves, by God. The General's had one of his turns."

It was a comfort to know this wasn't the first such turn he had had. I noticed that all the servants seemed to know what to do. Phillipe brought brandy and Sandeep blankets; and a few minutes later Jian shuffled in with a couple of hot water bottles which he tucked carefully among the blankets that enveloped the General's torso. "You feel better, sir, yes?" he said encouragingly.

"Yes," agreed the General. His voice was only a croak, but he did look better. As Jian turned to go, I saw the Little Fellow's scared face peeping around the doorframe. The General saw it, too, and mustered a smile. "Come here, boy," he croaked. "It's all right. Not got my marching orders this time."

The Little Fellow returned his smile and came forward to sit on the sofa beside him. "You ought to be in bed," said the Major, albeit in no very critical tone.

"It's all right," said the General. "Let him be." I noticed he had regained his old authoritative manner.

"But you ought to rest, sir," urged the Major.

"Well, I am resting, aren't I? Don't be an old woman, Major."

"I think you should be in bed yourself," persisted the Major, "sir."

The General said he would do very well as he was. "*If* I can get some peace and quiet," he added in a meaning voice.

At this hint, we all got up to go. The General, however, indicated that the Little Fellow might stay. "*You're* all right," he told the boy. "You can keep your mouth shut, can't you? *You* know how to follow orders. Not like these others."

Looking highly delighted, the Little Fellow nodded and sat back on the sofa. I reflected how fickle were the ways of men. It might have been I stroking the General's brow, but he clearly preferred the ministrations of his grandson. "Pour me a glass of water, lad," he was saying as we left the room. "And pass me the brandy decanter."

⇥ ⇤

Once in the hall, I realized that I was now stranded at Cincinnatus for the night, unless I borrowed the General's carriage to get back to the Priory. Either alternative presented a dilemma. As I was hesitating over the question, the Major invited me into the kitchen for a drink. "I don't know about you," he said, "but I could use a spot of brandy myself at this point."

Glad to postpone my decision, and feeling really in need of stimulant, I went along to the kitchen with him. It was a white-washed room, meticulously clean but barer than most such offices. We sat down at the kitchen table, and the Major poured us each a glass of brandy, adding soda to mine at my request. Without asking, Jian fetched us a plate of his glutinous cakes. Knowing by this time what to expect, I found them quite toothsome.

The Major sipped morosely at his brandy. "D'you suppose the old man's going to let Mr. Alexis pull the wool over his eyes again?" he asked me, after a few minutes had gone by. "Damn it all—beg your pardon, ma'am—dash it all, he saw for himself how the fellow was tricking him!"

"It may not matter," I told him honestly. "Some people won't accept the evidence of their own eyes. Not if it conflicts with their beliefs."

The Major let fly with some pithy and profane epithets. "I do beg your pardon, ma'am," he said, "but this business has me that provoked! I hate to see the old man bled."

I told him not to despair. "I don't think the matter is settled one way or another," I said. "The great thing with a man of the General's temperament is to not argue with him. Just give him time to think it over and draw his own conclusions. He's not a fool, after all."

"No," agreed the Major, but there was an inflection in his voice that betrayed a hint of doubt.

"You think he *is* a fool?" I questioned.

The Major made a despairing gesture. "There's fools and fools," he said. "You know what I mean, I daresay. A man can be no end sharp-witted in one way, and the most damnable fool in another. Begging your pardon, ma'am," he added belatedly. "But you heard him going on and on about Hannibal this evening, and if that isn't foolishness, I don't know what is."

"I noticed he wasn't willing to accept any substitute," I said, smiling at the recollection. "But really, I don't know that there's anything extraordinary about that. Hannibal is one of history's great military geniuses. Nobody else has ever gotten elephants over the Alps. And he had some other clever tactics, too. The General was telling me about them the last time I was here. He's obviously a great admirer."

"Aye, so he is," agreed the Major, "but he didn't used to be so single-minded about it. It's only the last six months or so that he has been. I blame Mr. Alexis for encouraging him."

"Well," I said, "he didn't seem to be encouraging him tonight."

"No, he didn't," agreed the Major. There was a pause, during which his brows slowly drew together. "And that's rather queer, when you think of it," he said reflectively. "Why would he encourage him all this time, and then try to shut him down?"

I don't pretend to be a real psychic, Dear Reader, but I do assure you that when the Major spoke these words, I felt a real thrill of fear and foreboding. "Why would he?" I repeated. "*Why* would he?"

The Major stared at me. "I don't know," he said. "D'you think it matters?"

"I think it might," I said, rising to my feet. "Let's go and ask."

The Major accompanied me back to the parlour, but with a reluctant air. "Do you really think we ought to disturb him?" he asked, as we stood together outside the parlour door. "After all, he was in a pretty bad state not so long ago. Needs his rest."

"We won't disturb him if he's resting. But I think we ought to at least see."

Obediently, the Major cracked open the door. He applied an eye to the crack, then flung it open with a startled oath. "He's gone!" he exclaimed.

It was true, Dear Reader. A heap of blankets lay on the sofa; the brandy decanter and glasses stood on the table, but the General was nowhere to be seen. Neither was the Little Fellow. But the French window stood suggestively open, swaying on its hinges in the night breeze.

The Major gazed at it blankly. "That's odd," he said. "Deuced odd. Why would he go outside at this time of night?"

As if in answer, we heard a voice raised in the distance. "Stop," it shouted. "Stop!"

# CHAPTER TWENTY-FIVE

Neither the Major nor I hesitated for a moment. We were through the window and out on the lawn in a twinkling.

From there, we might have been puzzled where to go, but just then came another shout, followed by a third shout, much louder than the other and expressing itself as a kind of prolonged roar. It sounded rather like a wounded bull, Dear Reader. I had no difficulty recognizing the General in a fit of temper.

"The hothouse!" I said, pointing.

"Yes," said the Major. "I can see a light over near the potting shed. But what on earth can the old fellow be doing?"

I could imagine several things, Dear Reader, but my imaginings fell well short of the reality. For when the Major and I arrived at the potting shed, we found the doorway blocked by none other than Inspector Harper. "Keep back," he said, casting a harried look over his shoulder. "Keep back, for God's sake. He's got the boy in there—and a knife."

At these words, it was the Major's turn to roar. He sprang forward and tried to charge through the door, but the Inspector caught and held him back by main force. "Don't!" he said. "Didn't you hear me? He's threatening to kill the boy."

"I heard you," said the Major. His face was ghastly pale. "What can we do?"

The Inspector looked from one to the other of us, as though evaluating our utility in a crisis. "For a start, you might try to convince him to let the boy go," he said. "That's what *I've* been trying to do."

"You've no right," said the General's voice behind him. "No right to be here in the first place, sirrah, and no right to interfere. This is a private matter, on private property."

"You are mistaken," said the Inspector, wheeling to address him. "Murder isn't a private matter."

"It's not murder," said the General, sounding frighteningly matter-of-fact. "It's a sacrifice."

Rising onto tiptoe, I could see him where he stood with his back to the potting bench. The Little Fellow lay on the bench behind him, a small and pathetic figure. His eyes were closed, but I could see the rise and fall of his chest that indicated it was a drugged sleep rather than death. Still, death was hovering dangerously near. I could see the knife in the General's hand as he pointed it at the Inspector for emphasis. I was reminded of Isaiah on the church window and of Reverend Douglas's scriptural reading, and at that moment the whole business fell into place. "Tophet," I said. "False gods. Good heavens!"

"*Not* false gods," asserted the General. "Only forgotten. Moloch." He spoke the name with great solemnity. "Hannibal knew his power—so'd his father. And the power's still there if you know how to get it."

"Sir!" said the Major, who was now weeping in an agony of paternal anxiety. "You wouldn't kill your own grandson?"

"I'd rather not," said the General. His voice was mildly regretful, Dear Reader: no more. "But it's necessary, I tell you. That was the mistake I made with the others. The other boys," he clarified. "They were all defectives in some way. I picked 'em on purpose, thinking to kill two birds with one stone."

We all stared at him speechlessly. He clicked his tongue and went on, with an air of condescending to lesser intelligences. "It's just like gardening. You've got to root out the weak stock. All three of those boys were weak stock, with two of 'em budding criminals, and the other a cripple. And all like to be a charge on the public in the future, if something wasn't done. So Shaddock fetched them for me, and I did it." His expression became introspective. "Of course I see now that I made a mistake. It stands to reason that blood's all-important in those sort of matters. The better the sacrifice, the more power's in it. Same as in the Bible, y'know: the lamb without spot."

"But your own grandson," repeated the Major. "Your own grandson!"

The General frowned. "You mustn't think it's a painful death," he said. "I drug 'em first, so they don't feel it. It's an easier death than what I've seen many a man suffer."

"Then why don't you take it yourself?" inquired the Major in a steely voice. "Sir?"

The General frowned again. "That would hardly answer the purpose, would it?" he said sharply. "*I'm* the one who needs power. You don't know what it's like. Feeling your strength diminish year after year—your health crumbling away—all your powers growing less. I'd do anything to get 'em back." With which definitive statement, he turned back to the bench and raised his knife.

The Major leaped forward, and so did the Inspector. But someone else got there first. There was a flash of movement, and suddenly the knife was on the floor, and the General was held tight in the grip of a tall figure I recognized, belatedly, as Phillipe.

"Phillipe, b'God!" said the Major. "And not before time, either." He let out a laugh I would have called hysterical, Dear Reader, had it been credible to suppose he possessed a uterus.

"Yes, sir," agreed Phillippe. His own manner was quite tranquil. He looked down at the General, addressing him in a mildly reproving voice. "You must not struggle, sir," he said. "I shall be obliged to hurt you if you do."

The General gave up the struggle, which was a most unequal one in any case. When he spoke again, his voice was calm. "Where'd you come from, Phillipe?" he inquired. "I didn't see you."

"I came through the side door," said Phillipe. "I heard voices and came to see what was happening."

"Well, you can let me go now. In fact, I *order* you to let me go!"

Ignoring him, Phillippe turned to address the Major. "If you will take the boy into the house," he said. "He should see a doctor, I think. And so, too, should the General. Obviously he is not well."

"Damn you," roared the General. "How *dare* you disobey a direct order? You can leave my service this instant, Phillipe!"

"Very well, sir," said Phillipe, but he didn't release his grip. This caused the General to renew his struggles. As he thrashed about, he roared out threats in which the supernatural was mingled ludicrously with the mundane. We were all to be arrested; we were all to be sued; we were all to burn in the fires of Moloch.

"Try to hold him still," said the Inspector, eyeing him with concern. "I'll see if I can put the handcuffs on him. He's a danger to himself as it is. If we can get the doctor here, perhaps he can administer a sedative."

Just then the General went suddenly stiff and silent. "He's shamming," said the Major sharply. "Don't be fooled, Phillipe. It's all a trick."

Phillipe looked down at the figure in his arms. "I do not think he is shamming, sir," he said.

Phillipe's diagnosis was confirmed by the doctor. "Apoplexy," he told us, with a shake of his head. "And not unexpected, either. He had an attack early this year, if you'll recall."

"A mild one," said the Major.

"A mild one," agreed the doctor. "Made very nearly a full recovery from it, too. But that won't happen this time." He looked at the Major kindly over his spectacles. "There's no point in giving you false hope, Major. I've left some medicine and given instructions to your servants about diet and massage and so forth, but it won't make any difference. He might linger on a few days or even weeks, but it can only be a matter of time."

The Major sustained this news without flinching, Dear Reader. But there was anxiety in his next question: "And the Little Fellow?"

"The boy? Oh, the chloral's already wearing off. He'll be right as rain tomorrow, I daresay." The doctor readjusted his spectacles to regard the Major curiously. "How did he come to take chloral hydrate in the first place?"

As the Major did not seem inclined to speak, the Inspector answered for him. "We think his grandfather must have had a bottle of the stuff," he told the doctor. "Somehow the boy appears to have got hold of it."

"Boys will do that," agreed the doctor. "Into everything at that age." But he cast a shrewd look at both the Major and the Inspector as he left the room. It was no wonder, of course, for he knew the Inspector from his previous visit. He himself had examined the remains of the three murdered boys, and he also knew Shaddock had been in the General's employ. Under the circumstances, it wouldn't have taken much to put two and two together.

The Major said as much after the doctor had gone. "It's good of you to try to hush it up," he told the Inspector. "But I don't think it's any use. The sawbones, there: you could see he guessed what had happened. And there's the servants, too. A thing like this is bound to get out. It's too good a story not to."

"Probably," agreed the Inspector. "In any case, I must make a full reporting of the matter to my superiors. But it's likely they would be willing to suppress some of the details for the sake of you and your family."

The Major said fatalistically that it didn't matter. "Bound to get out," he repeated. "And maybe it's just as well. Been too much secrecy about this business as it is. To think the old man was at the bottom of it! It's got me fair knackered." He rubbed a hand over his face, which was still a little pale. "I think I need another drink."

I felt I could use one, too, Dear Reader, and since the Inspector was now technically off duty, he agreed he might have one with us. "Speaking of duty," I said, as we sat in the parlour with our drinks, "how did you come to be here in the first place, Tom? I had no idea you were even in Ainsworth!"

He contemplated me with a smile. "You remember I spoke of intuition before," he said. "Well, the more I thought about your coming here, the more I felt I ought to be here, too. So I came."

"You might have told me!"

"I intended to, if I got a chance. But you'll understand my position was rather delicate. I hadn't any official sanction to be here, and no more than suspicion to go on. For the most part, I've been dodging around trying to keep you in sight while trying to stay out of sight myself."

The Major had listened to this exchange with astonishment. "I say," he said, "it sounds as though the two of you know each other pretty well! Do you both work for the Yard, then?"

"Not I," I said. "Not officially, at least."

The Major looked at me inquiringly. The Inspector was looking at me, too, in a way that made me rather uncomfortable. "The connection is—er—personal rather than professional," I said.

It was obvious I couldn't leave it at that. Indeed, something in the Inspector's gaze compelled me to come clean, as the saying is.

I took a deep breath. "In fact, I have been deceiving you, Major. My name is not Letitia Blackwood. It's Mrs. Thomas Harper."

The Major exclaimed at the idea of our being man and wife. "And here I thought you and the General might make a match of it," he said.

"That was never a possibility," I said, avoiding the Inspector's eye. "Just as well, perhaps, as it turns out!"

When I risked a look a few minutes later, he was smiling as if to himself. I was glad it pleased him, Dear Reader. As a married person, one must make these concessions from time to time, and the present circumstances did seem to warrant it. Still, I didn't mean to make a habit of it. Being honest and aboveboard is a fine thing among people one can trust, but I count a very small proportion of humanity in that category. In any case, I had sailed so long under false colours that it felt extremely odd to do anything else.

In the meantime, Phillipe had come into the parlour. He and Jian had been assigned the job of nursing the General while Sandeep was tending to the Little Fellow. It appeared there was some question about the details of the arrangement which he wanted to discuss with the Major. "No, that will do very well," said the Major, once he had heard Phillipe out. "I'll be along to take my turn nursing, too, once I've done discussing the matter with Mr. and Mrs. Harper."

Phillipe turned to contemplate the pair of us. "Mr. and Mrs. Harper?" he inquired politely.

"Oh, aye: they're married," said the Major, with a wave of his hand. "Surprising, ain't it? Turns out they both work for the Yard."

Of course this was an exaggeration, but I let it pass, Dear Reader. So, too, did the Inspector. But I noticed that Phillipe, as he turned away, had a very faint smile on his lips. It looked as if the Major's words had confirmed some private conclusion. And very likely they had. It is difficult to deceive intelligent servants.

# CHAPTER TWENTY-SIX

After Phillipe left, the three of us continued our discussion. I was eager to learn how the Inspector had arrived on the scene in such a timely fashion.

"All I did was follow you," he explained. "To the Priory first, because that's where you were staying. I wanted to be on the spot in case of developments."

A memory stirred in my mind. "I saw you!" I exclaimed. "As we were leaving in the carriage, I saw you standing under the archway to the stable. But I didn't realize it was you. I thought it was Mr. Alexis."

He threw me a look of humourous reproach. "I can't say I relish that comparison," he said. "Especially considering how he looked the last time I saw him! Thrashing around on the floor like a dog in a fit."

"You saw that?" I exclaimed. "But how?"

"I was lurking outside, peering through the window. Trying to peer, anyhow. For a while, it was too dark to see anything. And then, all of a sudden, it wasn't." He smiled in recollection. "You'll have to show me how you played that trick. It appeared to be very effective."

"Only partly effective," I said ruefully. "It convinced everyone else that Mr. Alexis was a fraud, but not the General. Still, he was obviously shaken by it. And it was at that point that the Major and I thought we ought to get him home."

The Inspector nodded. "When your party broke up, I was uncertain what to do," he said. "But since it appeared *you* were going to Cincinnatus, I decided I'd better go along with you. I had a bicycle I'd borrowed from the landlord at the Hound and Huntsman, so I rode along to Cincinnatus, concealed the machine near the stable, and reconnoitered. The windows were open, so I could see and hear pretty well what was going on. The General seemed to have had some kind of attack, and it appeared you were all ministering to him."

"Yes," I said. "It appeared to be a severe attack, too—although the sequel would indicate otherwise."

The Inspector looked sober. "I almost left at that point," he said. "It didn't look as though anything else was likely to happen. Fortunately, I decided to stick it out a while longer. It was only a few minutes later that I saw the General come through the French window and make off toward the hothouse. That astonished me, for I'd supposed he was too ill to move, let alone take a nighttime stroll."

"It astonished us, too, when we found he was gone," I said.

"Shamming," said the Major grimly. "He must have been shamming all along."

"Possibly," agreed the Inspector. "At any rate, I was perfectly astounded to see him come through the window. He was having a lot of trouble walking, and I thought at first he was just unsteady on his feet. Then I realized he was carrying the boy. I'm sorry I wasn't quicker about intervening," he said, looking apologetically at the Major. "But as I mentioned before, my position was somewhat equivocal. You saw what he was like when I was here before, and I had a warrant that time. I felt it behooved me to go cautiously."

"Oh, aye: no doubt about it," said the Major gloomily. "He'd have made out you were the guilty one, if you hadn't actually caught him in the act."

"I'm afraid so," agreed the Inspector. "That's why I was slow in acting. The fact it was dark didn't help, either. Until he lit a lantern, I couldn't see what he was doing—and once I *could* see, he already had the knife in his hand. I let out a shout, which stopped him for the moment, but then we were at a stalemate. I couldn't get any closer without him threatening to kill the boy outright, and at that point, I couldn't doubt he meant it."

A groan escaped the Major's lips. "What a beastly business," he said. "Gives me the jimjams just to think of it. I hadn't any idea the old fellow'd gone off the rails that way. His own grandson! It beggars the imagination."

"No one could have imagined such a contingency," agreed the Inspector. "It's one of the strangest cases I've ever handled. I suppose madness must be the explanation—madness combined with senile decay, perhaps. But I still am not quite clear as to why it took that particular form. All that business about Hannibal and Moloch and human sacrifice . . . as you say, it beggars the imagination."

"I think *I* understand," I said. "And it's all down to Mr. Alexis."

The Major pushed back his chair with fire in his eye. "*That* fellow?" he said. "If you mean to say he's the one who nearly got the Little Fellow killed—"

He did not finish the sentence, but it was obvious Mr. Alexis was in mortal danger himself at that point. Begging the Major to calm down, I hastened to explain.

"From what you have told me, the General made a habit of consulting ancient military leaders at the séance table," I said. "Not just Hannibal, but Alexander and Julius Caesar and so forth."

The Major nodded. "A regular fancy of his."

"Mr. Alexis knew that, of course. In order to play his part, he studied those men in detail. He would have made notes about their lives and military campaigns. Then, during his sittings, he would give out the information as though the man himself was speaking at first-hand."

"Aye," agreed the Major. "I attended a couple of his sittings last summer, when he first came to stay with us. It was Julius Caesar then—supposed to be, anyway. Awful nonsense I thought it, but the General lapped it right up and kept coming back for more."

"I think that's where the problem arose," I said. "With men like Julius Caesar, Mr. Alexis had lots of material available. Caesar wrote his own memoirs, as well as being written about by other people in both ancient and modern times. But that's not true of Hannibal."

"No," agreed the Inspector, who had been following this discussion closely. "As I recall, only a few of the ancient historians give any real account of him. And nothing he wrote himself has survived."

"Exactly," I said. "And that means Mr. Alexis started running out of material very quickly. So, in order to supplement his scanty supply of historical accounts, I think he turned to fiction."

"Fiction?" repeated the Major. "You mean like stories?"

"I mean novels," I said, "and one novel in particular. All that stuff he was roaring out about the fires of Moloch—it reminded me of something, and now I've remembered what it was. Are you familiar with Gustave Flaubert, the French writer?"

"Yes, of course," said the Inspector. The Major looked as though he wasn't, but nodded anyway.

"Most people know him as the author of *Madame Bovary*," I said, "but he also wrote a novel set in ancient Carthage. It's called *Salammbo,* and it's very dramatic—almost excessively so. There's one climactic scene in which the ancient Carthaginians, threatened with disaster, sacrifice hundreds of their children and burn their bodies to propitiate their gods. It's described with a wealth of gory detail, and I'm afraid Mr. Alexis must have thought it was just the thing to liven up his séances with the General."

"The *bastard*," growled the Major. "The bloody, *bloody* bastard. Begging your pardon, ma'am."

"If it's any consolation, I don't believe he realized that the General was taking his words as a working strategy," I said. "Not at first, anyway."

The Inspector agreed that this was reasonable. "The first murder, in May, must have been in the nature of an experiment," he said. "The victim in that case was Georgie Hubbard. I think we may assume the experiment was successful. Or rather, that it coincided with an improvement in the General's health and made him *think* it was successful. Because he went on to repeat the experiment twice more, as well as attempting it a fourth time tonight."

The Major was staring straight ahead of him with a transfixed expression. "He had a bad turn around the end of April," he said. "Dismissed his doctor—said he'd doctor himself from now on. Good God! If only I'd realized. But I'm not a brainy chap, more's the pity. I never guessed he'd taken to murder."

"None of us guessed it," I said, "and no wonder. By having Shaddock procure his victims and then dispose of their remains, he could keep his own risk to a minimum."

The Inspector looked a little dubious at this statement. "I'd say bringing Shaddock into the business increased his risk rather than diminishing it," he protested. "From what we saw and heard tonight, it would appear the General himself did the actual killing. That means Shaddock might easily have turned Queen's evidence instead of hanging himself."

"Yes, but if it came to Shaddock's word against the General's, he could easily lay it all in Shaddock's dish," I said. "Probably he counted on that in choosing Shaddock in the first place. He prided himself on being a judge of men, and events would seem to show he was right. From everything I've heard about Shaddock, I gather he was equal parts ignorant, unprincipled, and mercenary. The perfect tool, in other words, for the General's purpose."

"Still, it must have been a tense business for him when I showed up with the warrant," said the Inspector. "He might have guessed Shaddock would make away with himself at that point, but he couldn't have been sure."

I cast my mind back to the night when the General and I had watched the moving lights among the trees. "He hid it pretty well," I said, "but you could tell he was anxious. Of course, I just assumed it was because one of his men was being arrested."

"He must have been wondering if *he* would be arrested, too," said the Inspector. "As would have happened if Shaddock chose to implicate him rather than taking all the blame on himself."

"I'll wager he took steps to make sure that didn't happen," I said. "The delay with the warrant—don't you suppose he took advantage of that to get word to Shaddock? By springing the news on him suddenly, and pointing out how the evidence implicated him alone, he could stampede him into taking his own life rather than waiting for the Law's slower processes."

"Possibly," agreed the Inspector. "Or it may be he merely suggested Shaddock clear out before the police came back with the warrant. I've thought all along that must have been Shaddock's original plan, based on that half-packed valise. But the police were watching for just such a move, and I expect Shaddock became aware of it at some point. Realizing he couldn't escape, he must have lost his nerve and decided suicide was the best way out."

"Which would have suited the General's purposes even better," I said. "Dead men tell no tales."

"Quite right. And once he knew Shaddock was dead, he put the chloral hydrate in the cottage," said the Inspector. "He had to wait until later that night, and he either didn't realize the police had already searched the place or calculated that it didn't matter. Which it didn't, as it turned out."

"No," I agreed. "But he must have fetched it away later, judging by tonight's events."

We both glanced at the Major, who groaned. "What about Mr. Alexis?" said the Inspector. "Do you think he was he a tool of the General's like Shaddock?"

"No," I said. "I think he only provided the inspiration. And I believe he did that quite innocently in the beginning. But I'm pretty sure he came to suspect, in time, what was happening. Probably around the time Peter Dray disappeared."

"But you don't think he was directly involved in the disappearances?"

"No, I think he was probably appalled when he realized what he had inspired. Not enough to disclose it to the police, of course, but enough to try to stop it. During these last few weeks, he's taken steps to distance himself from the General. He left Cincinnatus and moved to the Priory, and tonight, when the General tried to get him to summon Hannibal again, he put him off."

The Major said that for his part, he still regarded Mr. Alexis as guilty. "Even if all he did was fill the old man's head with a bunch of damnable notions, that makes him responsible in *my* book," he said stubbornly.

"But not legally responsible, I think," I said.

We both looked at the Inspector, who weighed the idea with judicial impartiality. "If you're right in what you say," he told me, "I doubt it's actionable. Still, I'd like to talk to him."

"You'll have to do it quickly, then," I said. "Lord Rodney wants him gone from the Priory by tomorrow morning."

The Inspector said admiringly that I was a quick worker. "Perhaps I'd better go over to the Priory tonight, then," he said. "It's still fairly early, and I need to talk to Lord Rodney anyway."

"To apologize?" I inquired in an innocent voice.

He tried to frown, Dear Reader, but was betrayed by the twinkle in his eyes. "A policeman has to suspect everybody more or less," he said. "Which you know perfectly well. If I had to apologize every time I made a mistake of that sort, I'd never be done with it."

The Major, who had caught only part of this, was looking gloomier than ever. "If we're speaking of mistakes," he said, "nobody's made more mistakes than I have. I should have seen what the General was up to and put a stop to it."

"But you did," I said. "You sensed Mr. Alexis was having a harmful effect on him, and you enlisted my help to put a stop to it. You got us all invited to that sitting tonight, which was crucial in uncovering the truth. If you hadn't done that, we might never have known the whole story. Or worse yet, we mightn't have known it till the General claimed another victim."

The Major seemed a little consoled by this idea, Dear Reader, but said he still blamed himself. "This never would have happened if Lily were alive," he said mournfully. "Of the two of us, she was the one with the brains. And there was nobody like her when it came to managing the General." He looked very sad. "I feel I've let her down . . . let her *and* our boy down. Nearly got him killed, by God."

The Inspector and I did what we could to reassure him. We pointed out that the boy was safe now and would likely remember little of what had transpired. He thanked us but said the business had been a lesson to him. "Fact is, I've been thinking it's time I married again," he said. "And this tears it. The Little Fellow needs a mother, and I need someone with more brains than I've got, so I don't make more of a muck of raising him than I've already done." He smiled, looking absurdly shy. "Think I've found just the woman to suit us both. *And* I've about got her convinced to take the job on."

I was pleased to hear it, Dear Reader, though a little surprised to learn he considered brains to be one of Ellen's qualifications.

Between you and me, I wasn't sure he was going to the right market for *that* commodity. But I reminded myself that men frequently deceive themselves in the women they marry. Quite possibly, a woman with heart would suit him just as well.

⋙⋘

Before the Inspector and I left Cincinnatus, I had a private word with Phillipe. I had a proposition to make him, and though I feared it was a lost cause, I could not depart without at least trying.

I began by telling him how impressed I had been by his quick thinking. Then I pointed out that, according to the General's own words, he had been relieved of his employment. "That being the case," I went on hopefully, "I wondered if you might like to come to work for me?"

He smiled, but I could tell it was going to be a refusal even before he opened his mouth.

"I thank you very much for the compliment, madam," he said, "but I feel it is my duty to remain with the General. He is dying, you know." He looked suddenly solemn. "I could not think it right to abandon him now, whatever wrongs he may have committed. This does not shock you, I hope?" He paused to survey me for evidences of shock.

"No," I said. "I'd say it's perfectly natural. You've known him a long time. No doubt this business has been a shock to you, as to all of us, but it wouldn't erase everything that came before."

Phillipe nodded. "He was a great man once," he said. "A very great man. Though not, *entre nous*, perhaps a good one."

I said that seemed to sum it up pretty accurately. "But what will you do once he is gone?" I asked. "Will you remain here with the Major and his son?"

Phillipe hesitated. "I think not," he said. "I have an affection for them, you understand—naturally I have. But being in service does not altogether suit me. Thanks to the General's generosity, I have a good amount of money saved, and I think of going into business. I would prefer some business where I may be independent."

I could understand *that*, Dear Reader, and said so. "I suppose you will be leaving Ainsworth, then. I am sure living here must often be difficult for you. London would likely be easier—and *entre nous*, Paris easier still."

Surprisingly, he refuted this statement, Dear Reader. "For myself, I would rather remain in Ainsworth," he said. "I have friends here whom I would be sorry to leave."

"Well, I am very glad to hear it," I said.

I *was* glad to hear it, Dear Reader, though also a little surprised. Still, it had been an evening of surprises all around, and that was scarcely the greatest of them.

# CHAPTER TWENTY-SEVEN

The Inspector and I didn't leave Ainsworth until the following day. We were both kept busy in our separate ways right up until the time the train departed.

I spent the morning at the Vicarage, while the Inspector spent it informing Lord Rodney, the Ainsworth constabulary, and the local magistrate of the General's rôle in their local mystery. All of them were shocked speechless on hearing the news. He had also to meet with Mr. Alexis, who was *not* shocked speechless, but loudly insisted that he was innocent of any wrongdoing.

"Did you believe him?" I asked as we sat together on the train, being borne London-wards.

"No, I didn't," said the Inspector. "Almost certainly he was an accessory after the fact. Possibly even before the fact, too. It would depend on when he first caught wind of the General's activities. I'm sure, in my own mind, that he guessed long ago that the old man was murdering those children in the style he himself had suggested. But we'd have a devil of a time proving it."

"So you let him go?"

"With a warning to mind his step in the future. *And* a suggestion that England might not prove very congenial for his activities after this. He was talking about returning to Vienna when I left. To hear him tell it, he and the Austrian Empress are like brother and sister."

"It's possible," I said, fair-mindedly. "There's no reason royalty can't be as foolish as anyone else."

The Inspector said there was plenty of evidence to prove that, at any rate. "In regard to *Salammbo*," he went on, "you were right about its being a source of inspiration in this business." Opening his bag, he produced a leather-bound copy of Flaubert's work. "I taxed Mr. Alexis with it, and he finally admitted it. He'd bought this back in the spring, when the General's fancy first turned lightly to thoughts of Hannibal. Later, after he moved to the Priory, he hid it in Lord Rodney's library. That, to my mind, proves his guilt. Otherwise, why conceal the thing? But I don't think it's anything the law can prosecute him for."

"Has Lord Rodney relented toward him?" I asked.

"Quite the contrary. After hearing that Mr. Alexis actually inspired the murders, he's more up in arms than ever. Surprising, really, for I'd thought he was rather a soft fellow." The Inspector smiled in a shame-faced way. "But he's on the warpath now, and no mistake."

"Miss Douglas was pretty fierce about it, too," I said reminiscently. "There'd be another 'Hanged Man' in Ainsworth if she had any say in the matter."

"That 'Hanged Man' business is another thing," said the Inspector, who was obviously still fretting about his inability to bring Mr. Alexis to book. "If he prophesied Shaddock's suicide, that proves he must have had some idea of what was going on at Cincinnatus even after he left it."

I said I didn't see it that way. "Mr. Alexis deliberately distorted the meaning of that card to make it fit Shaddock's suicide,"

I explained. "It made him seem spiritually omniscient to Lord Rodney, who didn't know any better. But in fact the card's real meaning is quite different—and also quite eerily apposite. In the *tarot divinatoire,* 'The Hanged Man' is usually interpreted as a sacrifice."

The Inspector, with typical doggedness, argued that in that case, Mr. Alexis had deliberately obscured the card's real meaning to hide his own guilty knowledge.

"Possibly," I said. "But coincidence would explain it pretty well, too. Or simply a case of the Lord working in mysterious ways. Like Reverend Douglas reading that passage about Tophet and false gods at Evensong on Friday."

The Inspector had not heard about that incident, Dear Reader. When I described it to him, he agreed it was a remarkable coincidence. "Almost too much of a coincidence," he said, his mental wheels visibly turning as he tried now to fit Reverend Douglas into his theory of the crime. "I can't see why he would make his knowledge public if he had any rôle in the business, but there's no denying criminals do foolish things sometimes. And I know you thought at one time he might be involved."

"Because he was short of money," I agreed, nodding. "And because his sister had spoken of disgrace. But it turns out his problems were caused by something else entirely. While I was at the Vicarage this morning, Miss Douglas told me in confidence that her brother has always had a weakness for gambling. Recently, he was tipped off on what was supposed to be a sure winner in a horse race and bet a year's income on it, only to see his horse limp in dead last."

"I see," said the Inspector. "Not a crime, but something a lot of people might regard as disgraceful in a minister of the gospel. And certainly it might prompt said minister to reduce his household expenses."

"It might, but it's not going to," I said. "There was a reprieve at the last minute. Miss Douglas's great-uncle died, and it turns out he made her his sole heir. It's not a great fortune, but it will support both her and her brother, and *she* will hold the purse-strings. I expect they will go on much more comfortably after this."

The Inspector said cynically that any man who was reliant on his sister for financial support could hardly be called comfortable. I retorted that if the man was foolish enough to gamble away his substance in the first place, he might thank his stars he had *anyone* willing to support him. "True," agreed the Inspector in a pacific voice. "At any rate, it means Mrs. Mason won't be turned adrift in the world along with the rest of the Vicarage staff."

"As to that, I don't think she will be at the Vicarage much longer," I said. "She was horrified to hear how close the Major came to losing the Little Fellow. Of course the idea of his being a poor motherless boy worked on her sensibilities anyway. And the Major has been steadily chipping away at them on his own account. As he himself would say, this tears it. She was already putting on her bonnet to call on him when I left."

The Inspector said it was a pity it took something so grievous to bring them together. "They've both had to suffer over this business," he observed. "I'm afraid there'll be more to suffer once word of the General's guilt gets about. As the Major said, it's too much to expect that people won't talk about it."

I pointed out that without a trial, the talk wouldn't be as bad as it would be otherwise. "The General is already under sentence of death," I noted. "So there's no need to hang him."

"*If* he dies," said the Inspector. "But if he should make a recovery, we'd have to go forward with the prosecution."

"The doctor didn't seem to think there was any chance of that."

"Perhaps not. But I can't disregard the possibility that he's shamming, just as he was after the séance."

"I know the Major thought he was shamming," I said, "but the more I think about it, the more certain I am that he wasn't. His colour, his breathing, and his pulse were all very bad. I think he was genuinely unwell."

"Then how do you explain his being spry enough an hour later to drug the boy and haul him out to the potting shed?'

"I think it was a last, desperate attempt to vindicate his actions," I said. "His last stand, if you will. He'd just been brought face to face with evidence that his spiritual guide was a fraud. He had to decide whether to face up to the truth, or go on denying it. A better man might have faced up, but General Whitmore chose rather to shut his eyes and compound his error."

"A better man would never have committed that sort of crime in the first place," said the Inspector sternly. "No matter what the incentive."

"In nineteenth-century England, that's true," I agreed. "But the ancient Carthaginians considered it a perfectly acceptable way to attain divine favour."

"That's not just fiction?"

"I'm afraid not. Flaubert was inspired by the work of French archaeologists in Tunisia, who found evidence of wholesale child sacrifice.[12] If you'll pass me that copy of *Salammbo*, Tom, I'll translate the bits that deal with the subject."

For the next hour or so, I read him the more lurid parts of *Salammbo*, which caused him to say that in his opinion, Flaubert had a lot to answer for.

"That's hardly fair," I protested. "Authors can't be held responsible for the silly things weak-minded people might do in response to their work.

"Silly things," said the Inspector with a snort. "Is *that* what you call them?"

---

12  This is one of the instances where Madame Fox seems to show true psychic ability. Flaubert's novel was published some decades before archaeological evidence confirmed the scope of Carthaginian child sacrifice.—*Ed.*

"Lunatic, if you prefer," I said. "But in any case—" I paused, looking at him provocatively over the top of the book, "—in any case, you should have guessed early on that the General was mentally unstable."

"*I* should have guessed?" he repeated. "How?"

"He wanted to marry *me*," I said.

To my disappointment, Dear Reader, he refused to be drawn on this subject. Instead he embarked on a discussion of whether the General fit the criteria of insanity as described by the M'Naghten Rules.[13] "He knew what he was doing, all right. And the fact that he kept his rôle in the business secret and put the blame on Shaddock means he knew what he was doing was wrong. It was he who put that bottle of chloral in Shaddock's cottage, after the fact—and he who took it back later, once the excitement had died down."

"But if I were called as a witness," I countered, "I would have to testify that I heard him deny outright that he was committing murder. He called it a sacrifice rather. And the Carthaginians thought it an honour to sacrifice their children to the gods."

We were still arguing the case when the train pulled into Waterloo Station. We continued to argue all the way to Wimpole Street. When our cab drew up in front of the Temple, however, I was distracted by the sight of not one but two carriages already drawn up at the curb. Looking up at the windows, I could see lights burning in the Spirit Parlour.

"What on earth?" I exclaimed. "Can Susan be conducting a sitting in my absence?"

---

13 The M'Naghten Rules allowed insanity to be used as a defense if "at the time of the committing of the act, the party accused was labouring under such a defect of reason, from a disease of the mind, as not to know the nature and quality of the act he was doing; or, if he did know it, that he did not know he was doing what was wrong."—*Ed.*

"Do you want me to come in with you and see?" asked the Inspector.

"No, I'm sure it's nothing I can't manage, Tom. Go on to your own flat. You didn't get any sleep last night, and I'm sure you would like to rest. We can—*ahem*—meet later."

With a nod, he picked up his bag and headed toward the building's other entrance, which was decorated with a large set of teeth that slowly opened and closed with mechanical regularity. Our building housed a dental office as well as the Temple of Spiritualism, and I had been instrumental in making the dentist's entrance more conspicuous as a way of keeping his customers away from my door. The word "DENTIST" was emblazoned in electric light bulbs above the teeth. As electricity was a new development in our quarter, quite a few street urchins and idlers had gathered to gape at both teeth and sign. I paused to admire them myself before letting myself into the Temple with my latch-key.

Susan had evidently been on the watch, for she came hurrying down the corridor to meet me. "Thank God you got my telegram," she said. "I don't know what we would have done if you hadn't got here soon."

"But I didn't get your telegram," I said. "What is happening?"

As I spoke, a loud moan came from the direction of the Spirit Parlour. I turned a startled gaze in that direction. "It's all right," said Susan. "It's just Mrs. Clarke."

"Mrs. Clarke," I repeated.

"Yes," said Susan. "She's in the Spirit Parlour with Mr. Clarke and the doctor."

I stared at her. "You don't mean—she's not—?"

"Yes," said Susan with weary satisfaction. "She's having her baby. Or babies, as the case may be. Between you and me, I'm thinking it must be twins. Jenny and I have a bet riding on it. She's that enormous."

I paid no heed to this latter statement, being still focused on Susan's earlier one. "Mrs. Clarke is having her baby," I repeated. "But do you mean to say she's having it *here?*"

"Yes," said Susan, rather defiantly. "She is."

"*Why* is she having it here? I am sure *I* made no such arrangement!"

"No," agreed Susan, "but you've got her convinced that this is the only place in London safe from 'malign influences.' And now the baby is actually on the way, she's in mortal fear something will go wrong. Her husband's as bad as she is—worse, in fact. There's nothing he can do at this point except see that she's happy. So he kept offering me more and more money, until I was ashamed to keep saying no."

"How much money did he offer?" I demanded.

She told me, Dear Reader.

"Well," I said, "that is . . . very satisfactory. Very satisfactory indeed." I had got hardly any sleep the previous night and was weary from my journey besides, but business is business, after all.

"Tell Jenny to make me some coffee," I said, picking up my bag. "I'll go and change my clothes and wash up a bit. I'm dusty from traveling and in no condition to preside over a solemn ritual."

"You needn't hurry," Susan called after me. "It's been going on for hours now. And the doctor reckons it will be at least a couple more hours before the baby comes."

⇥ ⇤

In spite of Susan's advice, I changed very quickly and hurried down to the Spirit Parlour. On the threshold I paused, startled at its changed appearance. Susan and Jenny had removed the table with the Spiritograph—into my study, as I later learned—and they had set up a camp bed in its place. It stood in the centre of the room under the hanging lantern. The alabaster lamps that lined the walls were all lit and glowing, and there was a sweet scent in the air that indicated Susan had been dispensing our best floral essence with a lavish hand.

Mrs. Clarke lay on the camp bed, with her husband seated on one side of her and a man I took to be the doctor on the other. A few basins, towels, and blankets stood on a table near to hand, along with the doctor's bag. I advanced toward the group, feeling a little nervous, but taking care not to show it. "Good evening, Mrs. Clarke," I said, kneeling down beside her.

She turned a wan face to me, trying to smile. "Madame Fox!" she exclaimed. "I'm so glad you are here." Susan was right: her belly was perfectly enormous, and if she wasn't having twins, then it was as gross a case of misrepresentation as I had ever seen.

Mr. Clarke, meanwhile, had sprung to his feet. "Thank heaven you are here," he said. "Take my seat, Madame Fox—yes, please do. I know Drusilla will go on better now you are here."

The doctor gave me a brief, disparaging glance as I took the chair. When he spoke, his voice held a note of exasperation. "She's going on perfectly well as it is," he said. "I tell you there's no need to be alarmed, Mr. Clarke. Everything is progressing just as it should."

Mr. Clarke didn't look as though he believed it, Dear Reader. His face was quite as wan as his wife's. "But it's been hours," he protested. "Hours! Shouldn't the baby have come by now?"

"No," said the doctor impatiently. "I told you that before. This is your wife's first baby. First babies always take a long time coming. You might as well sit down and compose yourself. In some other room, perhaps," he added pointedly.

Just then Mrs. Clarke gave another moan. Involuntarily I flinched, whereupon the doctor threw me a look of contempt. As for Mr. Clarke, he started back as though he had been struck. "There!" he cried. "There!"

I wasn't sure whether he meant the words as comfort to his wife or accusation toward the doctor, Dear Reader. Possibly he didn't know himself, for the next moment his eyes rolled up in his head and he slid to the floor in a heap.

The doctor made an impatient noise. "Now look at that," he said. "Two patients rather than one. All I need right now!"

"Is he hurt?" cried Mrs. Clarke, trying to see above her own belly. "Oh, Alfred, are you hurt?" Her voice sounded hysterical.[14]

"I'll see to him," I said soothingly. "Rely on me, Mrs. Clarke."

I may not have much experience with childbirth, Dear Reader, but I have lots of experience with fainting. I went to the door to summon help. Evidently Susan had been watching through the ventilator and had beaten me to it, for when I opened the door Jenny and Sam were standing there. They came in, picked Mr. Clarke up by the legs and shoulders, and bore him away to the Sitting Room. I went along to direct the operation.

"Smelling salts," I told them, as they settled him onto the sofa. "And brandy. Try to keep him in here," I added in a lower voice. "I don't think he's doing either himself or his wife much good in there."

I returned to the Spirit Parlour and took Mrs. Clarke by the hand. "There," I said, smiling. "You needn't worry about him any-more. He is in good hands. Let us concentrate now on bringing this new soul into the world."

"From a place of Light and Beauty," agreed Mrs. Clarke in a weak voice. "Surrounded by Beings wise and understanding."

The doctor threw us both derisive looks, but I didn't pay him any heed. Grasping her hand, I spoke at length about spheres within spheres and Light and Beauty and Understanding. I described the Bright Beings surrounding her and their eagerness to render her aid. After a while, Susan, without any instruction, began sound-ing a few chimes *extempore.* Mrs. Clarke continued to groan when the labour pains came, but in a more resigned and muted way. I

---

14 We can presume with certainty that *she*, at least, had a uterus.—*Ed.*

stroked her hand and encouraged her to breathe deeply, and the doctor put in an instruction of his own now and then. As time went on, I thought he was regarding me with more approval—if not as an actual help, then at least as no positive hindrance.

I will say right now, Dear Reader, that having witnessed the miracle of birth, I feel completely vindicated in my decision to remain childless. Nothing in the *world* would make me go through that amount of pain and labour and indignity. Still, I am obliged to admit that seeing a new human being brought into the world is an awe-inspiring spectacle. Mr. Clarke was there to share it with us. He came staggering into the Spirit Parlour—well steeped in Spirits himself, by the smell of him—just as the climactic moment arrived. "I'm here, Drusilla," he declared dramatically. "I'm here."

His wife's reply was a piercing cry, which was joined presently by another, shriller cry. A moment later the doctor stood up jubilantly holding a small squirming bundle in his arms.

Both Mr. Clarke and I stared at it in fascinated horror. "Is it . . . all right?" ventured Mr. Clarke, after a moment.

"Of course it's all right," said the doctor testily. "A fine healthy boy. Take him from me, would you? I rather think—yes, indeed!" Hurriedly he knelt again before Mrs. Clarke.

Mr. Clarke and I looked at the baby. "I didn't know they were so small when they first arrived," he said in a hushed voice. "Or so messy."

It was true, Dear Reader. Rather than coming from a place of Light and Beauty, the baby appeared to have come from a place of blood and mucus. Still, you could see that once it was cleaned up a bit, it wouldn't be bad-looking. Thankfully it had quit crying for the moment.

Then we heard a baby crying again—only it wasn't the same baby. Mr. Clarke and I looked at each other, then down at the doctor, who was busy again with Mrs. Clarke. A moment later, he stood up, holding *another* squirming bundle.

"Twins, by God!" said Mr. Clarke in a stunned voice.

Susan had won her bet, Dear Reader. I made a mental note to congratulate her later.

As for the doctor, he still seemed preoccupied with Mrs. Clarke. He thrust the second howling baby at me, so that I had no choice but to take it. That is how I learned, the hard way, that a satin evening dress is not the proper thing to wear to preside over a childbirth. As I was being well paid for the evening's work, however, I chalked it up to experience.

"Twins," said Mr. Clarke again, "Drusilla, we have twins!" He turned to his wife in excitement.

Mrs. Clarke appeared not to have heard him, Dear Reader. Her face was shiny with sweat and set in lines of grim determination. "Yes," said the doctor encouragingly, "yes, yes!" And then, once again, there was the sound of a baby crying.

# CHAPTER TWENTY-EIGHT

Susan ended up losing her bet after all, Dear Reader. It was triplets rather than twins. The doctor said that the babies, though small, were remarkably strong and healthy.

"That's a rare thing," he told us. "A very rare thing." With a grudging smile, he added, "Maybe there's something in your Spirits after all."

"Of course there is," said Mrs. Clarke, who was gazing down at two of her sons with a beatific smile.

"Of course there is," echoed her husband.

Jenny threw me a smile. She was holding the third baby, which she had just finished bathing in accordance with the doctor's instructions. I noticed she kept looking down at the thing with the same fatuous expression Mrs. Clarke was wearing. A premonitory tingle shot down my spine. Still, I reminded myself there was no use borrowing trouble. Time enough to cross that bridge when we came to it.

"It's not many women who present their husbands with three sons at one go," continued the doctor. "A family ready-made, by Jove!"

At these words, Mrs. Clarke's face fell ludicrously. "Sons," she said. "Sons! Three of them and all boys." She looked at me with contrition. "And here we were wanting to name the baby after *you*, Madame Fox."

The irony of this had already occurred to me, Dear Reader. There would be no Baby Seraphina. It had been a fifty-fifty chance right along, of course, but with three babies in the equation it seemed less like chance and more like some kind of celestial joke. I took it good-humouredly, however, saying I was only glad the babies were well and strong.

About their strength there could be no doubt, judging by the amount of noise they made. Just so soon as one of them quieted down, another would start squalling.

At this point, I was eager to get them all off the premises, not only because of the noise, but because every moment Jenny spent with the babies was clearly infecting her further with a desire for one of her own. It was no use, however. A celebratory spirit had seized the whole party. No one seemed to hear my hints about the lateness of the hour, or the need for all of us to seek our beds. I finally gave up, called for champagne all around, and sat down to wait it out.

The Inspector found me hours later in the Sitting Room. He was wearing his dressing gown over his shirt and trousers, and I could tell from his amused expression that he was already in possession of the facts.

"I fell asleep waiting for you," he explained. "And when I woke up and found you still hadn't come to bed, I thought I ought to see what was keeping you. This is a new development, isn't it? Your Temple has become a crèche!"

"I'm surprised you *could* sleep," I said sourly. "Or that anyone in the building could! I'm only waiting for the dentist to come complaining about the noise."

The Inspector said that his patients had disturbed me so often that a little turn-about seemed fair play. "But the junior Clarkes aren't making any noise at present," he said. "Jenny showed them to me in the parlour just now, and they were all sleeping as sweetly as cherubs."

"So much the worse," I retorted. "The less trouble they appear now, the more she will think she wants one."

"It did rather look that way," said the Inspector apologetically. "She had Sam in there, too, looking at them."

"Damn," I said.

I poured more champagne into my glass, then offered him some, too. He refused, however, saying it was almost breakfast time. "I'll be obliged to go along to the Yard soon," he added, with a glance at the sitting room clock.

"I'm so sorry, Tom," I said. "It's too bad that this should have happened to disturb you, after all the disturbance of these last few days."

He sat down beside me and took my hand in his. "As to that," he said, "they're rather different propositions, aren't they? I'm quite glad to share in other people's happiness for a change. Mostly it's other people's troubles I get to share. In this case, the one might be said to counterbalance the other."

I knew what he meant, Dear Reader, for I had been feeling it, too. After the dark business of Ainsworth, it was strangely affirming to see new life born into the world. Yet I couldn't delude myself that it had been a straightforward exchange of souls. The three boys who had been dealt a poor hand at birth and a worse one in death didn't bear any relation to the three born tonight into an atmosphere of love and privilege. And who was to say that love and privilege would endure even for them? There was no guarantee that these three new souls would live longer or happier lives than the others.

I expressed these sentiments aloud, as best I could. "I don't know why anyone would want to bring children into the world," I said. "How do they dare? Even if the children themselves turn out perfectly, the world itself is so . . . imperfect."

"I know," he said. "I feel the same way. Being a policeman, it's natural that I should, perhaps." His mouth curved into a reflective smile. "But I find it rather encouraging that other people want to do it. If nothing else, it shows I'm doing my job. The public feels secure enough to bring new and vulnerable beings into the world, and hopeful enough about the future to trust that nothing terrible will happen to them."

Perhaps this is the proper way to look at it, Dear Reader. I am not a believer myself in the Eternal Progression of Mankind, or the idea that we are steadily evolving from Lower to Higher Spheres. But sometimes I wish I were.

⇥⇤

In the aftermath of these events, I am happy to report that life at the Temple of Spiritualism has resumed its normal course. Still, there have been some interesting after-effects that I must detail here.

For one thing, the Clarkes have generously lain the whole of the credit for Mrs. Clarke's safe triple delivery to me, with the result that I now have a steady stream of would-be clients seeking help with their own issues of generation.

"It's very provoking," I told Susan. "You'd think I was some kind of fertility goddess. I don't mind it so much when the baby is already conceived, but when I am asked to preside over the conception itself—well, I feel I must draw the line there!"

With a grin, Susan observed that there looked to be a lot of money in it. She was right about that, Dear Reader. If I were less scrupulous, I might re-christen my business the Temple of Hymen and grow rich renting out Celestial Beds in the good old style of charlatans past.[15] Still, that would likely put me on a course of

---

15  A most lucrative enterprise, as Madame Fox notes. London's Temple of Health and Hymen, c. 1781, charged £100 a night for the use of their Celestial State Bed.—*Ed.*

collision with the Law, which would be inconvenient seeing I am married to one of its representatives. On the whole, I believe I will stick to my present calling.

On the subject of marriage, Ellen and the Major have indeed become husband and wife. The General passed quietly away not long after their wedding and left most of his estate to the Little Fellow, who is now, at Ellen's insistence, called by his proper name of David. I will not belittle the nature of her grief by suggesting that the acquisition of a step-son could ever make her forget the loss of her daughter, or of the boy she befriended. But she is one of those who finds happiness in loving and serving others. That being the case, it seems likely she will be as happy as most of us in this imperfect world.

Ellen's was not the only union to come out of the business. Felicity informed me recently that Sally, her former protegée, had also married. "And you'll never guess who the bridegroom was," she said. "Do you remember the General's coloured manservant?"

With a sense of fatality, I asked if she meant Sandeep. She said no, it was the African fellow with the French name: "Phillipe, that's it."

Well! You could have knocked me over with a feather, Dear Reader. When he said he had friends in the village, I hadn't an idea he meant Sally—or that he meant friends in such a particular way.

On further questioning, I learned that the General had left Phillipe a handsome legacy which, together with his savings, enabled him to buy the Hound and Huntsman. It is now called the Two Drums and is, by all accounts, quite a transformed place. It has become a popular resort for travelers, and though the local populace initially harbored a degree of suspicion—and a lingering prejudice—toward its formidable proprietor, this has largely been done away with by the excellence of its beer. Sally, it seems, numbers brewing among her other accomplishments. She would appear to be as intrepid in her way as her stalwart bridegroom. I wish them both well, though I can't think married life will be easy for them. Still, I can say from first-hand experience that a few differences between husband and wife need be no impediment to happiness.

＝⤙⤚＝

Speaking of my own marriage, I still have made no general announcement, but I did summon up the courage to tell Susan about it privately. She crushed me by saying she had known it all along. "We all knew it," she told me. "Sam and Jenny, too."

"How could you know?" I demanded. "How?"

"We know what the Inspector's like," she explained. "As soon as we heard he was moving into the building, we guessed you must be married. No matter how besotted he might be, he wouldn't ever countenance irregular goings-on of *that* sort."

"That's all you know," I shot back. "As it happens, he *did*—"

At this point I broke off in some confusion. Susan, however, smiled in a superior way. "If he did," she said, "I notice you're married now, all right and tight. So I'd say that proves my point, wouldn't you?"

As she was exactly correct in her surmises, I did not dignify her comment with any reply. I merely informed the Inspector that he need not blush any longer to meet Jenny's eye. He said that was very satisfactory.

＝⤙⤚＝

I still use the name of Seraphina Fox professionally, though I have left off using Letitia Blackwood. My stay in Ainsworth has, I feel, compromised that name beyond repair. I am presently looking for another name, suitable for those occasions when I need a convenient *alias*. At the moment, I am favouring Laura Baldwin. The Inspector, predictably, had his own suggestion: "You wouldn't find it easier to just to call yourself Mrs. Thomas Harper?"

I said no, I wouldn't want to take a chance of compromising that name, either. It was a diplomatic answer, Dear Reader, but also a true one. Some things are too important for any compromise.

Thus, it follows by a curious twist of fate that Ainsworth is now the one place in England where I can comfortably appear in the character of a respectable married woman.

It gives the place a certain charm, Dear Reader. And the Douglases are always pleased to receive the Inspector and me at the Vicarage. The last time we were there, Reverend Douglas proudly showed us a new stained-glass window which now occupies the church's east wall across from Abraham and Isaac. This window bears an image of Christ among the children which Lord Rodney commissioned as a memorial to the lost children of Ainsworth.

If you look closely, Dear Reader, you will see that one of the boys gathered around the Christ has a bulldog jaw and a catapult tucked in his back pocket. Another is conspicuously missing his front teeth. A third leans upon a crutch. And there's a little girl, too, seated on the Christ's knee, that Miss Douglas assures me is the image of Becky Mason.

I may say that this circumstance has mellowed some of Miss Douglas's antagonism toward Lord Rodney. She admits that he has shown taste in his tribute and generosity in the way he has helped the boys' families. I praised his gift, and him, in unstinted terms. Only later did it occur to me that the features of the Christ, as depicted in the window, bore a certain resemblance to Lord Rodney's own.

It might be coincidence, Dear Reader. Likely the artist who created the window did not even realize it. But if he did (and speaking strictly between ourselves), I do feel he might have chosen a worse model.

Just don't tell Miss Douglas I said so.

## The End

# ABOUT THE AUTHOR

Joy Reed is the author of 16 romance novels, an award-winning master's thesis, and the Seraphina Fox mystery series. Her works have been published around the world and translated into four languages. She is a voracious and indiscriminate reader, a collector of unconsidered trifles, and a historian specializing in the Bleeding Kansas era. Ms. Reed lives with her long-suffering husband and an undisclosed number of cats and tarantulas in the Greater Little Rock area.

You can read her musings about life and literature on her blog BookJoy: http://bookjoy.livejournal.com/